Wild Wild Death

CASEY DANIELS

BERKLEY PRIME CRIME, NEW YORK

THE BERKLEY PUBLISHING GROUP
Published by the Penguin Group
Penguin Group (USA) Inc.
375 Hudson Street, New York, New York 10014, USA

Penguin Group (Canada), 90 Eglinton Avenue East, Suite 700, Toronto, Ontario M4P 2Y3, Canada
(a division of Pearson Penguin Canada Inc.)
Penguin Books Ltd., 80 Strand, London WC2R 0RL, England
Penguin Group Ireland, 25 St. Stephen's Green, Dublin 2, Ireland (a division of Penguin Books Ltd.)
Penguin Group (Australia), 250 Camberwell Road, Camberwell, Victoria 3124, Australia
(a division of Pearson Australia Group Pty. Ltd.)
Penguin Books India Pvt. Ltd., 11 Community Centre, Panchsheel Park, New Delhi—110 017, India
Penguin Group (NZ), 67 Apollo Drive, Rosedale, Auckland 0632, New Zealand
(a division of Pearson New Zealand Ltd.)
Penguin Books (South Africa) (Pty.) Ltd., 24 Sturdee Avenue, Rosebank, Johannesburg 2196,
South Africa

Penguin Books Ltd., Registered Offices: 80 Strand, London WC2R 0RL, England

This is a work of fiction. Names, characters, places, and incidents either are the product of the author's imagination or are used fictitiously, and any resemblance to actual persons, living or dead, business establishments, events, or locales is entirely coincidental. The publisher does not have any control over and does not assume any responsibility for author or third-party websites or their content.

WILD WILD DEATH

A Berkley Prime Crime Book / published by arrangement with the author

PRINTING HISTORY
Berkley Prime Crime mass-market edition / January 2011

Copyright © 2012 by Connie Laux.
Interior text design by Laura K. Corless.

ISBN: 978-0-425-24582-8

BERKLEY® PRIME CRIME
Berkley Prime Crime Books are published by The Berkley Publishing Group,
a division of Penguin Group (USA) Inc.,
375 Hudson Street, New York, New York 10014.
BERKLEY® PRIME CRIME and the PRIME CRIME logo are trademarks of Penguin Group (USA) Inc.

PRINTED IN THE UNITED STATES OF AMERICA

10 9 8 7 6 5 4 3 2 1

Dead Man Talking

"There's no savoring the Pepper Martin series—you'll devour each book and still be hungry for more!"
—Kathryn Smith, *USA Today* bestselling author

"My favorite ghost hunter, sassy Pepper Martin, is back in another hauntingly good mystery."
—Shirley Damsgaard, author of *The Seventh Witch*

Night of the Loving Dead

"Gravestones, ghosts, and ghoulish misdemeanors delight in Casey Daniels's witty *Night of the Loving Dead*."
—Madelyn Alt, national bestselling author

"Pepper proves once again that great style, quick wit, and a sharp eye can solve any mystery." —*Publishers Weekly*

"Pepper is brazen and beautiful, and this mystery is perfectly paced, with plenty of surprise twists." —*RT Book Reviews*

"[A] well-plotted paranormal mystery that . . . shares some answers that fans have had since we first met this entertaining character, and adds several surprising twists along the way." —*Darque Reviews*

continued . . .

Tombs of Endearment

"A fun romp through the streets and landmarks of Cleveland . . . A tongue-in-cheek . . . look at life beyond the grave . . . Well worth picking up." —Suite101.com

"[A] PI who is Stephanie Plum-meets-*Sex and the City*'s Carrie Bradshaw . . . It's fun, it's 'chick,' and appealing . . . [A] quick, effortless read with a dash of Bridget Jones–style romance." —PopSyndicate.com

"With witty dialogue and an entertaining mystery, Ms. Daniels pens an irresistible tale of murder, greed, and a lesson in love. A well-paced storyline that's sure to have readers anticipating Pepper's next ghostly client." —*Darque Reviews*

"Sassy, spicy . . . Pepper Martin, wearing her Moschino Cheap & Chic pink polka dot sling backs, will march right into your imagination." —Shirley Damsgaard, author of *The Seventh Witch*

The Chick and the Dead

"Amusing with her breezy chick-lit style and sharp dialogue." —*Publishers Weekly*

"Ms. Daniels has a hit series on her hands." —*The Best Reviews*

"Ms. Daniels is definitely a hot new voice in paranormal mystery . . . Intriguing . . . Well-written . . . with a captivating storyline and tantalizing characters." —*Darque Reviews*

"[F]un, flirtatious, and feisty . . . [A] fast-paced read, filled with likeable characters." —Suite101.com

Don of the Dead

"Fabulous! One of the funniest books I've read this year."
—MaryJanice Davidson, *New York Times* bestselling author

"There's not a ghost of a chance you'll be able to put this book down. Write faster, Casey Daniels."
—Emilie Richards, *USA Today* bestselling author

"One part Godfather, one part Bridget Jones, one part ghost story, driven by a spunky new sleuth . . . A delightful read!"
—Roberta Isleib, author of *Asking for Murder*

"[A] humorous and highly entertaining expedition into mystery and the supernatural."
—Linda O. Johnston, author of *The More the Terrier*

"A spooky mystery, a spunky heroine, and sparkling wit! Give us more!" —Kerrelyn Sparks, *USA Today* bestselling author

"[F]unny and fast-paced; her sassy dialogue . . . her bravado, and her slightly off-kilter view of life make Pepper an unforgettable character . . . The only drawback is waiting for book two!" —*Library Journal* (starred review)

"[A] fun cozy with a likeable heroine and a satisfying plot."
—Suite101.com

"Fans of Buffy ought to enjoy this one." —MyShelf.com

I don't know if there's some publishing rule against
dedicating two books in a row to the same person.
I only know that without Leslie Wey,
this book would not exist.

Thank you, Leslie, for welcoming me into your home,
introducing me to all your wonderful
friends (furry and human),
and showing me around New Mexico.

You, girlfriend, are the best!

Acknowledgments

Is there really a curse on Cleveland sports teams?

Years of disappointing win/loss records and dashed hopes here on the north coast make people think so, and there's even a legend to back them up.

It all starts with a Native American chief named Joc-O-Sot, who lived from 1810–1844. The chief performed in Wild West shows and while on a trip abroad, he became ill. He desperately wanted to return to his people and be buried in Minnesota, but he only got as far as Cleveland before he died. Local tales say that he haunts the city and that he's the one whose curse keeps the Cleveland Indians from winning a World Series.

Is it true? I can't say, but I do know that on a visit to Joc-O-Sot's grave, I commented that I was surprised some rabid baseball fans haven't dug him up and taken him out of town. I was only kidding, of course, but the idea struck a chord and became the basis for *Wild Wild Death*. With any luck, what happens in these pages will be the fictional catalyst that will realign the universe and take care of that pesky curse. If the

Acknowledgments

Cleveland Indians win the World Series anytime soon, I am more than happy to take credit for helping out.

There is also historical fact behind the labor troubles mentioned in the book. The Streetcar Strike of 1899 began in June, and as management tried to replace striking workers, riots broke out and explosives were planted to destroy streetcars and tracks.

A writer's brain plays with facts like these, molds and shapes them to become part of the fiction that turns into a book. Nowhere is this more evident than in my creation of the Taopi.

There are many different Pueblo Indian tribes living in the Southwest. Taopi is not one of them. They, too, are an invention of my imagination as is a pueblo on Wind Mountain. In fact, I didn't know there was a town in Minnesota called Taopi until after I had created my fictional tribe, or that the town was named in honor of an Indian chief who once lived there. Coincidence considering how Joc-O-Sot figures into this story? I can't say. With the help of Jody Coffman, a Taos Indian I met while visiting the Southwest, I have tried to incorporate the customs and beliefs of real Pueblo peoples into the story. Any mistakes are the fault of a girl from Cleveland who doesn't get to New Mexico nearly often enough. I'm also grateful to Jody and her mother-in-law, Judy Coffman, for introducing me to the wonders of frozen avocado pie. Yes, I know . . . sounds terrible, right? Do yourself a favor, find a recipe online, and give it a try.

It was on a trip to New Mexico back in 2009 that I first visited Bandelier National Monument and the remarkable pueblo ruins there. It is truly an incredible place and I en-

Acknowledgments

joyed scrambling up into the ancient pueblos and getting a glimpse of how the inhabitants lived many hundreds of years ago. As interesting as the entire place was, the memory that remains clearest to me is that of the kiva. As we entered the area, it was late in the afternoon and there were few tourists visiting. That may have been because of the weather. Dark clouds gathered overhead and thunder growled, echoing off the steep cliffs. As we approached the sacred kiva, I knew we were not alone. The spirits of the pueblo's ancient inhabitants were surely all around us. In researching the Pepper Martin mysteries, I have visited many haunted places and participated in paranormal investigations, but nowhere have I felt the presence of spirits as distinctly. New Mexico is known as the Land of Enchantment. Bandelier is proof.

Prologue

I t's tough to decide what to wear to a body snatching.

On one hand, there's the whole thing about being inconspicuous and blending in with the shadows. On the other . . .

Truth be told, in my heart of hearts, I feared the night might end with questions, accusations, and yes, mug shots. If that was the case, I didn't want to go down in history in the Cleveland Police Department arrest records archives looking like some frumpy reject.

I compromised, and even though it was a sticky night, I chose jeans for practicality along with a black jersey T. Good camouflage and flattering lines, and both looked just right with the oversized Jimmy Choo multicolored print tote I slipped on my shoulder. What private investigator for the dead could ask for more? Since it started to rain just as I left my apartment, I grabbed Quinn's blue windbreaker, too, and shrugged into it. If worst came to worst and I ended up against a wall with hash marks on it, I could always take off the jacket for the pictures.

Without going into the ugly details, let's just say that getting over the stone wall that surrounded Garden View Cemetery wasn't the most graceful thing I've ever done. It was also more exercise than this girl is used to, and by the time I finally had both feet on the ground of the place I used to work, I was breathing hard. As much as I hate to admit it, I may have been sweating, too. Well, just a teensy bit. No matter. Within a couple minutes, I was outside the marble mausoleum where Chester Goodshot Gomez rested in peace—but hopefully not for long.

All I had to do was figure out which of the keys I stole from Ella fit the mausoleum door.

Long story. For now, let's just say I'm not cut out for a life of crime. Especially when it comes to stealing from fluffy, lovable Ella. I swear, the guilt was what made my hands shake and my heart beat a jackhammer rhythm. Then again, thinking that Dan Callahan's life depended on me and what I was about to do didn't do much for my composure, either.

The very thought made me feel as if I'd chugged a Slurpee. Or maybe that frozen-stomach sensation came when I heard the crunch of car tires against the road that wound through this section of the cemetery with its century-old mausoleums and headstones that stood as tall as my five feet eleven inches. Security, and yes, I was on a first-name basis with the entire crew. Something told me that did not mean they'd take it kindly if they found me lurking there in the middle of the night.

I darted to the far side of Goodshot Gomez's mausoleum, flattened myself against the marble wall, and waited for the white patrol car to cruise by. They were on a forty-five-minute schedule so I knew exactly when they'd be back. By the time they were, I planned to be long gone.

Keeping the thought firmly in mind, I clenched my pocket-sized flashlight between my teeth and tried key after key in the rusted lock on the mausoleum door. When one finally fit and the ancient lock clicked open, I took a second to congratulate myself. Right before I stuck my head into the mausoleum.

"Hello?" Okay, it might have been crazy for anybody else to peek into a musty tomb and call out a greeting, but in my world, it's just common courtesy. "Hello? It's me, Pepper."

No answer. And no sign of Goodshot.

So far, so good.

Not that I have anything against Indians or anything. It's just that this was not the moment to run into the former Wild West show star who'd died in a tragic accident in Cleveland and—

How do I know? About Goodshot?

Well, like I said, I used to work at Garden View, and not just answering phones or selling plots or anything like that. I was the one and only full-time tour guide at the historic cemetery, and I'd brought plenty of people past this mausoleum.

I knew Goodshot's story, all right. It went something like this.

1

July 17, 1899

"I don't know, fellas . . ." With a slow look around at the buildings that ringed them like the rocky cliffs of an arroyo, Chester Goodshot Gomez took a long draw on his Cuban cigar and released the smoke in a series of O's that weren't as lazy as they were just plumb weary. "All this talk of streetcar riots and unions and management scrapping with workers . . ." He shook his head, his eyes on the spot not twenty feet away where a man in a dark cap stood square in the center of a set of streetcar tracks that glinted in the afternoon sun like twin butcher knives. The man was handing out flyers and urging the folks who passed to support his cause and avoid riding something he called the Big Consolidated Line.

"We've only been in this town for a day, and I'm tired of the bickerin' already." Goodshot took a last puff on his cigar, tossed the butt onto the sidewalk, and ground it

under the heel of his leather boot. "Heard someone talkin'
this morning. Those union types, they used explosives last
night to demolish some streetcar tracks not too far from
here." Chester sighed. "I can't help but think . . . life, it
was never so complicated back on the pueblo."

"It might not have been complicated, but you're forgettin', my friend, you always said as how it was plenty bor-
ing." Thad Jenson, tall and lanky, slapped Goodshot on
the back. "Ain't like you to talk like you's hankerin' for
what's past."

"Yeah, what's got into you?" With his thumb and forefinger, Rawley Moran snapped his Stetson back on his
head and tipped his craggy face to the sunshine that poked
its way between the shadows of the two buildings across
the wide, public green space from where they stood. He
laughed, coughed, and pounded his chest. "You gettin'
homesick in yer old age?"

"Nah!" It was true, or at least Goodshot liked to think
it was, so he sloughed off the comment like it was nothing
more than a fly bite. "Just ponderin', is all. Thinkin' about
how cities is—"

"Big? Excitin'? Filled with pretty women?" Thad
caught the eye of one such lady as she passed and she giggled, the sound as delicate as the clink of champagne
glasses. But then, like so many city ladies, she probably
wasn't used to the sight of two cowboys and an Indian out
on the street together. Thad grinned, and Goodshot couldn't
blame him. He'd caught a whiff of the woman's lavender
scent, too. "A visit to the nearest saloon will change your
mind and get you back to thinkin' about what's really im-

portant in life." The young cowboy looped an arm through Goodshot's.

"Like tonight's show," Rawley added, falling into step beside them.

To Goodshot's way of thinking, they were probably right. The show was what mattered. But then, Colonel Brady's Wild West Stampede of Rough Riders and Ropers was the place he'd called home ever since he left the New Mexico Territory. He'd been young then, restless and bored growing corn and tending sheep the way his ancestors had done for a thousand years. He craved adventure, excitement, and in all the days he'd spent traveling and the nights he'd performed, he'd had no complaints. Hell, to his way of thinking, his life was just about perfect.

He'd been around the world twice, eating at the grandest restaurants, staying in the nicest hotels, being appreciated—a smile touched Goodshot's lips—by some mighty fine women, too. He loved the exhilaration of a show, racing Tandy, his mustang, around the ring to the sound of the crowd's applause. It was satisfying, sure enough, almost as agreeable as the fact that big-boned, booming Colonel Brady paid him a whole two dollars a week more than the Anglos who performed alongside him. Then again, as the longest-performing ridin', ropin', shootin' Indian in the show, Goodshot was its main attraction and he loved the attention.

Oh, how Goodshot loved the attention!

Automatically, he fingered the heavy buckle on his snakeskin belt. It wasn't every day a scrappy kid from the pueblo ended up on the other side of an ocean he couldn't have imagined as a boy, having tea with the queen of England, and not every man did she present with such a token of her admiration.

Sure enough, his life was falling into place, just the way he always dreamed it would.

Still . . .

With a shake of his shoulders, Goodshot twitched away his misgivings. He could not so easily be distracted from his errand.

"Hold on there, boys." He locked his legs and refused to budge another inch. "We come out to the post office, remember. I promised Brady we'd mail these for him." He took a fat pile of letters from his pocket. "I don't want you two gettin' me blind drunk so I'm forgettin' what I was supposed to do."

Like he knew they would, Thad and Rawley laughed and Goodshot pulled away and marched past the man with the flyers.

"Don't ride the streetcar today," the man said, stepping into Goodshot's path. "Sir, show your solidarity with the workers of this town. Please, don't ride the streetcar today."

Goodshot paid him no mind, heading instead into the imposing building with the U.S. flag studded with its forty-five stars hanging outside.

When he came out again, he had a letter in his hand, and a funny feeling in the pit of his stomach that reminded him of the time he rode his first bull.

Thad had just tipped his hat to a woman in a yellow gown, and he settled it back on his head and narrowed his eyes, studying Goodshot. "You look like you swallowed a rattler back end first. What's that you got?" He leaned forward to catch a glimpse of the letter, but since Thad could barely sign his own name, much less read other people's writing, Goodshot didn't pay him any mind.

Rawley was another matter. He could not only write his name, but he had actually been known to read whole, entire books. He cocked his head, curious. "Who'd be writin' to an old In'jun like you anyway? Unless it's some pretty señorita, eh? Maybe remindin' you that you was supposed to be comin' back to her?"

"Or tellin' him he's got a passel of kids he should be supportin'." It wasn't Thad's laugh that snapped Goodshot out of his thoughts, but the way Thad poked him in the ribs with one elbow.

"This here letter, it came from the Taopi pueblo." Goodshot held up the envelope and explained for Thad's benefit. "It's been followin' us from town to town. See here, next to my name, it says 'Saint Louis,' then 'Chicago,' then 'Cincinnati.' All the places we done shows. It's been tryin' to catch up with me. I wonder who even remembers me back in New Mexico."

"Then you'd better go on and open it and find out," Rawley suggested.

Goodshot knew he was right. Just like he knew it was foolish to suddenly feel so jittery about something as fiddling as a letter.

Except he'd never gotten a letter from home before.

Not in the twenty years he'd been away.

His fingers trembling, he tore at the envelope, unfolded

the single sheet of paper inside, and scanned it. With each word he read, his heartbeat raced as fast as Tandy around the ring.

He finished, and somehow found his voice. "I need to get home," Goodshot told his friends. "Now."

"Hold on there, amigo." When Goodshot made a move to cross the street, Rawley put a hand on his shoulder. "You can't just up and say you're leavin' for New Mexico. What about Colonel Brady?"

"Yeah." Thad didn't look indignant or even confused. Nope. If Goodshot had to put a name to the twist of the kid's mouth and the look in his eyes, he'd call it disappointment. For that, at least, he owed Thad an explanation. For being the best sort of friend any man ever had, he owed Rawley, too.

Goodshot had already folded the letter and tucked it in the pocket of his plaid shirt. He touched a hand to his heart. "A long time ago," he said, "before I left the pueblo . . ." He chewed his bottom lip. Though he had no qualms about donning feathers and war paint for the part he played in Colonel Brady's show, he didn't often discuss his past or the customs of his people. It wasn't that he was embarrassed by his upbringing. Or ashamed. It was just that in the life he'd chosen—in the world he'd escaped the pueblo to be part of—a man's past didn't matter so much as his plans for the future. When Goodshot envisioned his future, it included a comfortable house in a place that had running water, a supply of fragrant cigars, and enough female companionship to keep him happy—

and not make him feel obligated in any way. His future? It had never included the pueblo.

At least not until that moment.

He thought about the best way to tell his friends the story and decided on the quickest and simplest.

"There is a legend in my tribe," he said, "about a silver bowl. It's many hundreds of years old, and when the Spanish conquistadors came, my people knew they would steal it because the bowl is not only beautiful, it is valuable. My people hid it, and it stays hidden to this day. It is only brought out and used for ceremonies."

"So you're goin' all the way back to New Mexico on account of a bowl?"

"It is sacred," Goodshot said, ignoring Thad's question. "Magical. And only two people in the tribe are allowed to know where it is kept. The shaman, he is one. And in my generation . . ." He wasn't sure why the words didn't want to leave his lips, only that they felt heavy and odd, like he was talking in his native tongue again, and these two Anglos couldn't possibly understand. "When I was a boy, I was told where the bowl is kept." Like he had that day he'd taken one last look over his shoulder at the home of his ancestors, he shrugged. "My mother's brother, he is shaman of the tribe. It was because of that relationship that I was entrusted with the secret. It was a great honor. One I didn't understand. One I didn't care about. When I left the pueblo, I took the secret with me, and now, my mother's brother . . ." Again, he touched a hand to his shirt and the letter in his pocket. "He was killed in a fall from a cliff. Some months ago. That was when this letter was written and it has been followin' us from town to town ever since. The new shaman says I must get back to the pueblo, to the New Mexico Territory, and share the secret."

"Send him a telegram!" Thad laughed, but Rawley knew better. He and Goodshot had known each other for just about longer than Thad had been alive.

"Give the man room," Rawley said, sticking out an arm to hold Thad back when Thad made a move to corral Goodshot. "If he says he needs to get back to New Mexico, then he needs to get back to New Mexico. Only Chester . . ."

Rawley never used Goodshot's given name, and it was that, more than anything, that pulled Goodshot's attention from the thoughts that raced through his head. He'd need a train ticket, and he'd have to talk to Brady. Yes, of course he had to talk to Brady first thing. He wasn't worried about Tandy; Rawley would take good care of his horse. But there were other things to consider, and many miles between him and the pueblo.

Rawley seemed to be reading his mind. He patted Goodshot's arm. "You be careful, you crazy ol' In'jun. And you make sure when you're done talkin' with that magic man of yours, you meet up with us again. We're headin' to Philadelphia, remember. And on to Boston from there."

"And the women in Boston . . ." Thad gave him a wink. "I hear there's nothin' they like better than Indians."

Goodshot would keep that in mind. As soon as his

mind had a chance to settle down, that is. For now, he was caught in a swirl of thoughts and unfamiliar emotions. He'd never shared the secret of the ceremonial bowl's existence with any other man. Why would he? Once he shook the dust of the New Mexico Territory from his boots, he was certain the shaman would reveal the location of the bowl to some other member of the tribe.

Yet it seemed he had not.

His mother's brother had faith in Goodshot—in his memory, in his devotion to his people, in the fact that someday Goodshot would return. It was a faith the old man took to his death.

A faith Goodshot had never had in himself.

He twitched off the thought just as a streetcar clattered to the corner, and the man in the cap hurried past. "You don't want to ride the streetcar," he said, plucking at Goodshot's sleeve. "Not today."

Goodshot pulled his hand from the man's grasp. He wasn't concerned with the streetcar, with the union, or with management or unfair business practices. That's what he wanted to say.

He never had the chance.

No sooner had the streetcar clacked to a stop than a deafening roar split the afternoon and a burst of black smoke, fire, and searing heat exploded from the tracks.

In that one instant, Goodshot heard the high-pitched screams of the women, and the cries of men. He thought he heard a whirring sound, too, like the air racing past him, as fast as an arrow shot from a bow.

He didn't feel himself get lifted off the ground by the force of the explosion, and he never realized he landed a full twenty feet away until his spine accordioned in on itself and cracked, and his breath whooshed out of his lungs along with an animal cry of pain. The world erupted into stars and sunlight that burst behind his eyes one second, and the next, dissolved completely, lost in the utter blackness that enveloped him.

"Chester? Chester, can you hear me talkin'?"

Goodshot had no idea how long he'd been unconscious; he only knew that Rawley's voice finally penetrated the darkness. Though they felt as if they were weighted with lead, he managed to open his eyes. He saw Thad bent over him on one side, Rawley on the other. There were smudges of soot on both their faces.

"Damn it, Chester, what'd you have to go and get in the way of that explosion fer?" Rawley swigged his nose, but then, there was a lot of smoke in the air.

"I . . ." Goodshot tried to swallow the sand in his throat. "I . . . must get . . . New Mexico."

"Don't worry about that, pard'ner." Rawley again. He stroked Goodshot's shoulder and put something soft under his head. "You got plenty of time to get back to that pueblo of yours."

"But the bowl . . ."

"We'll go. We'll tell the shaman for you." Thad looked to Rawley for verification, and Rawley nodded. "All you need to do is tell us where it is, Goodshot. Where is the bowl hidden?"

He tried to shake his head, but it refused to move. "Can't find . . ." A wave of pain shuddered through Goodshot like the molten lava he'd heard spewed from volcanoes on South Seas islands. He closed his eyes against it and forced himself to think. To concentrate. This was important.

When he opened his eyes again, he saw that the dirt on Thad's face was streaked with tears. He didn't need a kid like Thad to tell him he was dying.

"Can't tell." His voice scraped out of him and he felt blood at the corner of his mouth. "Must show. But if you take my body . . ." Another spasm of pain erupted somewhere between his heart and his stomach at a place on his shirt that felt wet and sticky.

"Sure we will." Rawley grabbed his hand. "Of course we will."

"The shaman . . ." This time, the blackness that enveloped Goodshot didn't feel endless and empty. There was warmth beyond its darkness, and familiar faces he knew he'd see if he could just lose himself long enough in the blackness to look for them.

He would, he promised himself. He would see them all. But not yet. Not until . . .

A cough wracked his body and Goodshot's eyes flew open. "My bones must be taken to the pueblo," he said. "My bones . . . my bones will lead the way."

"Whatever you say, pard'ner." The words were right, but Rawley's expression was all wrong. He didn't understand, not really.

"You must!" Goodshot wrapped Rawley's fingers in a death grip. "If you don't . . . if you leave me . . . if I am not with my people . . ." His gaze wandered to the sky above them. His voice drifted with it, his words gurgling on the blood that filled his mouth. "If you do not . . . I will curse the city where you leave my bones."

W as there really a curse?

There were times I sure believed it. Like when I realized there was some sort of critter nest in the far left corner of Goodshot's mausoleum. Twigs, branches, leaves. No sign of said critter, but I wasn't taking any chances. I skimmed the light of my Rayovac around the interior of the mausoleum and got a move on, before whatever squeaky thing that shared this space with Goodshot's remains decided to make an appearance.

Just like I knew the story of the Wild West star interred here, I knew the lay of the land. Though most mausoleums are essentially big stone boxes that contain niches in the walls where the coffins are kept, this one was a little different. We're talking fancy and, for its time, expensive, too. There was a narrow winding staircase just to the right of the stained glass window opposite the door. A staircase that led down, underground, to where Goodshot's coffin was displayed on a sort of platform.

"Bier."

In my head, I heard Quinn's voice correct me.

I told it to shut up, and myself to get moving, and in another minute, I was at the bottom of the wobbly stairway, my hands filthy from its rusted rails, my heart pounding like the bass line in a rap song, and the light of my flashlight trained on Goodshot Gomez's final resting place. Lucky for me, the coffin was old and made of wood, and wood does not last long in a climate like Cleveland's. It wasn't hard to get the latches undone. As for lifting the lid . . .

I drew in a long breath and held it until my lungs were ready to burst. There couldn't be all that much left of the old guy, I reminded myself. In fact, I was counting on it. Otherwise, I would have brought a bigger tote bag. Even so . . .

I braced myself, wondering what I'd find staring back at me, and threw open the lid of the coffin.

Maybe I was a little too enthusiastic.

The old bier creaked and tilted and I watched in horror as the coffin began a slow slide. I darted forward and caught hold of it. A slick and very quick move. Maybe a little too quick and slick.

I dropped my flashlight, stepped on it, and my ankle buckled. My feet slid out from under me, and before I could say *Colonel Brady's Wild West Stampede of Rough Riders and Ropers,* I was falling through the darkness, not sure which direction was up and which was down. I only knew that by the time I landed on my butt—hard—on the dirt floor, the coffin had already tipped and was headed straight for me.

I think I screamed. I know I threw my arms over my head to protect myself.

Good thing, because that coffin came down right on top of me. The wood was old and mushy. It splintered into a million pieces.

Curse? Yeah, I think it's safe to say that, at that particular moment, the curse was at work. Just like it had been a week earlier when this whole crazy plan to steal Goodshot Gomez began.

"I swear, this team is cursed!" Quinn Harrison had been up on his feet, cheering along with the rest of the baseball crowd, and now he plunked down in the hard-backed stadium seat, reached for the paper cup he'd left on the cement floor between us, and took a long swallow of beer.

When whatever had just happened happened, I'd been busy looking over the manicure I'd given myself that afternoon so, honestly, I couldn't say if the above-mentioned whatever was good or bad. My first clue came when I saw the deep vee creased between Quinn's eyes. He was pissed.

About something that happened.

Or didn't happen.

"Can you believe it?" The inning was over, and Quinn had time to reflect on the . . . whatever. He shook his head and his inky hair glinted in the last of the evening sun that streaked over the scoreboard on the other side of the stadium. The sunlight added shadows to a face that was as gorgeous as ever but pinched by the pain he lived with every day, and the strain of a brutal five-times-a-week rehab schedule he insisted on keeping because he was jonesing to get back on the job.

"That ball had home run written all over it, and their center fielder never should have been able to jump like that and catch it. Damn!" He slapped a hand against the leg of his jeans. "The Cleveland Indians are cursed."

"You got that right, brother!" The man sitting behind us leaned forward and put a hand on Quinn's shoulder. Not a good move. Even I knew that. A cop is a cop is a cop. Even a cop who isn't working at the moment because he got shot a couple months earlier and is still out on disability leave. Always suspicious—even when there was nothing to be suspicious of—Quinn shrugged out from under the man's hand, spun in his seat, and gave the guy a quick once-over.

Apparently, the Cleveland Indians ball cap, red sweatshirt with the big blue *I* on it, and bag of peanuts in his hand indicated the man seated behind us was one of the good guys. Quinn didn't so much smile at him as he rumbled—in a friendly sort of way that made it clear they were in this together. "It happens every year." Quinn's face was somber when he and the man exchanged knowing looks. "Spring training comes and the team looks great. Then the season starts and they play like—"

"Yeah, like I said." The man's sigh rose into the clear blue sky over our heads, an unheard prayer. "They're cursed."

The next inning was about to start and the players came onto the field. Grumbling, Quinn turned back to the game. "I thought this summer was going to be different."

This, I understood.

I thought this summer was going to be different, too.

It was my turn to sigh. Not that I was about to let Quinn hear the frustration that bubbled in me like the fizz in the Diet Pepsi I was drinking. Pepper Martin does not keep her opinions—or her feelings—to herself. Unless those opinions and feelings reveal her weaknesses.

And when it came to Quinn and what had happened a couple months before . . .

Okay, I admit it, I was feeling . . . well, maybe *weak* wasn't the right word. Maybe *helpless* was more like it. Or *frustrated*. Or *sick and tired of beating around the bush and always ending up back where we started*.

Yeah, that was it.

Sick and tired of beating around the bush and always ending up back where we started, I turned in my seat just enough to make it clear to Quinn that I wasn't as interested in watching our pitiful team drag its way through to another loss as I was in talking.

To him.

Now.

I put a hand on the arm of his navy windbreaker. Sure, it was summer. But this was Cleveland, and there's an old joke in these parts about how if you don't like the weather, all you have to do is wait around for a minute. True to form, it had been in the eighties earlier in the day and who could blame me for being thrilled about showing off the

21

scoop-neck, ruffle-front, multicolored sundress I'd gotten for a steal at Filene's Basement.

Then, just an hour before Quinn picked me up for the game, a front blew through and a wind off the lake brought cool Canadian air streaming our way.

"It's not about warmth," I'd told Quinn when he warned me I'd be more comfortable at the stadium near the lake-front in jeans and a sweatshirt. "It's about fashion."

I was fashionable, all right.

As long as nobody noticed the goose bumps that marched up my arms.

But have no fear, even the shiver that raced over my nearly bare shoulders wasn't enough to distract me. I leaned in close so Quinn couldn't fail to catch the scent of my Happy perfume. "We need to talk," I said.

He slid me a look. For about a second and a half. That was when he went back to watching the game. "About . . . ?"

It was my turn to grumble. "You know what it's about. About how you got shot by that murder suspect."

"He's behind bars where he belongs and I'm fine." That was that. Or at least that's the message he sent since Quinn never bothered to take his eyes off the field.

But I am a redhead, remember, and not so easily put off.

I tightened my hold on his jacket. "That's not what I'm talking about and you know it. You know it, because I've tried to talk to you about this like . . ." I really didn't have to stop to consider how many times I'd brought up the subject because I figured, by now, we were talking dozens. At least. I paused, anyway, the better to draw out the drama while the pitcher threw, the batter didn't swing, and the umpire called a ball, a decision the Indians fans around us disputed loud and long.

"I've tried to talk to you about this since it happened," I reminded Quinn even though I shouldn't have had to. "I'm not talking about how you got shot. I'm talking about how when you got shot, you died. For just a couple minutes, anyway. I'm talking about how I was home that night, and how you showed up in my living room and told me what happened to you. I'm talking about those few minutes, Quinn. You know, when you were a ghost."

"Did you see that?" Quinn was out of his seat faster than should have been possible for a guy who'd been mortally wounded just a few short months before. His groan was echoed by those of the other fans seated around us. He dropped back into his seat. "An error. The guy hit the ball and it went right through the third baseman's glove. A frickin' error."

"You mean *another* error." The fan in the row behind us threw his scorecard on the ground in frustration. "That's the second one this game and the second time the White Sox have scored thanks to the fact that our guys can't catch a ball."

"Or a break," Quinn growled.

The guy behind us agreed. "Hell, that's no surprise. We haven't won a World Series since 1948. And it's all because of that damned curse."

Not my problem, though from the way he nodded in agreement, Quinn apparently thought it was his. "That Indian," he said, and since he glanced at me when he said this, I figured he wasn't talking about one of the players on the field, "the one who put the curse on Cleveland. He's buried in your cemetery, isn't he?"

This time, I had no reservations about showing my ticked-off-ness. Quinn should have known better than to bring up a subject that was still plenty sore. I narrowed my eyes and shot him a look, my teeth clenched.

"It's not my cemetery anymore."

"Of course. I know that." This was his way of apologizing, and it wasn't good enough. "I keep forgetting you got laid off."

"Dumped, you mean." I crossed my arms over my chest. It was the perfect way to display my displeasure, and besides, it helped keep me a tad warmer. "When you get laid off, there's some expectation of getting called back to work. Garden View Cemetery—"

"Don't take is so personally. You know what Ella says—"

"That the cemetery is cutting costs. Sure." I knew this like I knew my own name, because in the two months I'd been out of work, I'd heard Ella, my former boss, tell me all about it with tears in her voice every time she called me. Which was every day.

Sure, I understood the party line. Times were tough. Budgets were tight. Costs had to be kept in line, and around Garden View, that meant getting rid of staff.

Me.

That didn't make the sting of losing my job any less painful. Not that I'm a geek like Ella and actually like working in a cemetery. But there is the whole paycheck thing. Getting by on my unemployment check and the monthly payment I still got from helping out a ghost's granddaughter a couple years back wasn't easy. It was putting a cramp on my lifestyle, not to mention my ability to stay fashion-forward.

"Besides, Goodshot Gomez isn't buried at Garden View, he's interred."

Quinn finished watching the next play before he asked, "Who?"

"The Indian." I sounded as exasperated as all the baseball fans around me. For all different reasons. "You're the one who brought it up."

"The curse. The Indian." Quinn nodded. "The one in your cemetery. The legend says that with his dying breath, he said he had to be taken back to New Mexico, and if he was buried anywhere else, that place would be cursed."

"Only he's not . . ." I controlled a screech, but just barely, and used my best tour-guide voice. I congratulated myself—two months and I could still fake my way through sounding like I knew what I was talking about. "Technically, Goodshot Gomez isn't buried. His casket is kept in a mausoleum. That means his body isn't in the ground. It's inside this fancy-dancy little marble building. He was in town as part of some Wild West show, you know. And he died here. And his friends left money at Garden View so the cemetery would keep his body until they came back for him and took him to New Mexico." Even when I had a tour group in front of me, this was always an *Ew!* moment for me, and I shivered now like I always did back at the cemetery when I told the story. "Only they never returned for him. Nobody knows why. And there was this mausoleum that somebody had built and never finished paying for so the cemetery used Goodshot's money and put him in there. His casket is kept in the mausoleum on a sort of platform."

"I think it's called a bier."

"How would you know that?"

A smile tugged one corner of Quinn's mouth. "I hang out with a cemetery tour guide."

"A former cemetery tour guide."

He patted my knee. "Former cemetery tour guide."

"Who talks to the dead."

It wasn't exactly subtle, but I was long past toeing the line. For my sake as well as for Quinn's. I am not, after all, stupid. Deep in my heart, I know that people have to accept me for who I am without external proof. I wish Quinn would have just believed me back when I finally admitted that I keep getting mixed up in his cases because I've got this goofy Gift and it's nonreturnable and the ghosts I deal with tell me they'll haunt me for the rest of my life if I don't help them. But that wasn't how it worked, and then Quinn finally did have . . . well, I guess it wasn't living proof . . . but it was proof. That's for sure. He did finally have proof that I was telling the truth, and it was time for him to man up and admit it.

"We've got to talk about it, Quinn," I said. "When I told you I talk to the dead and solve their mysteries, you walked out on me, remember?" I guess he did because his green eyes flashed. "But then you died. And you were a ghost. At least for a little while. And you came to me and you told me where the cops could find the guy who shot you. I couldn't make up that kind of information and get it right, could I? That proves the experience was real. That I really do talk to the dead. We need to talk about this, Quinn, partly because I need to hear from you that you don't think I'm a nutcase, but mostly because you can't keep something like this bottled up inside you. You were dead!"

"As dead as this team, and it's only June!" I guess while I was busy passionately defending my position, some more bad stuff happened out on the field because Quinn slumped back in his seat and the people around us groaned, got to their feet, and headed for the exits. "Another loss for the record books," he said.

And another go-nowhere, solve-nothing, can't-get-passed-it conversation between me and the guy I once thought was the man of my dreams.

There was no use prolonging the evening; I got to my feet, too, and headed up the steps to the main concourse of the stadium with Quinn right behind me. At the top of the steps, a brisk breeze whipped my curly hair and a new batch of goose bumps erupted up my arms and across my shoulders.

Quinn's not a cop for nothing. He's pretty good when it comes to noticing things. "Here." He already had his windbreaker off and he draped it over my shoulders. "I'm tired of watching you shiver, so don't give me any bull about who might see you looking like a dork in my jacket."

I was too chilly to argue.

I slipped my arms into the jacket, snapped it shut, and

warmth enveloped me along with the scent of Quinn's expensive aftershave. My mood brightened. At least for as long as it took us to get out onto the street. Right outside the stadium, there was a knot of people around a man with a microphone and a woman dressed in a buckskin dress and a feathered headdress.

"I could put a stop to the curse," the woman said. Her dark hair was done up in braids that hung over her shoulders, and she had a dozen strands of beads around her neck that reminded me of the jewelry Ella liked to wear. She was holding a smoldering bunch of smelly herbs and she raised her arm and waved the smoke toward the stadium. "I come here every game and do my best to try and clear the bad vibrations around the team, but if the cemetery where Goodshot is buried would just allow me to perform a corn ceremony at his grave, I know I could lift the curse. The city of Cleveland needs my help. The Cleveland Indians need my help. I'm pleading to the people in charge of the cemetery. If you'd just let me in to do the ceremony, I can turn this city around!"

"Let's see what this disappointed Indians fan thinks." The reporter was in front of me and his microphone was in my face so fast, I never had a chance to duck out of the way. Too bad. At least then I could have shrugged out of Quinn's jacket so I didn't look like a complete fashion moron on the eleven-o'clock news.

As if things could get any worse, the reporter's eyes lit the moment he looked me over, and I knew what it meant. He recognized me from that wacky PBS cemetery renovation show I'd been involved in the year before. Sure, it was nice to know I was still something of a cult celebrity. Not so nice when I realized I was about to be put on the spot.

Wearing a man's blue windbreaker.

"Talk about luck! This is Pepper Martin." The reporter's smile was as bright as the lights of the TV camera. "She works at Garden View Cemetery, where Goodshot is buried. Tell us, Pepper, what's the cemetery going to do? Do you think Morning Dove here . . ." He glanced toward the Native American who I'd bet any money wasn't a real Native American at all. "Do you think she can lift the curse? Can you help us out, convince the people at the cemetery that we need her? You could be a hometown hero, Pepper."

Did that pause mean I was supposed to say something?

I scrambled, thinking about how I could get out of this tight spot by telling the world how I was low man on the totem pole (no Indian puns intended) and how I'd been unceremoniously tossed out of my cemetery job on my blue windbreaker–covered butt in the name of profits. I would have done it, too, except that I knew the reporter was from the station Ella watched every night. And I wouldn't embarrass her for all the world.

"I can't speak for the cemetery administrator," I said, pulling out that tour-guide voice again and giving the reporter a wide smile. Maybe if people concentrated on the seven thousand dollars of teeth straightening in my mouth, they wouldn't notice the fashion faux pas that was my attire. "And I certainly can't speak for Ella Silverman, the cemetery's community relations manager, either. But I would like to remind your viewers that there's no way to prove that there really is a curse."

"A curse? Sure there's a curse. And somebody needs to do something about it."

Saved by the guy behind me who piped right up, his voice so passionate, the reporter had no choice but to swing his way. Glad to be off the hook, I stepped back to Quinn's side to watch.

The guy was in his twenties, short, round, and wearing an Indians T-shirt and flannel pants with Chief Wahoo, the team's mascot, all over them. "That curse is what's keeping us from winning," he said, his face as red as his shirt.

"No way we should have lost tonight," the tall, thin kid next to him said. "We had our best pitcher on the mound. Winning should have been a sure bet."

"There's no such thing as a sure bet," another guy with them grumbled. "Not when it comes to this team."

The reporter signaled to his cameraman to stop filming. "That's great," he said to everyone, and no one in particular. "Thank you all. And Morning Dove"—he turned to her—"when Garden View lets you in, you'll let us know, won't you? Hey, talk to Pepper here. I bet she can arrange . . ." By the time he got that far, I was already marching down the street for all I was worth.

It wasn't until Quinn and I stopped at the next corner to wait for the light that I realized the guys who'd been on camera with us were right in front of us. And that I knew one of them.

"Brian?" I turned for a better look. The last time I'd seen him, Brian was decked out in one of those vests fishermen wear, the kind with about a hundred little pockets all over them. But then, he'd needed the flashlights, batteries, notebooks, and such he'd brought along because we were on a ghost hunt. I was trying to solve the forty-year-old murder of a rock star, and Brian and his merry little band of buttinsky ghost hunters had been invited along by Dan Callahan, a paranormal investigator friend/boyfriend/almost lover of mine. "Brian, it's me, Pepper. We met—"

"Of course. I thought you looked familiar." Brian stuck out his hand, I introduced him to Quinn, and he told us the guys who'd been on camera with him were John, the round guy in the flannel pants, and Gregory, taller, thinner, and decked out in just as much Indians gear. There was a fourth man in the group, too, a quiet guy by the name of Arnie. Done with the introductions, Brian got right to the meat of the discussion.

"Maybe you can do something, Pepper. You know, about the curse. You work at that cemetery and . . ."

I might not want to admit my unemployment on the nightly news, but I knew I had to come clean with these guys. It was that, or they'd bug me forever about getting them into Goodshot's mausoleum.

I told them the bad news—no job, no influence, no corn ceremony—and watched their expressions fall.

"We're doomed." Arnie shook his head. "If we can't lift this curse, the team is never going to get any better."

Quinn sized them all up in his usual eagle-eyed way. "You're really serious fans."

"You got that right." John stuck out his left arm, backside up. His wrist was tattooed in red and blue. THE TRIBE WILL RISE AGAIN, it said in thick, block letters right above 1948.

"We've all got them," Brian said, and he and Gregory and Arnie showed off their matching tattoos. "We figured it was the least we could do to show our solidarity with the team."

"Yeah, the team." John's shoulders drooped.

The light changed. We crossed the street and said good-bye to the guys outside the bar where they went to drown their baseball-induced sorrows. Quinn drove me home, relatively silent. At least about what mattered.

He talked about the game. And about Brian and the guys and how refreshing it was to still find fans who were committed to the team. He talked about going to rehab the next day and hinted that he could leave from my apartment—if I'd let him stay the night.

Two could play the same game, and besides, I wasn't ready to hop back into bed with the man who'd smashed my heart into a million pieces with his skepticism. We had a long way to go, Quinn and I, before we were back to where we'd once been.

When we pulled up to my apartment building, I gave him one last chance to make a move. No, not that kind of move. A move in the right direction. "If you want to come in and talk about what happened to you outside that ware-house a couple months ago . . ."

My offer dangled in the air between us for a few seconds. "I think you're right," Quinn said and my spirits rose. He was finally going to open up about what it was like to be dead and how lousy he felt to have ever doubted me. "It's getting late and I'd better get home." He gave me a quick peck on the cheek. "I'll call you."

"Sure." My smile was brittle, but honestly, I got out of the car and he drove away so fast, I doubt Quinn noticed.

Grumbling, I unlocked the door and went into the building. What I needed was a little therapy in the way of Ben and Jerry's Crème Brûlée.

That, and something that would distract me from the sad realities of unemployment, baseball, curses, and a TV appearance that would do nothing for my reputation—not to mention my image.

3

Exactly one week to the day later, I got a kick-in-the-pants reminder about that ol' *be-careful-what-you-wish-for* saying.

I asked for a distraction?

Sure, the Universe responded. Here's a doozy.

As these things so often do, it started out simply enough, with me heading down to the lobby of my apartment building that afternoon to pick up my mail. My unemployment check was there, and for that, I was grateful. I set it on my dining room table, where I could admire it, and promised myself a trip to the bank first thing the next day. A couple other things arrived along with the check, including a box wrapped in brown paper, a couple advertising flyers, a card from my mom in Florida, and . . .

A postcard fluttered out of the pile and hit the floor and

I bent to pick it up and froze, pikestaffed by the photograph that was looking up at me.

"Dan!" I scrambled for the postcard and the photo of Dan Callahan, brainiac scientist, paranormal investigator, husband of the late Madeline who, as it turned out, was a ghost who stole my body for a while and used it to get her jollies with him when those jollies should have been mine.

Shaggy-haired, cute-as-a-button Dan smiled back at me.

Let's face it, I'm not usually unhinged by cute. After all, I'm used to Quinn, who's got the whole gorgeous thing down pat, is as hot as freshly poured Boule espresso, and packs as much of a punch (both literally and figuratively). Normally, just looking at Dan wouldn't have made my knees weak and my hands shake. Chalk it up to the stress of the last few months. And to surprise, of course. The last I'd heard from Dan, he was heading to England to delve into some woo-woo mystery or another and drown his sorrows about finding out his late wife was really a scumbag murderer.

Knees shaking and hands trembling, I dropped down on the couch and flipped over the card, fully expecting some foreign postmark. It looked like a lot had happened since that winter in Chicago a couple years earlier; the card came from New Mexico.

"Going to be in Cleveland in a few weeks." Out loud, I read the message written in his loose, scrawling handwriting, and the prospect of seeing Dan again shivered in my words. " 'I've got some exciting news to share. Let's plan to get together as soon as I arrive.' "

By the time I turned the card over again, I was smiling as broadly as Dan was in the photo. New Mexico? Maybe. I took a closer look at the photo and the sweeping panorama of mountains behind Dan, and all I could tell was that it had been taken in a place with a lot of rocks and dust. Dan, dressed in jeans and a T-shirt with a smudge of dirt across the front of it, was standing in front of some ruiny-looking thing, half building, half cave, that was totally nasty looking.

His right hand was raised in a friendly greeting, and on his wrist, he was wearing a watch with a wide silver band.

It was clearly Native American and not my style, but that didn't mean I wasn't intrigued as I always am by things that are pretty and valuable. I squinted for a better look at the band engraved with mysterious-looking symbols and studded with teardrop-shaped bits of turquoise.

Southwestern, certainly. New Mexico.

But coming to Cleveland.

Soon.

As distractions went, this was a pretty good one, and I thanked the Universe appropriately even as I set the postcard against the lamp on the table next to the couch, the better to see Dan and consider what his coming to town might mean. To me. To my future. To my Gift.

It's not like we're a couple or anything. I need to make that perfectly clear.

Pepper Martin and Dan Callahan had never been anybody's idea of a pair.

Not officially, anyway.

There was a time, and a place, and one brief shining

moment when I think that was actually meant to be, in spite of the fact that when we first met, all Dan wanted was the chance to study my brain and figure out how my Gift worked. But then Madeline swooped in and took over my body, and the golden opportunity for a Pepper and Dan hookup passed us by.

By that time, he'd figured out that it was actually true—that I could communicate with the dead and that I had been in regular contact with Madeline—and Dan was thrilled. It proved a theory he'd always believed: that there is life after death and that those on This Side and those on the Other are connected.

But things are never that simple. Not when it comes to living with the dead. Once the whole ugly truth came out about what a liar Madeline really was, and how she'd played Dan for a sucker, and how I almost got poofed into permanent oblivion thanks to her, the way he handled things said a lot about Dan.

He didn't try to pick my brain. Or use me as some sort of psychic guinea pig. In fact, he didn't ask any questions or try to delve into the mystery of my Gift at all.

He left town.

To give me some space, he said.

And himself some time to recover from the trauma of it all.

Not bad, huh? I mean, in a knight-in-shining-armor sort of way.

See, Dan is one of the good guys. Even if he does have lousy taste in wives. And soon—I checked the postmark again; the card had been mailed four days earlier—soon, I'd have a chance to see him again.

Jazzed at the prospect, I opened and read Mom's card (there was a kitten on it, designed to cheer me up), and finished with that, I turned my attention to the brown-paper-wrapped box.

I hadn't ordered anything online, so I wasn't waiting for a delivery, and since there was no return address on the box, I used my detective skills to narrow the field as to where the package might have come from. The postmark was smudged and unreadable. I shook the box and was rewarded by a dull thud. Something inside, and not something big. But then, the box was only the size of those rectangular ones that new checks come in.

I am not a big believer in premonitions and weird stuff like that. Sure, I talk to ghosts, but that has more to do with the bad luck of the draw than it does with ESP. Still, a shiver like the touch of a dead hand crawled up my back.

"Dumb," I told myself, and ripped the brown paper off the box.

Three cheers for me in the deduction department; it was a box from old checks. I lifted the lid. There was a folded piece of paper inside.

Another chill on the back of my neck.

Another reminder to myself that if I could deal with the dead but not departed, I could certainly handle a letter.

I unfolded the paper and saw the blocks of words, cut out of a newspaper and glued to the page:

If U Want 2 C Dan Callahan alive, follow instructions exactly

Bring Chester Goodshot Gomez (the name was written with a Sharpie, but then, I don't suppose they're common words in a newspaper) *2 Tres Piedras, New Mexico. Instructions @ gas station*

U have 7 days

It was a joke.

It had to be.

Only I wasn't laughing.

Especially when I realized there was something under the tissue paper wadded at the bottom of the box. I plucked it out, and found myself staring at a watch with a silver band.

Yeah, that one. A band engraved with mysterious-looking symbols and studded with teardrop-shaped bits of turquoise.

The moment I walked into her office, Ella's face lit up with a grin as bright as the sparkly yellow beads she was wearing with her orange dress. She was so obviously pleased to see me, I almost felt guilty for being there.

Almost.

I braced myself for what I knew what was coming, and managed one deep breath before she leaped from her chair and wrapped me in a hug that made the air whoosh out of my lungs. When she stepped back to look up and take a gander at me, there were tears in Ella's eyes.

"It's so good to see you," she crooned and sniffed. "I was afraid we'd never see you here at Garden View again, that you'd never want to come back. I mean, after the way we treated you."

"*You* didn't treat me any way. You were only doing your job. The cemetery had to cut staff. No hard feelings."

Lie No. 1.

I was still plenty pissed at Garden View in general and Jim, the cemetery administrator, in particular, not so much because he eliminated my job but because, before he did, he actually had me doing things like plucking staples out of old memos to save paper and helping to pick up garbage on the grounds of the cemetery.

I mean, really. If you're going to fire somebody anyway, it seems more than cruel and unusual to make that same somebody go through all that first.

I bit my tongue and kept my lips clamped shut. The last thing I was there to do was stir up trouble. Or upset Ella.

Pasting on a smile, I untangled myself from her maternal hug and strolled over to her desk. Ella's office at the cemetery was bigger than the one I used to occupy down the hall, but just barely. Her desk near the window was always picture-perfect, in a Martha Stewart sort of way. Cute china teacup. Cute mouse pad that featured a cute photo of a cute puppy. Cute pictures of her three teenaged girls.

Except today, Ella's office reminded me a lot of my old office.

And not in a good way.

"Don't pay any attention to the mess!" Ella raced over

to the guest chairs, unpiled a couple mile-high stacks of papers from them, and plopped them down atop the about-to-topple pile already on her desk. "Come on, sit down. Make yourself comfortable. I'm so happy to see you here again." She could have fooled me since there were tears streaming down her cheeks. "This is where you belong, Pepper." When I didn't move fast enough, she patted the seat of the empty chair. "Tell me what's been happening with you and why you stopped in."

I sat as instructed, mostly because I knew if I didn't, she'd bug me forever. In her own, fluffy Jewish-mother sort of way, Ella is every bit as persistent as the ghosts who promise to haunt me if I don't help them.

"I was just driving by," I said, and yes, it was Lie No. 2, but it's not like a person can just march into another person's office, blurt out one huge lie, and get away with it. Lies are delicate creatures, and they need a framework if they're going to stand. As the world's only private detective to the dead, I'd long ago come to accept lying as a fact of my life. Building up to the big lie . . . that was a skill. One I was getting very good at. "I thought I'd stop in and see how you were doing."

"Me?" Ella dug through her purse and pulled out a lace-edged handkerchief. She touched it to her already-red nose. "I should be asking you that, Pepper. How are you? Any luck finding another job?"

She was so darned concerned, I didn't have the heart to tell her I hadn't exactly gotten up the energy to send out my résumé yet. There was the whole thing with Quinn I'd been dealing with, and the whole bit about how, aside from the lack of money, I wouldn't mind taking the summer off. Now there was Dan to worry about, too.

I tucked the thought away so my expression didn't betray me.

"Something will turn up," I said, forcing my shrug to look unconcerned. "It always does."

"You're so brave." She pulled in a breath that escaped her on the end of a sigh. "And so considerate, asking about me. I'm . . ." Ella glanced at the devastation that had once been her pristine office. "What with doing your job and mine, filling in for Jim when he's busy, picking up some of the slack because Jennine out at the front desk has had her hours cut, and helping out with the groundskeeping work so we don't have to pay the landscaping crews overtime . . . I'm afraid I'm getting a little behind and feeling a bit overwhelmed." Her lower lip wobbled, and Ella fanned one hand in front of her face. But then, I could sympathize—the office was stifling.

I glanced at her window, open maybe an inch and a half.

Ella followed my gaze and chirped in the way she always does when something's bugging her and she won't admit it. "Don't get the wrong idea. The heat in here isn't a problem. Really. I'm comfortable. I was actually cold this morning."

I pinned her with a look. "It's got to be at least ninety degrees in here, and let me guess, Jim won't let anyone turn on the AC because he doesn't want to pay for the electricity. And he won't let you open your windows more than that because . . ."

"Dirt." Ella's shoulders drooped. "If we open the windows, who knows what will blow in from the outside, and then the office will get dirtier and we'll have to pay the cleaning crews more and . . . well, enough of that nonsense!" Ella popped out of her chair. There were a couple plastic grocery bags on the floor near where I was sitting and she scooted around to the other side of the desk to get at them.

"This is so lucky, you showing up here. I was going to call you this afternoon and ask if I could stop by your apartment on the way home this evening. To chat. Like old times. I thought maybe I could convince you to stop by for dinner one of these days. You know, I have been calling and inviting you and I'm sure you're busy. Yes, of course, you're busy, a young woman like you always has so many things to do. I understand. Of course, I understand."

I carefully prepared Lie No. 3. "I'm sorry I haven't been as good as I should be about returning your calls. There's something wrong with my cell phone. I get some of your messages, really, and I keep meaning to call, but—"

She held up one hand to stop me. "No apologies necessary. You're a young woman with a busy life, and I'm sure you're spending time with that nice policeman boyfriend of yours."

Ella was on a roll, so I didn't bother to correct her. *Nice* had never been one of Quinn's strong points. Then again, I don't think *boyfriend* applied, either. A boyfriend was a man who wanted to share a woman's life and her dreams and even her goofy Gift if she happened to have one. In

44

all the time I'd known him, the only thing Quinn wanted to share was my bed.

"Well, who can blame you?" This time when Ella fanned her face, I don't think it had anything to do with the temperature in the office. "What with him being so dreamy and all. And how he almost died a couple months ago! I can see you'd want to spend a lot of time with him. And with looking for a job, of course. I'm sure you're taking hours and hours every day to pound the pavement and look for work. Oh, Pepper . . ." She bit her lower lip. "I wish I could do something to help you. Well . . . well . . ." Ella pulled in a bracing breath. "I have done something. Like I said, I was going to call you and stop by." Her shoulders back and both her chins lifted high, Ella held out one of the blue plastic grocery bags to me. "I know it's hard for you living on unemployment so I've gone through my closets. You know, to find some things for you to add to your wardrobe."

It was the wrong time to say, "*Over my dead body*," so I forced a smile, plucked the bag out of her hands, and held it close to my chest. If I didn't look . . . if I never opened it . . . I wouldn't feel obligated. Or guilty. Or horrified.

Then I could just stop at Goodwill on my way home and—

"It's not much, I know, but it's the least I can do for you, Pepper. When I think about you sitting at home with no job and us, here at the cemetery, and how we could use your talents . . . well, it just makes me crazy. That's why . . . well, I know you're going to love these things."

As fast as I'd taken it from her, Ella grabbed the bag back from me and dug around inside it. She came out holding a white peasant blouse embroidered with bright flowers at the neckline and cuffs.

White peasant blouse.

In Ella's size.

"Perfect for summer," she crooned. "And here's a nice little sundress that will look adorable on you. I mean, once you nip in the waist just a tad." Ella held up said object for me to admire. It was turquoise and three of me would fit into it. "Some night when that nice policeman wants to take you out and you're looking to impress him—"

I jumped out of my chair, snatched the sundress out of her hands, and folded it—carefully but quickly. Before anyone could see. And think that I might actually . . .

The thought turned my brain to mush and froze my insides. Before I could succumb, I blurted out, "That's so nice of you. But you really shouldn't—"

"I know. But I can't help myself. You're just like one of my girls, Pepper, and with all you did for Ariel . . ." Her expression softened into that squishy motherly smile she always has when she thinks about her youngest daughter and how the kid used to be trouble with a capital *T* and is now, thanks to me, an annoying overachiever whose sole goal in life is to become a librarian and be as geeky as her mother. "That's why I brought along another bag, too."

I was almost afraid to look, but at least while I did, I could set down the bag of clothes in the corner, where I could then pretend I'd forgotten it.

The second blue grocery bag contained five boxed macaroni and cheese mixes, two jars of spaghetti sauce, a couple boxes of pasta, and one box of hot chocolate mix. Yes, it was summer and hotter than hell. To Ella, nothin' says lovin' like hot chocolate.

It was ridiculous, but I couldn't help myself; my throat closed around a lump of emotion. "I couldn't," I said, handing the bag back to her and hoping she didn't hear the catch in my voice. "You and the girls need—"

"Not as much as you do." That was that, and to prove it, Ella crossed her arms over her chest. "The least I can do is help out. After all, I was the one who—"

Fortunately, the phone on Ella's desk rang so I was spared listening to how guilty she still felt about having to let me go.

I glanced at the clock on Ella's wall and thanked whatever guardian angel looked out for Gifted PIs. Right on time!

"What's that?" Ella spoke into the phone. "Can't he come here to my office? Oh. Sure. Of course. I'll be right there." She hung up and headed for the door. "Someone out in the lobby needs to see me," she said. "And whoever it is, he won't give a name or come down here. Has to see me out there. I'll be right back."

And by the time she was, I hoped I'd be done doing what I had to do.

What I was feeling more and more guilty about doing with every jar of spaghetti sauce and every (gulp) turquoise sundress.

47

What I had to do, anyway.

I told myself not to forget it, and before Ella's door closed behind her, I got to work. Somewhere in the office, I knew Ella kept the keys to the mausoleums that were no longer in family hands.

Yeah, like Goodshot Gomez's.

The trick, of course, was to find them.

I raced around to the far side of her desk and whipped open drawer after drawer.

Granola bars, bottled water, hand cream, paper clips, computer paper, appointment book.

"Keys," I grumbled to myself. "I need the keys."

When the desk yielded nothing, I zipped back to the other side of the office and tried the file cabinets. If I were Ella . . .

I drummed my fingers against the metal cabinet.

"If I were Ella," I said to myself, "I'd file keys under . . ."

I pulled open the drawer marked *H–L* and practically whooped. Right behind the divider with the *K* on it was a zippered pouch and inside was a key ring with a dozen or so keys on it, the kind that are old and clunky and heavy, complete with curlicues on the handles.

By the time Ella came bustling back into the room— her cheeks pink and her breaths coming in short, quick puffs—those keys were safely inside my purse and I was lounging in one of her guest chairs like I didn't have a concern in the world.

Guilt?

I didn't have the time.

Dan's life was hanging in the balance and Goodshot Gomez hadn't needed his bones for like a hundred years.

Tell that to my pounding heart and shaking hands.

"Well, that was odd." Thinking it over, Ella shook her head. "That was Reggie. You know, the Reggie you worked with on that cemetery restoration. He said he was driving by, and he stopped in to say hello. Well . . ." Ella's eyes sparkled, but that was no surprise. In spite of the fact that she's like twenty years older than him, Ella has had the hots for Reggie since the first day she saw him—sans shirt—at that oldy-moldy cemetery. It was a classic case of Mrs. Straight-and-Narrow being drawn like a moth to the flame of the ultimate Bad Boy.

And Reggie was one bad boy.

"I told him you were here," Ella said, "but he said he had to run."

"Reggie's a busy man." Which was why I was grateful he'd taken the time to help me out. "Most drug dealers are. Busy, I mean. Not men. I mean, maybe some of them are men, but—"

"Pepper, what on earth is wrong with you?" Ella put a hand on my arm. "You're as jumpy as a June bug."

I was, and I had to get away from Ella's mothering or I'd risk everything and blurt out the truth.

I gathered up my purse and headed for the door.

"Wait!" Her command stopped me cold just as I was about to make my escape. I cradled my purse in my arms and hoped she didn't hear the keys clinking inside. Ella bustled toward me. "You forgot the food." She handed me one bag. "And your new clothes."

I thanked her and got out of there as quickly as I could, and I hoped she didn't see the guilt written all over my face. Stealing from Ella made me feel terrible.

Of course, I'd feel even worse if I didn't do everything I could and Dan ended up dead.

4

By the time my head settled and I groped through the bits and pieces of Goodshot's shattered coffin to grab my flashlight, I was covered with cobwebs, dirt, and—

There was something on my lap, and I held my breath and shined my light that way.

Hand.

Skeleton hand.

My heart stopped. Which wasn't such a bad thing because when it banged to a start again, I choked on the bile that clogged my throat. If I wasn't afraid someone might hear, I would have let out a shriek full blast. The way it was, I stifled it, and my pitiful cry wobbled back at me from the cold stone walls.

My teeth gritted and my insides shimmying like my mother's legendary (and not for good reasons) lime-and-marshmallow Jell-O salad, I did my best to ignore the ick factor and used two fingers to pluck the hand off my lap. As quickly as I could, I shoved it in the pocket of the blue windbreaker, and before I could talk myself out of it, I skimmed my light around the underground chamber to see where the rest of Goodshot had landed.

His ribs were against the wall. What looked like leg bones were near my feet. His skull stared back at me from where it had come to rest near my right hand. In the trembling light of the Rayovac, those empty eye sockets were bottomless.

Creepy. Majorly. I was used to the dead, sure, but when I encountered them, they looked the way they had in life. Skin. Clothes. Hair. Just like the living, only they weren't, of course. And not a bone in sight.

Of course, if I was going to keep Dan alive, I couldn't let a few old bones stop me.

Using the bier as a prop, I got to my feet and reminded myself that the next time I burgled a body, I needed to bring along latex gloves. Too late now, so I got to work, opening my tote bag, plucking up bone after bone, stowing them all in my tote. Within a few minutes, I had every bone and was brushing off the dirt of more than one hundred years of entombment from my hands.

At the same time I limped over to the winding staircase, I prayed that no one would come down here to check on Goodshot anytime soon, just like no one had checked on him in years. I was all set to get the hell out of Dodge when my light hit the pile of rotted and shattered wood and glinted off something metallic.

Could anything gross me out more? I thought not, so I bent to poke through the rubble.

"Belt buckle," I crooned, and wiped it against the leg of my jeans. I knew the story, and it was that Goodshot got the buckle from Queen Victoria and that it was his prized possession. It only made sense he'd be buried with it.

The buckle was rectangular, maybe three inches across, and from the weight of it, I'd say it was the real deal, too. Intricately worked silver leaves and curlicues surrounded a golden star ringed with sparkly stones. Grime or no grime, I'd been raised right, and I'd been raised by a mother who expected turquoise Tiffany gift boxes for all occasions, and a dad who knew there would be hell to pay if they didn't show up; I knew diamonds when I saw them. The star was engraved, and I held my light nearer and bent closer for a better look at the initials, *VR*.

Okay, I wasn't at my best, what with being in a filthy tomb and having just picked my way through the earthly remains of Goodshot Gomez. But even I recognized that the initials didn't make sense. Goodshot's would have been *CGG* and the Queen's . . . well, *QV*, I suppose. But hey, who was I to question hundred-year-old customs? Instead, I stowed the belt buckle in my tote bag, too, suspecting that Dan's kidnappers might want more tangible proof than just some filthy bones. I'd had experience with murderers and traitors. I'd crossed paths with poisoners and plagiarizers and thieves. I had never dealt with kidnappers, but something told me they were not a trusting bunch. There were plenty of photographs of the Queen presenting that buckle to Goodshot, and in that moment, I decided to take along the Garden View pictorial guide that showed one of them. Along with the bones, the buckle should be enough to prove my sincerity—not to mention my felonious tendencies—and assure Dan's release.

If I could make it out of the cemetery before I got caught.

It was all the reminder I needed that I had to get a move on. I checked the time on my cell. Fifteen minutes before Security showed up.

The minutes ticking away inside my head, I got back outside, locked the door behind me, and breathed a sigh of relief. "Well, that's that," I told myself.

"Not exactly."

Honestly, by now, I should be used to the dead popping up out of nowhere. That didn't stop me from screeching and slapping a hand to my chest to keep my heart from pounding out of my ribs. That is, right before I turned around and found myself face-to-face with the one and only Chester Goodshot Gomez.

"What do you mean, not exactly?" So it wasn't an elegant introduction. Ghosts aren't big on small talk, and I didn't have time for chitchat, anyway. "I got your bones." To prove it, I rattled my tote. "And now I'm out of here."

He was a stocky guy of forty or so wearing a black-and-red-plaid shirt, jeans, and beat-up cowboy boots, and his terra-cotta skin was so crinkled from the sun, it reminded me of a rumpled blanket. Since he was a full head shorter than me, Goodshot had to step back to give me a careful once-over. He swept off his cowboy hat. His coal black hair was parted in the middle, braided, and the braids were wrapped in red fabric and hung down to the middle of his chest.

"You got nerve for a woman," he said. "I'll give you that. And you're sure a sight for these sore eyes. But you're not usin' your head, girl. Not if you think you can just waltz out of here and—"

I was way ahead of him, and not inclined to stand around shooting the breeze when my reputation, not to mention my crystal clear, unbesmirched, and unblemished arrest record might be hanging in the balance. I marched away from the mausoleum, heading back toward where I'd climbed the wall, and told him, "Not to worry. I brought a step stool with me. You know, to help me get over the wall and get in here in the first place. And I was plenty smart." This should have come as no surprise. For a few reasons:

1. He knew I could see and talk to him, and

2. There was only one person in the world who could, so

3. He must have known who I was.

Still, when it comes to setting the record straight, it never hurts to lay the groundwork early with ghosts. They're all about *please, please, please* when they need my help. And way too bossy when they think they've got the upper hand.

"I tied a rope to one leg of the stool." I dragged it out of the bushes where I'd hidden it and showed him. "When I got to the top of the wall, I hauled the stool up, then lowered it down here. I'll do the same thing now to get back to the other side. No muss, no fuss. And no more exertion than necessary."

"No sense, you mean." He didn't elaborate, just chewed his bottom lip, crossed his arms over his chest, and watched me position the step stool on a level spot so I didn't have to worry about nasty spills.

When I was done and realized he was still just standing there, still just watching, I threw my hands in the air. "What? You . . ." I stabbed a finger at him. "You're not happy."

"Happy's got nothin' to do with it. You stole my bones."

I never considered that he might be pissed, but dang, that clock was tick, tick, ticking away and I didn't have time for drama. "You haven't needed them for years," I pointed out. "And besides, stealing them, it's all for a good cause."

"I'm glad of that, at least." Goodshot's voice was husky and as mellow as smoke. That didn't take away the sting when he said, "Somebody's gonna come lookin'. You know, down in my tomb."

I hated to hurt the guy's feelings, but he hadn't had a visitor in years. "They're not—"

"They're gonna find that mess you left behind," he said, ignoring my protest completely. He paused. One heartbeat. Two. Needless to say, these were my heartbeats I'm talking about. "That is, if you don't put back those keys."

I was already on the first step of the stool, all set to climb the rest of the way, and I stopped dead in my tracks.

Dead being relative, of course. Just like the heartbeat thing. The keys were in my pocket—the one without Goodshot's skeleton hand in it—and I jingled them. Dang, how I hated it when ghosts one-upped me! Nothing good could come of the ghostly grapevine getting wind of the fact that I wasn't on the ball when it came to these sorts of things, so I scrambled to save face. "I'll just come by to see Ella again tomorrow and—"

It wasn't exactly the most pitiful suggestion in the world but that's how it looked when Goodshot shook his head. "Suspicious," he said.

"Okay. Yeah. Right. Two days in a row might be too much. But I could wait awhile. Until next week. And I could come then and—"

"Risky."

I blew out a breath of frustration. "Nobody's going to look for the keys before then. They never have."

"Which doesn't mean Ella's not going to look for something else and notice the keys are missing."

He was right.

Another thing I hate about ghosts.

That, and them coming up with ideas like, "You could go right now and put them back where they belong."

"Yeah, if I want to take the chance of getting caught." I whipped out my cell and glanced at the time. "Security is going to be by here in just a couple minutes, and when they're done here, they swing past the administration building. Since the building is locked up tight after hours, that means me breaking in. I don't have keys anymore,

you know. They took mine away when they canned me."
Just for good measure, I grunted. "Like I'd ever really
want to come back to this place."

"You are back."

I rolled my eyes. "I didn't have a whole lot of choice.
Just like you didn't when your friends left you here."

Goodshot shrugged. "I don't hold it against them. They
did what they could. And then they got busy and moved on."

A very good idea, and keeping it in mind, I moved on.
If I was going to end up spending the night in jail, at least
it wouldn't be because Security rounded a corner and
found me standing there talking to thin air. I wove in and
out of the maze of headstones, heading for the administration building with Goodshot trotting along beside me.
"I'm taking your bones to New Mexico," I told him.

His eyes sparked. "I always wanted to be buried with
my ancestors. You are the answer to my prayers."

Maybe. Maybe not. I wasn't about to tell him that burying him wasn't as important as making sure Dan stayed
alive. Besides, I had other things to worry about. Like how
I was going to get into the office. I jingled the keys in my
pocket and had a thought. "The window was open!"

Hope springing in my heart, I covered the distance to
the administration building in record time. Sure enough,
Ella's window was still opened a crack, just like it had
been earlier in the day. I squeezed my hands into the opening, braced them, and—

Broke a nail.

"Damn." In the meager light of the nearest security
lamp, I studied the damage.

Goodshot chuckled. "Women is women. No matter where or when. You ain't gonna let a little thing like that stop you, are you?"

I wasn't. To prove it, I tried the window again. This time, I was able to raise it a couple inches. "A little more," I grunted. "A little more . . ." Of course, just because the window was open didn't mean I'd have an easy time getting into it. I looked around, found a nearby trash can, and dragged it over.

"Bones and dirt and trash," I grumbled, climbing on the trash can. It shifted and I braced myself against the building. Before anything could happen that would involve more dirt and maybe me being found facedown in the grass by Security, I threw one leg into the office, hoisted myself onto the sill, and slipped inside.

Goodshot was already in there waiting for me.

"Must be nice to be a ghost," I grumbled. "And just poof everywhere you want to go."

"Never had no reason to prowl around watchin' the living world. Until tonight, that is." He grinned. "When you showed up and stole my bones. Of course, it's a might inconvenient not being able to touch things." He strolled over to Ella's desk and put his hand on her computer monitor. It whooshed right through. "I hear touching people isn't a good idea, either."

I wasn't about to give him the chance to demonstrate. See, I knew from experience that the touch of a ghost can freeze a person to the bone.

Keeping my distance, I hurried to the other side of Ella's office, slipped the keys back into the file drawer

59

where I'd found them, and dragged myself back outside through the window, closing it down behind me. Goodshot was waiting for me by the road, but as I made a move to start across, he put a hand in the air to stop me.

"The automobile that patrols, it's getting nearer." Like one of the Indian scouts in an old Western movie, I expected him to put one ear to the ground and tell me just how far away Security was. I guess he knew it, too. He rolled his eyes and pointed. "Headlights," he said. "And they're comin' this way."

I was already standing in the center of the road when the glare of car headlights split the night. Blinded, I froze, and frozen, I was no match for the Security guard who threw open his door.

"Hey, you! Stop!" It was Mal Johnson. I recognized his voice as well as the silhouette of his barrel chest and stubby legs against the brilliance of the patrol car's headlights. I wasn't about to give him a chance to recognize me. I hunched into Quinn's windbreaker, hiked my tote up on my arm so I wouldn't lose any of the bones, and took off running.

"This way! Fast!" Goodshot moved like the wind. But then, he didn't have a body to worry about, or lungs that screamed for air. He raced ahead of me, waving me forward, and if I'd had any breath at all, I would have pointed out that we were moving farther from where I'd left the step stool, not toward it. The way it was, I didn't have the luxury. Mal might not be able to hear Goodshot, but he'd hear me for sure if I dared to open my mouth. I tried my best to keep to the shadows of headstones and angels and hulking mausoleums, Mal's huffing and puffing always just paces behind me.

"Take a sharp left turn when I tell you." Goodshot's voice hissed in my ear. "Get ready . . . now!"

I did as I was told and instantly felt the ground go out from under my feet. The grass was slick from the rain earlier in the evening, and my sneakers took to the hill like skis. I slid down, somehow managing to keep my body in balance and my mouth shut. At the bottom of the hill, I would have congratulated myself for making it unscathed if I hadn't heard Mal groaning and grunting behind me.

"Now here. This way!" Goodshot waved me forward. For a guy who hadn't bothered to emerge from his tomb to explore the cemetery before, he sure knew his way around. This was the oldest part of the cemetery and the terrain was bumpy. I tripped and nearly went down.

"Now here, to the right. Up this hill," he called.

Up a hill? I'd just come down a hill. But I think I knew what Goodshot had in mind.

I raced up that hill as fast as I could. Truth be told, that wasn't very fast. But it left lumbering Mal Johnson far behind.

A few more minutes, and I was back at the wall.

But not where I'd left the step stool.

"You'd better hurry, little lady. That man, he called in the cavalry."

I swung around just as a Cleveland Police patrol car cruised into sight.

Mug shots.

And now, the blue windbreaker was the least of my

worries. I was covered with dirt, my hair hung in my eyes, and my jeans . . . I glanced down to confirm my worst fear. Yep, they were ripped.

And I was going to look like one of those stoned celebrities when they stood me up against the wall.

I groaned and ran up and down looking for a foothold. I found one, finally, just as the cops stopped their car and flashed a high-beam light into the section. Lucky for me, there was an angel statue not far away. Its shadow kept me safely in the dark while I scrambled, grunting and groaning.

"Not fast enough!" As if I needed Goodshot to tell me. I dug my fingers into the moss that grew along the top of the wall and pulled for all I was worth. Still not enough to get me over the wall. I struggled and grunted and—

Flew over the wall as if I were as light as air.

I landed on the other side with less than grace. After my bones stopped rattling, I realized my feet were blocks of ice.

"You gave me a boost up."

Goodshot didn't take the blame. Or any credit. He wasn't wasting time, either. My Mustang was a couple blocks away, and when I hobbled in that direction, he came right along.

My hands shaking, I managed to get the car unlocked, got inside, and started it up. No easy thing considering I didn't have any feeling in my feet.

"Whoo-wee!" In the passenger seat, Goodshot grinned. "That's more fun than I've had . . . well, since I been dead!"

Keeping an eye on the rearview mirror, I peeled rubber,

and since it was after midnight and there wasn't any traffic, I didn't bother to stop at the stoplight at the nearest cross street.

This did not bother my passenger. But then, he was so busy looking out the window, I guess he didn't notice.

"Come on, little lady," he crooned. "It's time for us to git to the New Mexico Territory!"

I had never tried to get a bag of human remains past air-
port security—and I wasn't about to start now.

With Goodshot in the passenger seat next to me, I
drove all the way, and five days after I'd masterminded the
cemetery heist, we were cruising through the southern
part of Colorado. By that time, I was more than tired of
eating at fast-food joints, I'd had it with sleeping in mo-
tels, and I was sick of staring at my windshield.

A day of packing and planning back in Cleveland, then
sixteen hundred miles divided by sixty-five miles an hour
plus time out for eating, sleeping, potty breaks, and the
outlet mall we passed somewhere back in Nebraska that
called my name and was impossible to resist.

I'm no math whiz, but even I knew it added up to a lot
of hours.

Funny thing, though, with Goodshot along, I didn't mind nearly as much as I thought I would.

". . . and the horse wore the lady's hat!" He finished up another hilarious story about his days in the Wild West show, slapped his knee, and roared with laughter. At least for a minute. When we zipped passed a sign that said, WELCOME TO NEW MEXICO, LAND OF ENCHANTMENT, Goodshot's smile vanished. "I never thought I'd be back," he said, suddenly thoughtful. "And now, here I am. You taking me to the pueblo to be buried . . ." He sighed. "It's a wonderful thing you're doin'."

It wasn't the first time since we'd begun our road trip that he'd thanked me. This time, like all those other times, I pasted a smile on my face. But this time—unlike all those other times—I wasn't sure I was able to keep up what was feeling more and more like a scam.

On a dead guy I liked.

The thought ate away at my phony smile. Not to mention my conscience. Lucky for me, by the time it did, my GPS was telling me I was just minutes away from our destination.

Really? I glanced around at the craggy hills and low, scrubby plants that surrounded us and thought about that ransom note.

Tres Piedras, New Mexico. Instructions @ gas station

At least if nothing else, wondering how a gas station could exist in the middle of the rocky desolation gave me something to think about other than how burying Good-shot was the last thing I intended to do.

As it turned out, the gas station in question was situated at what I'd generously call an intersection. That is, where one godforsaken road crossed another that was just as empty, and a sign pointed east to Taos. One look at the pitted parking lot and rusted pumps and I was glad I'd filled up back in Colorado.

"Abandoned," I grumbled, slowing and pulling up beside the first pump. Maybe I'd seen too many movies, but this was not what I'd expected. I'd pictured arriving at some hubbub of a minimart and fill-er-up emporium, where I would be approached by a man in a hoodie who would be wearing a ski mask and using one of those Darth Vadar–like voice synthesizers. All breathy and scary-sounding, he'd demand that I hand over the bones, and when I did, Dan would emerge from the men's room, very much alive.

"Is there something wrong with your automobile?" Goodshot's question snapped me back to reality. "I hope not, because we're gettin' close. I recognize this place." He glanced around at the battered gas pumps and, beyond them, the cement block building that had probably once housed a coffee shop and now had a caved-in roof and windows spattered by the birds that made their nests in the nooks and crannies of collapsing walls. "Well, I recognize some of it. Not these crazy, modern places, but the land. Look! Over there!" Goodshot turned and pointed out the backseat driver's side window at the barren, cue ball–shaped peak that dominated the landscape. "That's Wind

Mountain. It has always been sacred to my people. We're close. The pueblo's just east of here, on the other side of the mountain."

"The pueblo, yeah . . ." I groaned and leaned my head against the steering wheel. "There's something I have to tell you," I said, only since my mouth was up against the leather, I knew he couldn't hear me.

And I couldn't sit there just a couple feet from the guy who was counting on me to make sure he rested in peace. Not when I was about to break his nonbeating heart.

I pushed open my door, got out of the car, and drew in a breath of dry, dusty New Mexico air. "It's like this," I said, and I didn't need to look; I felt a chill race up my arms and knew that, even though he hadn't opened the car door to get out, Goodshot was standing right next to me. There was no easy way to let him down and no better way to get this over with than to blurt it out. "I didn't steal your bones to bury them." When he didn't say a thing, I slid him a look. "Did you hear me? I said—"

"Back at the cemetery, you told me you were bringing my bones to New Mexico."

"Yeah, I did. And I wasn't lying. We're in New Mexico, right? Except . . ." I swallowed hard. "I'm not going to bury you here. I'm not going to bury you at all."

He waved a hand in my direction. "You're not talkin' sense. Why come all the way here if you're not—"

I told him. Fast, before I could change my mind. I told him about the ransom note. And about Dan. Well, not all about Dan. I left out the part about how before Dan's dead wife whooshed in and took over my body, I was about to hop into bed with him. Not relevant, and besides, it was embarrassing to think I'd had sweet, geeky—and very hot—Dan stolen away by a dead woman.

I finished up with the bit about the silver watchband. I even got my suitcase out of the trunk and dug through it so I could show him the watchband and the photo of Dan, just to prove I was telling the truth. When I was done, I held my breath, and glanced at him. "Are you pissed?"

His expression was unreadable. "You could have told me sooner."

"Then you would have been mad at me sooner, and I would have had to sit in the car with you all this time and feel bad."

"Do you? Feel bad?"

"I feel . . ." I pushed a hand through my hair. Humidity had always been my friend, curl-wise, and back in Cleveland, humidity was one thing I never had to worry about. Out here in what Goodshot called the high desert, it was a different story. In northern New Mexico, the air felt as empty as the rocky, tree-less, and very brown landscape. Already, my hair hung in my eyes, and I promised myself a trip to the local drugstore for ponytail holders as soon as possible. If . . .

I glanced around at the scrawny plants poking through the cracks in the beat-up blacktop, a weather-battered trailer a few hundreds yards away, the wasteland that surrounded us.

If, that is, I could even find a drugstore in this back of beyond.

"I feel responsible," I admitted, wishing Goodshot

would just fly off the handle and get the yelling over with. Then maybe we could put the entire I-told-you-the-truth-but-not-the-whole-truth-and-nothing-but behind us.

Instead, all he did was scrape a toe against the gritty ground. His cowboy boot didn't leave a mark. "What would kidnappers be wantin' with my bones?"

This I didn't know, and I told him as much. I told him, too, that I'd been over it a million times in my head and that it didn't make any more sense now than it did any of those million times.

Call me self-centered (not that anybody ever would), but if we were talking about my bones, I would have gotten a little defensive. I guess it's only natural people think of themselves as indispensable. And valuable. To think that our earthly remains were just part of some sicko joke was just too weird for words. The only thing I could think of . . .

"You cursed the city!" I reminded him, even though I shouldn't have had to.

"What'd you expect? I just got myself blowed up. Can't blame a man for being mad."

He scratched a finger along the back of his neck. "Don't make no difference, though, does it? What you're tellin' me is that I'm no better off now than I was back in Cleveland in that mausoleum. Can't believe kidnappers are goin' make sure I get back to the pueblo. They're gonna dump that bag of bones somewhere, fast. And I'm gonna be right back where I started from. You ain't goin' to do me any good."

Maybe it was just as well that he was being so restrained. I was emotional enough for the both of us. "It's not going to do Dan any good if some crazy kidnappers kill him," I wailed.

My words blew away on the never-ending wind and were lost in the silence that pressed against us.

Finally, Goodshot lifted his chin. "This Dan, he's your friend."

I nodded. "If Dan gets hurt . . . If he gets . . . killed . . . and I don't do everything in my power to try and stop it—"

"So you're comin' to Dan's rescue. Like the cavalry." Goodshot's solemn expression broke into a grin and he held up one hand and said exactly what I was thinking. "I know. Bad joke. Especially comin' from an Indian. Sorry. But true, huh? It's a rescue mission. And you're helpin' a friend." He took a long look around, drinking in every rock and scrawny shrub. "Guess it won't make that much of a difference. I've waited this long to get back to the pueblo, it won't hurt to wait a little longer."

I think maybe he saw the tears that filled my eyes, because he gave me another wave of the hand and turned his back on me. "You know," he said, "it's kind of like a treasure hunt. That ransom note told you to come here. So there must be something here . . ." His hands out at his sides, Goodshot spun around, taking in the abandoned gas station and the desolate hills. "You were brought here because you were supposed to find somethin'. And I'm guessin' the kidnapper chose this place because he figured nobody else was goin' to find it and nobody was goin' to disturb you while you looked."

"I hope you're right." Hands on my hips, I looked

around, too. "You don't think Dan is here somewhere, do you?" I started toward the dilapidated coffee shop, but stopped before I got too close. Who knew what was hiding in there! "Maybe they just want me to leave the bones and he's here and—"

"Too easy." Don't ask me how ghostly things work, but I heard Goodshot exhale the words and turned to find him puffing on a fat cigar. He stepped back, blew out a couple smoke rings, and studied the scene. "If I was gonna kidnap some fella—"

"I'd want to make sure I had the bones in hand before I released him." He nodded so I'd know I was following where his train of thought was headed. "Which means . . ."

"I'd leave a note. Or a clue of some sort." Another puff and Goodshot narrowed his eyes. "Here, maybe." He closed in on a piece of paper fluttering across the blacktop in the wind that hadn't stopped blowing around the gritty air since I stepped out of the car, but since he was unable to touch it, I was the one who ended up plucking the paper off the ground.

It was just a bit of newspaper, and I dropped it back where I found it and kicked it aside. That's when I noticed another scrap of paper stuck into the credit card slot on one of the gas pumps.

"Brilliant!" I told Goodshot, and reached for the note.

10 pm
Taberna Antonito, Colorado
After Tuesday?

Then u r too late
Dan is already dead

The words burned into my brain and my fingers trembled against the sheet of paper. It was Monday and I had made it just in time. If I hadn't gotten there . . . If I'd arrived after Tuesday . . . If I didn't have the bones with me . . .

I refused to let my brain go there. The important thing now was to follow the kidnapper's directions. I was close. Too close to let a couple little things like panic, worry, and I'm-so-scared-I-can't-stand-it stop me.

I looked north, back up the highway we'd just traveled south on. I knew that Colorado was about an hour in that direction, and I remembered the town of Antonito, all right. But then, it was hard not to remember the last place I'd seen anything that even sort of resembled civilization.

One main street, a grocery store, a couple bars, dust. Oh yeah, I remembered the dust. Colorado dust was a lot like New Mexico dust.

"And there was a motel back that way," I said before I glanced around again at the barren landscape. "That might be a better option than trying to find someplace to stay around here."

"Then what do you say? We'd better get a move on." Goodshot was already in the car. "I've always liked the idea of racin' in to save the day."

Yeah, I liked the idea, too. Especially considering that I was anxious to get this whole thing over with.

Bad enough I had to worry about seeing Dan alive again . . .

I wheeled the car around and headed back in the direction we'd just come while Goodshot stared out the passenger window, his gaze riveted to Wind Mountain.

Now I had to worry that even after I handed over the bones and saved Dan, I was still going to feel lousy about letting Goodshot down.

It wasn't like I actually saw a wolf or a coyote or a buffalo or anything. But the wide-open spaces, rocky hills, and dusty cliffs around Antonito looked like the kind of place I might, and I wasn't taking any chances that some wild beast would stroll into town. I insisted on a second-floor room at the motel. It overlooked the parking lot. At least I could easily keep an eye on the Mustang. Especially since mine was only one of three cars there.

The good news was that it was a short walk from the motel over to Taberna, the bar where I'd been instructed to meet the kidnappers at ten o'clock. Then again, it was a short stroll pretty much everywhere in town. Antonito was not exactly a bustling metropolis. Aside from a couple streets where adobe houses and aluminum-clad trailers sat side by side, Main Street was pretty much it.

It was already dark by the time I showered, changed, and headed out. A couple minutes before ten, Goodshot and I stood outside the door of the bar. I had the bag of his bones slung over one shoulder and a feeling in the pit of my stomach that was half nervousness, half guilt.

"If there was any other way," I told him.

"Don't worry." I think he would have patted me on the shoulder if he could have gotten away with it and not frozen me solid. "I understand."

"But you—"

"Me?" Goodshot didn't give me a chance to apologize again. With two fingers, he snapped his cowboy hat back on his head. "I'm headin' over to the local cemetery. I used to know a couple pretty little señoritas in this town. The way I figure it, I just might be able to catch up with them."

I watched him stroll down the sidewalk and heard him whistle some old song. By the time he got to the street, he'd completely melted into the shadows and the last note of his tune faded into the night.

I was on my own.

And if I thought about it much longer, I'd bolt for home. Ignoring the cha-cha going on in my chest, I pushed open the door. Inside the bar, the lights were dim, the country music was loud, and I was one of exactly four patrons. Two of them were old guys slamming down shots and beers at the bar. The other one was a hippie-type with long greasy hair and a scraggly beard. He was sitting by himself near the front window, sipping a beer and reading a book.

None of them looked like kidnapper material to me.

I slid into a booth in the farthest corner from the door and set my tote bag beside me on the vinyl bench.

"What'll you have?" The bartender was talking even before she was out from behind the bar, her voice loud

Casey Daniels

enough to be heard over the wailing of a steel guitar. She was forty or so, a stick-thin woman with bleached-out hair and the telltale pinched mouth of a smoker. She had a damp rag in one hand and she swiped it over the table, gave me a brief look, and did a careful once-over of the tote bag on the bench next to me. I understood her bag envy; I'd had the same reaction the first time I set my eyes on the glazed canvas bag with the studs on its straps.

The jukebox switched off, and she lowered her voice. "Dollar beer night," she said, her gaze still on the Jimmy Choo creation. "And if Ramon isn't snoozing in the kitchen"—she swiveled a look from the swinging kitchen door to me—"I can get you wings or a burger."

My stomach was in no mood for food. I opted for a Diet Coke and she was back in a minute with it. "My name's Norma," she said. "If you need anything, flag me down."

I knew I wouldn't, but told her I would. Then I settled back to wait.

According to the time on my cell phone, it was already a couple minutes past ten when the front door popped open and two men walked in. They were both wearing jeans, dark sweatshirts, sneakers. Oh, and plastic Halloween masks. The kind that stay on with those funny, skinny elastic bands that loop around the wearer's head.

Green skin. Big, dark eyes.

Aliens.

Yeah, that's right. I'd driven sixteen hundred miles to meet with a couple guys in alien masks.

They made a beeline across the room and slid into the bench opposite from where I sat.

76

"Are you kidding me?" I looked from one man to the other. "I kind of thought kidnappers would want to be a little more subtle. You don't think somebody's going to notice you two in that getup?"

"This is the Southwest." The taller of the two men used a fake, gravelly voice. Somewhere along the line, the elastic band had broken on his mask. The elastic was tied to a paperclip that was bent into a drunken figure eight and poked through one side of the mask. "Nobody around here is going to notice us. Heck, half the people here believe in aliens and the other half are aliens."

I guess he was right—not about how there are aliens in Antonito but about how nobody was going to notice two guys in goofy disguises—because Norma didn't bat an eye when she trotted over with a pitcher of beer and two glasses. She poured, spilled a little, and swiped at the puddle with her bar rag. Maybe it was the low lights, but I could have sworn that when she did, her hand brushed Tall Alien's arm, and not in an accidental sort of way. When she walked back to the bar, I kept my eyes on her.

"Did you bring me Chester Goodshot Gomez?"

Tall Alien's raspy question snapped me back to the matter at hand, and I put the bag of bones on the table between us. I did not, however, take my hands off it. "How do I know Dan Callahan is alive?" I asked him.

Tall Alien clicked his tongue. I bet he made a face at me, too, only I couldn't see it. "How do I know that's Goodshot Gomez in that bag?"

I tipped my head and forced what I hoped looked enough like a cocky smile to make them think I wasn't scared to death I'd do something wrong and Dan would pay the ultimate price. "You could go over to the local cemetery and ask him yourself," I said, batting my eyelashes. "He's visiting a couple old girlfriends. But if that doesn't float your boat . . ."

I kept my left hand on the bag and, with my right, reached into my purse and pulled out Goodshot's belt buckle along with that picture of Queen Victoria presenting it to him.

"The only place I could get the belt buckle was from his coffin, and if I was going to go through all that trouble, why would I bother to bring you someone else's bones? Now where's Dan?"

"The bones first." With one finger, Tall Alien tapped his side of the table.

I slid the bag of bones back my way and wrapped both arms around it. "Some proof that Dan's okay first."

"Told you she was smart!" This from Short Alien, who was instantly silenced by a look from the tall guy.

This time when Tall Alien tapped the table, it was with a little more force. "Bones," he growled.

I leaned forward, the better to pin him with a look. "Dan," I growled right back.

He let go a breath of exasperation and dug around in the pocket of his jeans. Only that wasn't so easy since he was sitting. He was forced to nudge Short Alien out of the booth, stand up, and fish through his pocket. He pulled out a photograph printed on computer paper and dropped it on the table and my heart thudded to a stop when I looked at it.

It was Dan, all right. He was bound and gagged and somebody was holding a newspaper with the day's headlines right behind him.

Since my stomach was in my throat, I couldn't exactly say anything, so I nodded to let Tall Alien know he'd convinced me. "When will I see Dan?" I asked.

He tapped the table one more time.

"How am I supposed to find him?"

Another tap.

I nudged the bag across the table, but still kept one hand on it. "I don't know what you have in mind, but if you could bury the bones over at Goodshot's pueblo—"

One more tap, this one far more impatient than the last.

I knew a game-ending move when I saw it.

With a sigh, I slid the bag across the table and Tall Alien reached out to intercept it.

That was exactly when all the lights in the bar went out.

"What do you mean, you lost my bones?"

Remember how Goodshot was cool, calm, and collected when I told him how I'd brought his remains to New Mexico but I wasn't going to bury them at the pueblo?

Yeah, me, too.

That's exactly how cool, calm, and collected he *wasn't* when I finally found him at the local cemetery and reported what had happened back at the bar.

"You had the bones. In that ugly bag of yours and—"

"Just for the record, it isn't ugly, and the bag's gone, too." Okay, it wasn't fair to get cranky with a guy who I'd just informed had all that was left of him vanish into thin air. It's not like I could help myself. Redhead, remember. And I loved that bag. "It wasn't a knockoff," I pointed out because, let's face it, Goodshot probably wasn't all that into fashion even before he was dead so he wouldn't recognize the genuine thing when he saw it. "It happened to be the real deal. And yeah, there were bones in it, but I was going to find a way to get it clean and—"

"Not just any bones. My bones!" When I found Goodshot, he was sitting on a headstone, charming the hell out of a sweet little señorita in a flowing red circle skirt and white blouse who he introduced as Anarosa Rodriguez. It was her tombstone he was sitting on. Watching him jump to his feet and shake his fist at me, her ghostly face went a little paler.

"Not a problem. I'm going to get them back." I said this to calm him down, soothe her worries, and convince myself. "I have to. Or Dan . . ."

I told myself it would get me nowhere, but I couldn't help but relive the scene back at the bar. Once the lights went out, they'd stayed that way for a minute or so, and in that time, it was impossible to see anything at all. What I heard sure wasn't encouraging. In the pitch darkness, the aliens across the table shuffled and grunted and banged into each trying to get out of the booth while the two old guys at the bar laughed and said something corny about ambience. And when the lights came back on again . . .

"What the hell!" Tall Alien looked down at the empty table between us and practically choked. He shoved Short Alien aside and hotfooted it over to my side of the table to check the bench next to me and under the table. "What the hell did you do with the bones?" he demanded.

"That was pretty much the question I was going to ask you," I bit right back.

"Well, I don't have them." Like it would prove the bag wasn't hidden about his person, he held his hands out at shoulder level. Call me a cynic, but that didn't exactly convince me. I checked his side of the table, just like he'd checked mine. I looked on the bench and under it, and behind it, too.

My Jimmy Choo bag was gone.

So were Goodshot's bones.

My heart beating double-time, I reminded myself to think like the detective I was and studied the scene for clues.

The two old guys didn't look like they had the energy to move fast enough to scoop up the bones and get back to their bar stools, and Norma was behind the bar, right where I remembered seeing her last before the lights went out. She mumbled something about how she'd have to talk to the bar owner and have him fix the old, temperamental fuse box, and poured each of the codgers another shot. They lifted their shot glasses in our direction, toasted, and drank 'em down. And that hippie in the corner? He just kept sipping his beer and reading, like nothing had happened at all.

That didn't keep me from racing over to the table where he was seated and looking under it, and all around it. I did that at every table, and behind the bar, too. No luck.

The bones had vanished.

Panic is an infectious thing. By the time I got back over to the booth where we'd been seated, the aliens had been through the bar, too, looking behind and under everything in sight, and Short Alien was wringing his hands. Tall Alien had his fists on his hips.

Never having been an active participant in a kidnapping, I wasn't sure of the protocol. Then again, I didn't much care. I closed in on both of them. "I kept my part of the bargain," I said, stabbing one finger at myself before I turned it on them. "Now you . . . You hand over Dan."

A snort escaped from behind Tall Alien's mask. "The deal isn't done."

Yeah, I was afraid he was going to say that. My temper hit the roof and I kicked the leg of the nearest chair. "I took the trouble to steal the stupid bones in the first place. I brought them all the way to this middle-of-nowhere hellhole. Why would I—"

"That wasn't the bargain. You were supposed to turn them over to us. You didn't. That's not my problem, lady. It's yours." Tall Alien gave Short Alien a nudge to send him to the door and Tall Alien was on his way over there, too, when he stopped, turned around, and came back to stand too close to me.

"I need those bones," he said. "And if you don't find them and bring them to me"—he leaned in even closer and his hot breath brushed my ear—"Your friend Dan is going to die."

It was a warm night there in the cemetery, but even so, just thinking about the steel edge in Tall Alien's voice sent a shiver up my spine and across my shoulders. I wrapped my arms around myself. "We're going to find your bones," I promised Goodshot. "We have to. Dan's life depends on it."

* * *

B rave talk, all right.

And by the next afternoon, it was looking more and more like nothing but wishful thinking.

I spent the day investigating. Or at least I tried to. I went to Taberna early only to find it was still closed. I went back later to talk to Norma, but it was her day off, and apparently, I do not have as honest a face as I always thought. A guy named Buddy behind the bar refused to give me Norma's address or her phone number, even when I did my best to flirt it out of him. He wouldn't reveal her last name, either, but hey, it's not exactly like it would have made a difference. I was pretty sure there weren't any phone books for a town so small, it shouldn't exist in the first place.

I hadn't seen Goodshot all day, and honestly, I wasn't all that disappointed. Bad enough we'd had that little tiff the night before. Worse, since I was getting nowhere fast when it came to keeping my promise to him about finding his bones. That being said, there are times when even the sharpest investigator can't go it alone. I was discouraged— not to mention hot, sweaty, and thirsty—and I needed someone to bounce ideas off. Back at home, I'd use Ella even though, more often than not, she didn't have a clue what I was talking about. Here in the boonies, a sidekick was a little harder to come by.

I headed to the cemetery.

Goodshot was there all right, this time with a blonde in a low-cut pea green gown who giggled and told me her name was Miss Kitty LaRue. Kitty was wearing too much lipstick, she had a phony beauty mark penciled on her chin, and her cheeks were painted a color that did not actually exist in nature. So not a good look, but I cut her some slack. The dead have enough to worry about.

"So?" They were passing a spectral bottle of whisky back and forth between them, and Goodshot took a long swig, wiped the back of his hand across his mouth, and fixed his dark eyes on me. "You find my bones yet?"

I guess the look on my face was all the response he needed, because he pushed away from the fence he'd been leaning against and sauntered over. "That bad, huh?" he asked, but he didn't wait for me to answer. Instead, he shuffled his boots in the dust.

"Been thinkin' about how I wasn't civil to you yesterday," he said. "And how that's not exactly fair seein' as how you're a woman, after all, and I should'a knowed better than to expect the weaker sex to do a lot of thinkin' when that's not what the Good Lord intended women for at all. And besides that . . . well, I just couldn't help myself, I'm mean about gettin' mad and all. It's not everyday a fella learns that all that's left of him has gone missin'."

Three cheers for me. Even though it would have been more than justified, I did not raise my voice. "Number one," I said from between gritted teeth, "that whole thing about being the little woman doesn't fly anymore, so get over it. Number two . . ." I thought about being stubborn, but since it didn't exactly fit into my purpose for coming over to the cemetery in the first place, I relented. "I accept your apology."

He took my lecture in stride, and when Kitty floated

over, he took the bottle from her, drank some down, and asked, "What'cha gonna do?"

Exactly what I was there to ask him.

What *could* we do now that I'd used up all my ideas, all my options, and every possibility I could think of?

Funny, on my way over to the cemetery, they seemed like the most natural questions in the world.

Standing there with two ghosts watching me with hope in their lifeless little eyes . . .

I lied and told Goodshot that I had a plan, all right, and that I'd continue putting it into action in the morning. Then I turned my back on him and dragged back to the hotel before he could ask me to elaborate. Truth be told, all I wanted to do was take a shower, climb into bed, and hopefully figure out some way to make sure Dan stayed alive.

Good idea.

I actually might have had the chance to make some sense of it all if I didn't scuff into my room, lock the door behind me, turn on the lights—

And find a man sitting in the chair next to my bed.

"What the—" I slapped a hand to my heart and sucked in a breath. Some of that reaction, I will admit, had to do with surprise. A little might have been because of fear. Most of it . . .

Well, far be it from me to be accused of being shallow, but I will say this—this guy was as yummy as a showcase chock-full of Godiva chocolates.

Eyes as dark as Goodshot's. Hair, too. Long and silky, pulled back into a tight ponytail.

High cheekbones. Dusky skin.

Native American.

Gorgeous Native American. Broad-shouldered, with a mouth that was rich and full and—

"What the hell are you doing in my room?"

It was a better than *What's your sign?* or *What are you doing later 'cause, see, I'm new in town and looking for some company.* I was glad the question whooshed out of me along with a breath of surprise and an indignant, "Who let you in here, anyway?"

Instead of answering, he stood. Taller than me. He was wearing dark pants and a tan shirt. Uniform. Badge. Gun.

Cop.

Which could have been good news if there was any way he could use his law enforcement connections to help me find Dan.

Or really bad news if someone back in Cleveland had gotten wind of the burgled mausoleum and my photo was now hanging in post offices across the country.

I swallowed a little too hard and backed up until my butt slammed into the door. "Wh-What do you want?" I asked.

"I hear you're looking for something."

So much for small talk. Perfectly at ease with himself, he stood loose-limbed, his feet slightly apart, his expression unreadable. Call me crazy, but I couldn't help thinking that if he was there to arrest me for the bone heist back in Cleveland, he might have had a hand on his gun.

But then, I was used to Quinn's way of doing things.

And Quinn had way too much testosterone. Even for a cop.

I didn't want to give this cop any ideas so I made sure I kept my eyes on his face, and away from that gun. "You must have heard wrong," I said.

"I don't think so."

"I do. I'm—"

"Not from around here. Yeah, I know."

I think this was supposed to be a compliment. I mean, what else could he have meant? After all, when he ran a quick but thorough look up and down my body, he no doubt noticed that I was wearing a brand of jeans they didn't sell south of the toniest shops in Denver, a tank top that didn't come from the local off-price emporium, and the cutest pair of peep-toe platform sandals this side of the state line. Either state line.

"You want me to be impressed by your law enforcement mojo, but my guess is there was no magic involved. You saw my car in the lot. Hard not to considering it's out there with a rusty pickup truck and a 'sixty-eight Volkswagen Beetle. The Ohio plates were a dead giveaway. I bet you already ran them."

"Bet you're right."

"And you found . . ." I couldn't afford to let him hear the tremor in my voice and catch on to the fact that there actually might be something to find so I laughed. "Nothing, right?"

"No open warrants. Should I check again?"

"Do I look like a criminal?"

"No, ma'am, you do not." He reinforced his opinion with a brusque nod, and the single light burning next to the bed reflected off his hair like liquid onyx.

Oh yeah, I was getting way too poetic. And it wasn't smart. I told myself to come to my senses and did my best to keep things light enough to prove I had nothing to hide, and serious enough for him to know I meant business. "Then it looks like you're wasting your time and we're right back where we started from."

"Yes and no. You're right, I am getting ready to say, 'I hear you're looking for something' again. And if I'm any judge of people at all—and I am, by the way—I'm pretty sure you're going to evade me on that subject again. Just like you did the first time. Even then, we won't be right back where we started from. Theoretically, we'll be in the same place, sure. But at a different time."

Just what I needed. An Indian philosopher cop.

It was best to set the record straight right from the start so I said, "I don't know what the hell you're talking about."

"He said that's what you'd say."

"He?" I guess it was too direct a question because when I stared at him for a couple seconds and he still didn't answer, I gave up with a sigh. I dropped down on the edge of the bed. "You're not making any sense."

"As much sense as you're making, here in Antonito, looking for something."

My smile was so stiff, it actually hurt. "Only I never said I was looking for anything."

"No, you didn't." He'd left a Stetson on the bed, and he

picked it up and dangled it with long fingers. "You don't have to. He told me that, too."

"The mysterious *he* again." I threw my hands in the air and got to my feet. There was something about this guy that made me feel as if electricity had been wired to my bones, and it wasn't just his crazy good looks. Heck, I'd met plenty of good-looking men in my time. I'd been sleeping with one before he went and got all stiff-necked and pissy when I told him I talked to the dead. I wasn't that easily charmed, and I was never that easily fooled. Well, except by Joel, my ex-fiancé, who turned out to be a total loser. But that's another story.

Still, my body hummed with something that was half expectation, half need, all warning.

For once, I listened.

I stepped back, my weight against one foot, and crossed my arms over my chest. "You want to talk, maybe we can talk. But you're going first. Who's been talking about me? About what I'd say? And do?"

"The shaman."

It was a word I'd heard before. But not one I'd ever paid much attention to. I leaned forward. "Sorry. I'm just a girl from back East. A shaman is—"

"A priest, of sorts. And a healer. In my tribe, he's also a go-between. You know, between this world and the world where spirits reside."

The little laugh I gave him along with a lift of my shoulders had always worked its magic on the weaker sex. And unlike Goodshot, I was not talking about women here.

"You're a cop, and I know cops. Cops aren't big into mumbo jumbo."

"I'm a cop, and I'm Taopi Indian. I guess you don't watch enough old Western movies. Indians . . ." His solemn expression never cracked, but his eyes narrowed just enough to make it look like he actually might know how to smile. "We believe all kinds of nonsense."

His voice was deep and thick, as intoxicating as brandy.

The better to make you spill all your secrets, my dear.

I told the voice inside my head to stuff a sock in it. I wasn't about to come clean about the bones and Dan. Not with a total stranger. For one thing, I didn't know if I could trust him. For another, if I admitted I was there to ransom a kidnapped friend, I'd also have to admit that I was doing it with bones.

The bones of a Native American.

Something told me he wouldn't think it was cool to find out where I'd gotten the bones, or what I intended to do with them. He hadn't said anything about the shaman seeing prison in my future, but I wasn't taking any chances.

I tossed my head. "Sorry. I still don't have any idea what you're talking about."

He didn't say a word, just stood there all calm and gorgeous. Like he had all the time in the world, and he knew I'd cave eventually.

Obviously, Mr. Philosophy had a lot to learn.

I kept my place, too, and stared right back at him. One minute. Two. The quiet pressed against my ears. My heart slammed my ribs.

When he finally moved toward the door, I flinched as if a gunshot had gone off.

"The shaman knows because he threw the bones. He saw a vision of you there. And he told me all about you."

"Ri-ght." I drew the word out into two syllables, and somehow, I managed to make it sound as cocky as I intended.

His hand on the doorknob, he paused. "You really shouldn't try to act so surprised," he said. "About the shaman. And the omens. And the spirit world. For one thing, you're not much of an actress." He opened the door and set his hat on his head. "For another . . . well, you of all people . . . you should know there are things some people see and others can't."

His words were still ringing in the air when he stepped outside and I kicked the door closed behind him.

I hoped he was out there listening when I turned the lock on the door. And the dead bolt, too.

7

Someone was watching me.

A chill snaked over my shoulders and settled at the back of my neck, and even though it was about one hundred degrees in the afternoon sun that baked Main Street, I shivered. While I was at it, I glanced around.

There wasn't much happening in downtown Antonito, and no sign at all of anybody who might want to take the least interest in me (well, except for the obvious reasons, of course). The two old guys I'd seen at Taberna a couple nights before were sitting on a bench outside the Hometown Food Market, chatting away. A late-model SUV rolled by and kicked up a cloud of dust, but the driver never gave me so much as a glance. Across the street, a couple women shuffled into Tom's Laundromat, baskets of clothes on their hips and whining toddlers in their arms.

Nothing out of the ordinary. Nothing fishy. Nothing weird.

Still, I couldn't get rid of the feeling I'd had since I left the motel that morning and started what was turning out to be the private investigator to the dead's version of Groundhog Day.

Same old, same old. Same old nothing, at least in terms of finding out what happened to Goodshot's bones or locating Dan.

Nobody in Antonito, it seemed, was willing to talk. But as sure as I'm Gifted (and I'm not talking just about the whole dead thing here, but about how I'm above average when it comes to mixing and matching separates into fabulous outfits), somebody had their eyes on me.

Hoping to catch whoever it was in the act and convince myself that my imagination wasn't running wild, I looked around again.

And saw the same no one and nothing I'd seen before.

Maybe I wouldn't have been so edgy if only I knew who I was dealing with. Kidnappers waiting for me to make a wrong move, and so, send Dan to his doom? Some ordinary person who hadn't seen this much style (not to mention peep-toe sandals this cool) in the hinterlands? Or was it that cop? The one who'd been in my motel room the night before?

If nothing else, at least that last thought got rid of the ice in my veins. All it took was the memory of that chiseled face and those eyes as deep as secrets, and my blood was boiling.

At least until I remembered all he'd said about shamans and seeing things that weren't there, and how had he known in the first place that I was looking for something? Delicious or not, this was one guy I had to be careful around.

"You lookin' for somethin'?"

Since Goodshot was behind me, it's not like I would have seen him when he poofed onto the scene, anyway, so of course I couldn't help but jump. I refused to turn around, though. If anybody noticed, it would be bad enough that I was talking to myself. It wouldn't matter which direction I was facing.

"Somebody's keeping an eye on me," I said, moving my lips as little as possible. "There was this cop in my room last night and—"

"He's going to help us find my bones?"

Since I'd been standing in one spot long enough—and since standing in one spot might look suspicious—I walked a little farther down the street. I stopped at an empty storefront and peered inside.

"I didn't tell him about the bones," I said to Goodshot. "I didn't know if I could trust him. He was—"

Trying to explain about things like the sensations that sizzled through me when that cop was near was not a good idea. Even under the best of circumstances. Trying to explain to a ghost how I spent the night dreaming about that killer body . . .

"He was an Indian," I said.

"Good, then maybe we'll finally have somebody with

some sense workin' with us. Unless you mean that's why you couldn't trust him? Because he's Indian?"

"Don't be ridiculous. You know me better than that. I'm an equal opportunity investigator." I moved on to the next storefront. It was empty, too, but once upon a time, it must have housed a beauty parlor. I pressed my nose to the window and looked inside at a couple chairs set in front of mirrors caked with dust. "I don't trust him because I don't trust him. I don't know him. For all I know, he could have been the one who stole the bones."

"Seems a might odd, don't you think? To steal them, and then to come talk to you about it?" Goodshot shook his head. "Don't make no sense."

"I didn't say it was true. I just said it was a possibility. Until I know what he's up to, I don't want to say too much. He said . . ." I weighed the wisdom of mentioning this next bit, but let's face it, it's not like I had a lot of choice. I was quickly finding out that the Great Southwest was a whole other world. One I didn't understand. If I was going to make sense of where I was and what was happening, I needed an interpreter.

"He knew I was looking for something," I told Goodshot. "And he mentioned a shaman. How—"

"No mystery there." Goodshot struck a ghostly match against the side of the building, and when it flamed, he lit a cigarette. "Shaman must have thrown the bones."

"That's what the cop said. But really—"

"You're standin' here talkin' to a dead man and you're gonna tell me you don't believe it?" The skin around Goodshot's eyes folded into a million little crinkles. "Shamans, they're powerful men. They walk in the spirit world. If you ask this policeman to take you to the shaman—"

"Not until I know if he's on the up-and-up. Then maybe . . ." Even I realized my statement left open the possibility that, somewhere along the line, I would not only get to see Mr. Tall, Dark, and Gorgeous again, but get to know him a little better, too.

This time the shiver that tingled through me had nothing to do with the sensation of being spied on.

"No luck on the bones, huh?" When I glanced to my right, I saw Goodshot puffing away. "So you were lying yesterday when you said—"

"I wasn't exactly lying. I was . . ." My shoulders drooped. "Okay, I was lying. I didn't have a plan. I didn't want to disappoint you. Or Kitty. She's an old friend, huh? Whatever happened to Anarosa, anyway? You'd better be careful, I've seen ghosts who are pissed. If those two ladies—"

"Not to worry." He dropped his cigarette and it vanished before it ever hit the ground. "Kitty's a professional, if you get my drift. She ain't goin' to get jealous over a little woman like Anarosa. And besides . . ." His face split with a grin. "I ain't headed out this afternoon to see neither one of them." Goodshot brushed his hands together and presto! he was holding a bouquet of summer flowers. "Used to be a schoolmarm in this town. Little lady by the name of Suzanna. Died in a fire at the schoolhouse, so I hear, and she's buried up at there cemetery, but I ain't seen her around. Thought I'd go over to where that ol' school used to stand and see if she's haunting it. You know how most ghosts is, can't seem to get what happened to them there at the end out of their heads."

"Some of them can't seem to get their conquests out of their heads, either." I grinned right back at him. "You were a playboy before there was even such thing as a playboy."

"Oh, I dunno about that!" Goodshot headed down the sidewalk. "As long as there have been pretty girls, there have been men chasing after them. Remember that, Pepper. Next time that policeman of yours comes around."

He didn't give me a chance to tell him that I didn't know what he was talking about. Or that he'd read me all wrong.

Then again, I guess he was tired of me lying to him.

"What are you gonna do, Pepper?" He called one last question out to me, and I looked up to see him floating down the street on a stiff wind.

And since I didn't have the heart to lie to him another time, I opted for the truth. "Grocery store." I pointed, and I didn't try to explain about how frustrated I was feeling about getting nowhere on my investigation so I just said, "Chocolate."

I watched Goodshot until he sailed around a corner, and when he was gone, I went inside the grocery store and grabbed a cart. While I was at it, I wanted to pick up some drinks to keep in my motel room and maybe some bread and peanut butter, too. There were only so many enchiladas a girl could eat, even if the diner attached to the local gas station did have the reputation for having the best ones in the state.

I wheeled up and down the aisles and I guess I was more upset about the case than I was willing to admit, because within a couple minutes, I had the whole comfort food thing just about covered: three Snickers bars, a bag of barbeque potato chips, and some of those pretzel nuggets coated with honey and mustard. Enough junk food to last me a couple days. With any luck, by that time, I'd have some idea what I could do to get Dan away from the kidnappers. After all, I liked Dan. No way he deserved to be bound and gagged and in the clutches of guys who were dopey enough to come to a handoff in alien masks.

I guess that's what I was thinking about as I stood in the snack-food aisle juggling a bag of tortilla chips while I decided if I wanted mild or spicy salsa. I'd just grabbed a jar of spicy (okay, Dan wasn't the only thing I was thinking about; I might have been obsessing about the hot cop, too) when I heard a commotion in the aisle that backed up to the one I was in. Grunting. Like somebody was trying to reach something on one of the upper shelves and couldn't. I was just about to go over there and see if maybe I was tall enough to help, when I saw a man's hand groping for a bag of Chips Ahoy.

"Damn," I heard him grumble. He made another stab and caught one corner of the package and the bag of cookies tumbled from the shelf. I heard his satisfied "Yes!" when he tossed it in his cart.

But I never moved a muscle.

I was rooted to the spot. Surprised. Angry. Completely blown away.

See, when he reached for that bag of cookies, the man's sleeve rode up his arm.

And that's when I saw it—a red and blue tattoo in block letters on the underside of his wrist. THE TRIBE WILL RISE AGAIN, it said, right above 1948.

The same tattoo ghostbuster Brian and his friends showed me the night Quinn and I went to the baseball game.

"Brian? And his Indians fans friends?" The words whooshed out of me at the end of the breath of surprise. At least I had the good sense not to talk to myself too loudly. I heard the guy in the next aisle push his cart on ahead and snapped to. I couldn't let him know I was there—or that I'd seen the telltale tattoo.

With one last regretful look at those Snickers bars, I left my cart right where it was and zipped out of the store. Lucky for me, I'd left my car in the Hometown parking lot when I started my pointless trek around town earlier that day, and now, I hopped in and slumped down in the driver's seat so I could watch the door of the grocery store and not be seen.

Then I waited.

Sounds easy enough. It might have been, too, if I wasn't so angry, I thought my head was going to pop off.

I remembered that ballgame and how Brian and his buddies had said something needed to be done about the curse Goodshot had put on the city and, hence, on its sports teams. They were rabid fans, sure, but I never imagined . . .

Automatically, my hands curled around the steering wheel, so tight, my knuckles were white.

Okay, I got it. I understood why people supported their favorite sports teams and why they wanted them to win. But would anybody actually go through the trouble of kidnapping someone (aka Dan) to make that happen? Would those same people then ask another someone (me, specifically) to mastermind a body snatching to win the kidnappee's freedom? Had Brian and his friends risked Dan's life and my spotless criminal record in the name of ridding the city of a curse they thought was keeping the Cleveland Indians from winning a championship?

It wasn't possible. I knew it in my heart, and not because I was all that well acquainted with Brian or his friends. I just couldn't imagine that anyone would be that bold. Or that desperate. Or that brainless.

Then again, the kidnappers had worn alien masks to our meeting.

Denial is a wonderful thing. I went right along believing no one was stupid enough to risk a person's life for the sake of a sports team for another five minutes or so. That is, until I saw Brian walk out of the grocery store.

Coincidence? I thought not. There was no way Brian and I would be visiting this godforsaken part of the world at the same time. Not unless he'd engineered my visit in return for Dan's life.

When Brian loaded his bags into a dark green Jeep parked on the street in front of the store and slid behind the wheel, I started my car and waited for him to make his move. And when he took off, heading north on Main Street, I stayed a couple car lengths behind him.

With any luck . . .

I sucked in a breath of dry desert air and told my brain not to get ahead of itself, but it was already too late for that; my mood brightened and my heartbeat sped up.

With any luck, Brian was about to lead me right to Dan.

Up ahead, the Jeep turned left, and since there was no traffic around, I waited a few seconds to follow. When Brian disappeared over a rise, I made the turn and trailed along after him, and within another minute or two, I had him in my sights again. He drove on, and I held back.

We played that game for a half hour, heading down one road after another, twisting and turning through the parched landscape. In a little while, I saw another WEL-COME TO NEW MEXICO, LAND OF ENCHANTMENT sign. Hey, I'd never been a whiz at geography, but even I knew that meant we were headed south. If I needed proof, I saw it up ahead in just a few more minutes when the smooth dome of Wind Mountain appeared, silhouetted like a brown egg against the cloudless blue sky.

All the while, I was careful, and I was sure there was no way Brian knew I was following him. I lagged behind, and when a van with Texas plates came rushing up to my bumper, I even let it pass and stayed back, the van between me and that green Jeep up ahead.

About an hour after we left Antonito, Brian turned onto a dirt road, stopped, and hopped out of the Jeep. It wasn't exactly like I could pull up next to him and ask what he was up to, so I hunkered down in the front seat and drove right on by. About a thousand yards down the road, I slowed and checked my rearview mirror. Brian had driven on, and for the first time, I had the luxury of taking a look at my surroundings and realized where I was—back at the gas station where I'd found the note instructing me to go to Taberna a couple nights earlier. I pulled into the pitted parking lot and swung around, and by the time I stopped at the turnoff where I'd seen Brian get out, the Jeep was already kicking up a cloud of dust on a winding road that led farther from the paved road and closer to Wind Mountain.

Since there wasn't a tree in sight, and no place for me to safely stay hidden, I waited until the Jeep disappeared behind an outcropping of boulders before I turned where Brian had turned. Not to worry, there was so much dirt trailing behind him, I knew I'd have no problem picking up Brian's trail. But before I'd gone even twenty feet, I saw why he'd stopped in the first place—there was a metal swing gate completely blocking the dirt road and a fence on either side of it that snaked along the main road as far as the eye could see.

Grumbling, I shoved my gearshift into park, climbed out of the Mustang, and stepped right on top of a rock. Peep-toe platform sandals, remember. Stylish for sure, but not exactly made for walking on the surface of the moon. My ankle twisted, and limping and cursing, I made my way to the gate. If I needed some sort of pass code or a key to open it, I was cooked.

Lucky for me, all I needed to do to open the gate was slide a huge metal bolt to one side and give the gate a healthy push. It swung open, and when it did, I limped back to my car and drove right through. I didn't bother to get out on the other side of the gate and close it behind me as Brian had. For one thing, I didn't want to risk another injury. For another . . . well, a girl never knows when she's going to need to make a quick escape.

From there, things got a little trickier. Following the Jeep on paved roads was a piece of cake, but on rough terrain, my Mustang was a whole lot like my shoes: made for the city, not the boondocks. I bumped over rocks and into ruts and through what looked like dried-up stream-beds and I had no choice, I had to slow to a crawl. It was that, or risk bottoming out the car.

All the while, I told myself not to worry. I could still see that giant poof of dust trailing behind the Jeep. All I had to do was keep it in sight and—

Bang! Hiss! Flap, flap, flap.

The not-so-encouraging sounds filled my ears and the steering wheel jerked in my hands. My poor car wobbled and tilted.

Flat tire.

"Damn!" I pounded the steering wheel, slowed down, and stopped, and all I could do was watch the cloud of dust in front of me get farther and farther away. Just like my chances of following Brian and finding Dan.

"Damn! It isn't possible. I've never had a flat and—"
Bang!

Another tire went, and my car sagged onto the dirt road.

Too mad to move, I sat there for a couple minutes, my

breaths coming in sharp, quick gasps, my brain cycling through my options. There weren't many. In fact, as far as I could tell, there was only one.

I pulled out my AAA card and my cell phone.

No signal.

"Who the hell ever decided that this place should be a place?" I screamed. "Who would ever want to live here? Who would bother to put a road here?" Since there didn't seem to be any point in sitting there waiting for answers, I got out of the car, and as long as I was hopping mad, I kicked the front left tire. Since it was already flat and I used the foot that wasn't attached to the ankle that throbbed, there was no further harm done.

Groaning, I leaned against the car and looked around at the nothing that surrounded me. No people. No houses. No traffic. Nothing but scraggly sage bushes, rocks, and more dust. If I was going to get back to the semicivilization that was Antonito, I was going to have to hoof it.

I grabbed my purse, and since it was late afternoon, the blue windbreaker I'd left in my car the night of the bone heist, too. After just a couple days in this part of the world, I knew that once the sun went down, the air chilled quickly. One last look in the backseat and the trunk, hoping for a pair of sneakers, and when I didn't find any, I headed out.

It didn't seem as if I'd driven on the dirt road beyond the gate for all that long, but getting back to the gate on foot took me forever. Then again, I was dodging potholes the size of some of the more elaborate gravestones back at Garden View, and more rocks that I swear were just waiting for me to make another bad move and twist my other ankle. As for the one that was already twisted, by the time I got back to the gate, I stopped to rest it. No way I was going to sit in the dirt, so I leaned against the gate, swiping my arm across my forehead to get rid of the sweat. I would have stayed longer if some furry creature didn't scurry by, just out of sight, but way too close for comfort.

The rest of my journey is best left undescribed. Let's just say it involved a whole lot more walking, a couple blisters, and a ride in a rusty pickup truck with a guy named Miguel, who in return for his kindness, asked for my phone number. What could I say? Miguel was insistent and he said something about not letting me out of the truck until he had my number in hand. I could only hope that when Ella started getting calls from this part of the world (and in Spanish, too), she'd understand.

By the time we rolled into Antonito, I was actually happy to see the place. I thanked Miguel (fast) and slid out of the truck, my hair in my eyes and my clothes caked with what felt like half the dessert. If I was paying more attention to my surroundings and less to my ankle and where I was going to get some ice to put on it, I would have noticed the police car parked nearby. As it turned out, it wasn't until I felt the familiar prickle of being watched that I realized I wasn't alone.

Oh yeah, it was Mr. Gorgeous Cop, all right, and he tipped his wide-brimmed hat back on his head and looked me up and down with something very much like pity in his eyes. I can't say for sure (what with the sweat and the hanging hair and all), but I think he might have been smiling, too.

"Come on," he said, opening the passenger door of the patrol car and urging me in. "It looks like we need to do some serious shopping."

He finally introduced himself in the women's clothing department of the twenty-four-hour Walmart in Alamosa, Colorado. He wasn't just a cop, he was the police chief of the Taopi Pueblo, and his name was Jesse Alvarez.

Gorgeousness aside, Jesse wasn't much when it came to fashion. At his insistence (and he was plenty insistent), I ended up buying two pairs of sturdy, off-brand jeans and four long-sleeve shirts. "Perfect," he said, "for scouring the desert, looking for whatever you're looking for."

Have I mentioned he wasn't exactly the type who beats around the bush?

He found out soon enough that I could be equally as stubborn. And that I had exacting standards. The stubborn part came when I completely ignored all the same old mumbo jumbo about the shaman and the throwing of bones and how, thanks to some mysterious message from the Beyond, he knew I was searching for something important. Like I'd told Goodshot, I didn't know Jesse well enough. Not yet, anyway. Until I did, I had to keep my mouth shut. As for the exacting standards . . . well, he learned about that as soon as he tried to lead the way to the shoe department. That's where I drew the line.

I understood the reasoning behind a pair of rugged cowboy boots. Honest! I even liked the idea of having a kicky little pair in my closet. But from Walmart?

I thought not.

Lucky for Jesse (who never would have heard the end of it from me if he'd pushed too hard), he had a leather-worker buddy back near Antonito who specialized in handmade boots. Lucky for me, Buzzard McGraw not only stayed up late, but was something of a god when it came to tooled leather. Jesse was pained and patient while I tried on boot after boot, but I refused to be hurried, and I was not about to settle. I finally chose a pair in goatskin. Fawn-colored, calf-length. They were burnished with a flame pattern that hugged the top of the foot and shot upward, wrapping around the leg. The design was artistic and intricate, lighter around the edges, darker in the center. Perfect for creating the illusion of a slim calf. Not that mine needed it.

I envisioned a stiletto-heel version of the boot that, for all his skill, Buzzard had never imagined, but he was willing to make it just for me. Jesse insisted (there's that word again) on the one-and-a-half-inch chunky Cuban heel already on the boots. Since my ankle was still tender, I let him win this round.

I fell instantly head over heels. With the boots, not with Jesse. That would only come later, though I had an inkling of it every time he was near and little skittles of electricity played across my skin. My gut told me he was one of the good guys, but I'd been fooled before. Sexual attraction is a powerful thing, and when it's crackling in the air, the line between reason and emotion is likely to get blurred. But during the night when my ankle throbbed and I tossed and turned and got up time and again to fetch ice from the creaking, clanking machine outside the motel office, I decided that if I still got good-guy vibes from Jesse the next time we were together, I would take a chance and tell him why I was visiting the Great Southwest. He was a cop, he might be able to help. Of course, he was also a Taopi Indian, like Goodshot, and I couldn't be sure how he was going to take the news of the body snatching. Then again, if it would help keep Dan alive, I was willing to take the chance.

The next morning my mind was made up and I was feeling better about life in general and my chances of helping Dan in particular. I was wearing the boots and they were dreamy, and comfortable, too. Turns out they provided perfect support for my tender ankle. I would have been on top of the world if I also wasn't dressed in those utilitarian but woefully unfashionable jeans along with a blue-and-yellow-plaid shirt that made me look like an extra in a high school–theater production of *Oklahoma*.

I limped a little closer to and then farther from the mirror atop the lopsided dresser in my motel room, trying to get a better gander at myself so I could decide if I was going to go for practicality or chuck the whole down-to-earth look and opt for my sandals, skinny jeans, and a tank top when I heard shuffling outside on the balcony that ran the length of the second floor of the motel.

I turned around just in time to see a shadow block the sunlight streaming in under the door. It moved quickly, and the next thing I knew, there was a single sheet of folded paper laying on the stained carpet. I raced to the window but I was too late. Whoever had been there was already gone.

For a minute, I stared at the paper. Which was silly, of course. I'd already figured it was from Brian the ghostbuster turned kidnapper. I already knew it was going to say something about Dan and the bones and—

My gulp echoed in the silence of my room, and the sound was enough to get me moving.

I reached for the paper, unfolded it, and read.

Dan 4 the bones
He still has a chance
But if u involve the cops
he will be dead 2 day

So I wasn't crazy when I thought someone had been watching me. Brian, and he'd seen me with Jesse.

Good guy or not, it didn't matter now. No way I could confide in Jesse.

He will be dead 2 day.

Just thinking about those words, my stomach went cold and my knees buckled. I sank onto the bed, but only for a minute, because that's when I came to my senses. I was the only one who could help Dan. I couldn't let him down. I had to find those bones, and I had to do it quickly. Before Brian and his alien buddies did something really stupid.

I would get right to work, right after I took the clothes I'd worn the day before over to Tom's Laundromat. The way I had it planned, while my dust-caked jeans were washing, I'd head over to Taberna. One of these days, I was bound to find Norma behind the bar. See, I remembered how she'd brought a pitcher of beer to the aliens even before they'd ordered it, and how her hand had brushed Brian's arm when she delivered the beer.

Oh yeah, Norma and I, we needed to talk.

I wadded my dirty clothes into a ball and headed across the street, and I was just pulling open the door to the Laundromat when a car pulled up alongside the cinder block building. Police car. With you-know-who driving.

I thought about that note that had been shoved under my door, the one that was burning a hole in the pocket of my no-name jeans, and even though I told myself it made me look weak and worried, I couldn't help it. I glanced around, wondering as I did if Brian had his eyes on me and, if he did, where he was watching from. I wasn't about to take any chances. When Jesse's window slid open, I hotfooted it into the Laundromat.

There was no back door so it wasn't exactly like I could avoid him completely, and that was too bad. I knew Jesse would come inside. He was a cop, after all, and cops don't give up easily. By the time he walked in, I'd already bought a packet of laundry detergent from a vending machine against the wall and thrown my clothes into a washer as far from a window as it was possible to get.

Jesse stopped just inside the door and looked me over. Since I was pretending to be busy watching the washing machine fill, I couldn't actually see this, but I could feel his eyes, everywhere they touched me. When I went right on ignoring him, he stepped closer. "Nice shirt," he said. "My mom has one just like it."

"Oh, thanks a bunch!" I threw my hands in the air, spun to face him—and caught the smile on his face right before he fought to hide it. "You got me," I said, turning back to the washing machine. "You knew you would, talking like that."

"But my mom really does have the same shirt. For what it's worth . . ." I heard his boots scrape against the beige linoleum and the long, low whistle that spoke louder than words. "You look a hell of a lot better in it than she does."

I pursed my lips to hide my own smile.

"If I didn't know better"—Jesse tipped his head back toward where he'd left his cruiser—"looked to me like outside there, you were trying to pretend you didn't know me."

There was nothing wrong with the machine, but I opened it anyway, rearranged the few things in there splish-splashing around, then closed the lid. "Why would I do that?"

"Just what I was wondering."

I knew Jesse was close, because the air heated and my temperature shot up along with it. I kept my hands flat on the washing machine in front of me and gave a little shrug that I hoped didn't draw too much attention to my bustline. "I guess I just don't think we have all that much to say to each other."

"Oh, I get it. Love 'em and leave 'em, eh?" When he chuckled, I looked up at him. "You got the boots you love, now you don't need me anymore."

"Maybe." Somebody had left a basket of clothes on the washer next to the one I was using and far be it from me to touch other people's clothes. I pulled out the towels, anyway, and one by one, folded them. "I didn't come looking for you yesterday, you were waiting for me when I got back here to Antonito. And you're the one who insisted we go shopping. So we went shopping. So maybe you're right." Could I sound convincing enough? I hoped so. I raised my chin. "Now I don't need you anymore."

"Except now I need you."

I dared to glance at him out of the corner of my eye, but I didn't dare ask what he wanted. I didn't have to. I already knew. He was going to press me for information I wouldn't give him the day before and I couldn't give him now. Not after this new threat on Dan's life.

"Sheriff over in Taos County is a friend of mine," he said, and I actually thought he was changing the subject until he added, "From what you told me about where you got stranded yesterday, I figured that's where you were. Gave him a call this morning and told him to be on the lookout for your Mustang. He called a little while ago, said they found your car, all right. They towed it over to the local station and they need you to call." He handed me a slip of paper with a phone number written on it. "You know, to authorize the work. You've got two flat tires you're going to need to replace."

"Which is exactly what I said. Two flats. I was out driving, taking a look around, checking out the scenery, and I had a freaky accident. Two flat tires at the same time."

"Only it wasn't an accident."

My mouth fell open.

So not a good look for me, so I snapped it shut, but only for as long as it took me to collect my thoughts. "Are you saying—"

"Somebody tossed nails on the road."

"It wasn't exactly what I'd call a road." He hadn't been bouncing in and out of the ruts like I had, so I figured I'd better point that out. "I guess I should have been more careful. Maybe there was some kind of construction going on or—"

"Construction? Out where you were? What do you think?"

"Then maybe . . ." I scrambled for anything that would help explain where I was and what I was doing there. Anything that didn't involve aliens. "Maybe a truck dumped its load."

"Only there's no reason a truck would need to be up

where you were. That road doesn't lead much of any-where."

"Then maybe—"

"Maybe you were following somebody who didn't want to be followed?"

Damn cops for all their insight.

I drummed my fingers against the washing machine, the rhythm keeping pace with the frantic thoughts spin-ning through my head like the laundry in the rinse water. "I don't know anyone around here I'd want to follow." I managed to say this at the same time I gave him a look that said *anyone* included him, and oh, how I hated having to do that! Bad enough Brian and his band of felons had risked Dan's safety. Now they were messing with my love life, and I didn't appreciate it. "I'm just a tourist, remem-ber. Just soaking in some of the local color."

"And if I'm any judge, getting yourself in a heap of trouble." He'd taken off his cowboy hat when he stepped into the Laundromat, and he set it on the closest washer. "I just thought you should know. About the nails, that is. You strike me as being a smart woman, but you may have underestimated whoever it is you're following. You see what I'm getting at, don't you? They know you're on to them. That's why they tossed those nails on the road. To flatten your tires. To strand you out there in the high des-ert. You're lucky that ol' truck came along and picked you up. The desert isn't a kind place, not if you aren't pre-pared. There are plenty of coyotes up that way, and moun-tain lions. Bears, too, though you don't have to worry about them all that much. Not unless you just so happen to step between a mother and her cub. No, the desert at night . . . it might be a pretty place, but it sure isn't a safe one."

I didn't point out that it wasn't all that great during the day, either. Heck, he lived around here. He should have already known that.

"I'm just saying"—he shuffled a step closer—"we'd be better off working together than we are working against each other. And in the long run, you'd be safer."

I sucked in a long breath, pulled back my shoulders, and faced him. "I appreciate it. I really do. And I wish I could help you. But you've got it all wrong. Thanks to that shaman of yours, you're concocting some mysterious story for me, but you see, there isn't one. You can't help me find anything, because I'm not looking for anything. And you can't keep me safe from anyone, because there's nobody I need to be kept safe from. So even though you think you know a lot about me—"

"You've heard the legend of the raven, right?" Jesse folded his arms across his broad chest and leaned back against one of the washing machines. "You know the story we Indians tell?"

I was so not in the mood for a cultural lesson. Not when, for all I knew, Brian was sitting in some nearby building watching us through binoculars and thinking we were talking about Dan. There was a bench along the far wall and I turned to head that way. "I really don't—"

Jesse's hand on my arm stopped me cold. Or I should say hot. Fire burned up my arm and puddled somewhere between my heart and my stomach. Maybe he felt it, too, because as quickly as he grabbed me, he let go and stepped back, and I swear, when he started to talk, he was a little winded.

"My people . . . they say that a raven is a magical bird. It sees the past. It sees the future. The shaman tells me you're a raven."

"What, so now you think I'm some kind of fortune-teller? Don't I wish! I could make a killing—figuratively speaking, of course—if I knew next spring's fashion trends before anyone else. But then, that's probably not what you're talking about. Is this just your way of telling me that I should know I'm getting into trouble and I should head back home where I belong?"

"Raven understands that sometimes there's more to the world than just what we see with our physical eyes. He's a messenger who brings word from the Other Side. Just like Raven sees the past and the future, he sees the living. And the dead."

I wrinkled my nose. "You can be really creepy. You know that, don't you?"

Jesse shrugged. "It's what the shaman tells me."

"That you can be really creepy?"

"That you are the raven."

"Sorry. My coloring is all wrong." I managed my sweetest smile. "And what does this have to do with you bugging me about looking for whatever it is you think I'm looking for, anyway?"

"I have no idea," Jesse said. "When I asked the shaman the very same thing, he told me I'd have to figure it out for myself." He plopped his hat on his head, sauntered to the door, and walked out. A minute later, I watched the patrol car cruise out of the parking lot and head south.

I let go a breath I didn't even realize I was holding. "Damn it!" I pounded the washing machine with my fist. "Doesn't it figure, just when I meet a guy who—"

"You like him, huh?" Goodshot popped up right on top of my washing machine. "You got good taste. He's Indian. Indian men make good husbands."

"I'm not looking for a husband."

He floated down to the floor. "Your boots say otherwise."

"My boots!" Honestly, I was so tired of men talking nonsense, I nearly screamed. I took out my frustrations on that pile of towels I'd just folded, slapping them back into the clothes basket I'd plucked them out of just a few minutes before. "I don't see how my boots—"

"A woman never wears boots that fancy unless she's out to get a man. You know how it works. He notices the boots, so he checks to see if her legs are strong, and that tells him if she's a hard worker." He skimmed a look over me. "After he looks over her legs, he studies her body. So he can judge if she'll be good at bearin' his children. From there, he has to figure out if that's the face he wants lookin' at him from the pillow next to him each mornin'. But believe me, Pepper, it all starts with the boots."

"Whatever!" I tossed the last towel in the basket. "Or it could be that a woman buys a pair of boots because she likes the boots. Period."

He scrunched up his nose and shook his head. "They ain't practical for ridin' or ropin'."

"Then it's a good thing I'm not going to be doing any riding or roping."

"But you are goin' be doin' some investigatin', right?" It wasn't what he said so much that got me interested as it was the gleam in his eyes when he said it. He had my attention and he knew it, and once he did, he went right on. "Figured you'd been so busy making moony eyes at that policeman, you hadn't heard the news yet. About that woman over at the saloon down the street, that Norma. She's dead. Local cops found her last night from what I heard. Strangled, right there in her own house. Can't imagine it has anything to do with my bones, but I figured as how you should know. I was over near her house—"

"You know where Norma lives?"

"Lived," he corrected me, and since he understood the difference between present tense and past in a far different way than I did, I let him. "Wouldn't have noticed at all except as how she lived right next to the cemetery. We were over there, me and Anarosa and Kitty and Suzanna. You know, shootin' the breeze and talkin' about old times. And we saw all the commotion last night. Pity, that Norma bein' such a young woman and all."

It was more coincidence than pity, and I'm not a big believer in coincidence. I spun the dial on the washer so that the water would drain and I could get my clothes out and toss them in a dryer. That way, when I got back, I could pick them up.

"The cops are there now?" I asked Goodshot.

He shook his head. "Been dead all day, pardon the pun. They took what was left of Norma away last night and locked up the house behind them. And I never would have even mentioned it to you, except that a little while ago, don't you know it, but a man showed up at the house. Not a policeman, somebody who didn't have no business there. I know this for a fact, because he didn't go in through the door. He broke a window round back and got in the house that way. Can't say what any of it means, or if it's important. But I thought you might like to know."

I think he realized he was right because I'd already raced out of the Laundromat and was waiting for him out on the sidewalk. Goodshot led the way to the ratty adobe right next to the cemetery. Anarosa, Kitty, and Suzanna (a pretty little blonde with a bowed mouth and a gosh-shucks looks on her face) were already there.

"He's still inside," Kitty whispered, though since she was dead and nobody could hear her except me, it didn't really seem to matter.

"We are watching him for you, yes." Anarosa's cheeks were pink with excitement. No easy thing for a ghost.

"Not very Christian of him." Suzanna's hands were folded at her waist, her jaw was tight, and that cute little chin of hers trembled with outrage. "Brazen as brass, that's what he is. He went into the house even though that sign there says it's a crime scene and no one's allowed in." I couldn't help but notice that when she pointed this out, she looked right at Kitty and Anarosa and batted the long lashes on her big blue eyes. No doubt, she was the only one of them who could read and she wasn't about to let them forget it.

"You guys cover the front of the house." I waved them that way. "Nobody's going to see you, anyway, and you can yell to me if he tries to get out that way. I'm going to . . ." I was already in stealth mode, stooped over, making my way along the side of the house. I reminded myself that they could be as loud as they wanted to be, but I had to whisper. "I want to see what this guy is up to."

Carefully, I raised myself up on tiptoe and looked into the window. Kitchen. Small, messy, and nothing going on in there. I flattened my back to the wall and moved on to the next window. This one was a combination living room and dining room and I had no better luck there. Cursing under my breath, I moved around to the other side of the house.

Norma's bedroom was painted a brassy shade of yellow and decorated with pictures of tropical islands torn from magazines. Water, water everywhere, and I guess I couldn't blame a woman who lived in this parched wonderland for craving blue ocean waves. Of course, it wasn't Norma's decorating talents (or lack thereof) that interested me nearly as much as seeing Brian inside her bedroom, rooting around in Norma's closet.

I kept low, peeking in through one corner of the window and watching as he tossed shoes and purses and a couple shabby sweatshirts over his shoulder and onto the floor. When he froze, his hand on something deep in the closet, I tensed and held my breath.

It came out in a whoosh of astonishment when Brian pulled my Jimmy Choo glazed canvas tote bag out of the closet. Grinning, he unzipped the bag, turned it over, and shook it.

Nothing fell out but a few flakes of dust.

Goodshot's bones weren't in there.

Not what I expected, and I will admit, I was puzzled. Brian? Not so much. Like he wasn't the least bit surprised, he slipped the bag over one shoulder, the better to hang on to it, and turned toward the door.

It is never wise to let emotion get tangled up in an investigation. I knew this in my head. Too bad it was so tough convincing the rest of me. Heck, I'd paid a lot of money for that bag. And I loved it. Nearly as much as I loved my new boots. Now Brian had the tote and . . . well, heck, there was no way I was going to let him walk away with it.

Anger pounding through me like each of my boot-shod steps in the dusty soil, I marched to the front of the house.

"Son of a bitch," I grumbled. "He's in there, all right, and he just found the bag. My bag. Your bones aren't in it," I added when Goodshot's eyes lit up. "So he must be looking for them in the house. Or for something else. Whatever it is, he's planning on taking it out of there in my tote bag."

I wasn't exactly surprised when Goodshot gave me a blank look in answer to this impassioned narrative. Not so Kitty. Her eyes narrowed and her painted mouth thinned. "Your bag, right? And it's something you took a fancy to the first time ever you laid eyes on it? That man in there has it?"

"You got that right, sister, and I'll tell you what, it proves Norma must have been the one who swiped Goodshot's bones when the lights went out, and she kept my bag as payment for her effort. Only I don't know what she did with the bones, or why Brian wants the tote bag." I sent a laser look at the door. "I do know there's no way that lowlife's getting out of here with my Jimmy Choo!"

With the ghosts trailing behind me, I stationed myself in front of the door. Of course, it didn't take but a couple seconds for me to come to my senses and realize Brian wasn't going to come out that way. He was going to leave the way he'd gotten in, through that broken window out back. En masse, we headed that way, and I'd just turned the corner to the back of the house when—

Well, I can't say exactly what happened because it happened so fast.

I only know that something came out of nowhere, something that felt like a piece of lumber. It smacked me right over the head.

My knees crumpled and I hit the dirt. The last thing I remember hearing was Brian's footsteps as he ran away. The last thing I remember seeing . . .

Goodshot, Kitty, Anarosa, and Suzanna hovered over me, wringing their hands and looking around for help they wouldn't have been able to summon even if they could find it. At least I think it was them. The ghosts faded, but not a little at a time like they sometimes do when I'm talking to them and they don't want to be bothered. They burst like bubbles, right in front of my eyes. First Suzanna. Then Kitty. Then Anarosa.

My eyes spun in my head and a burst of lights, like a galaxy of exploding supernovas, erupted across my field of vision. Through the blinding brightness I saw Goodshot. There one second. Gone the next.

I was all alone.

9

"Where's . . . Goodshot?"

That was my voice. Maybe. It sounded like it came from a cave, all muffled and echoey. Since it was barely more than a whisper, listening to it shouldn't have made my head hurt, but each word pounded through my brain in steel-toed boots.

"Goodshot?" In my small, rasping voice, I called out to him, but I didn't get an answer. My eyes were closed, but I turned my head against something warm and nearly fell right back into the blackness I'd been wrapped in. I was safe, only I didn't know safe from what. I was cared for, only I didn't know why or who could make me feel this way. I was comfortable. So comfortable, I was tempted to let myself float back into the blackness and forget whatever it was that was tapping at my brain, trying to get my attention. Too bad that whatever wouldn't let me. "Where . . . ? Goodshot? Kitty? Ana . . . rosa?"

"Whatever you're talking about, it doesn't matter right now."

Jesse's voice. Only it couldn't have been, because the last I remembered anything at all, I was back in the Laundromat pretty much telling Jesse to get lost. He drove away. Right before I went—

Norma's house.

Like a tsunami, the memories washed over me: Goodshot and the girls standing lookout at the front door. Me, going around the back, watching Brian take my tote bag out of Norma's closet. I was pissed. I remembered that loud and clear. I was all set to confront Brian, about the bag and about what the hell he'd done with Dan. And then—

Though they felt as if they were weighted down by bricks, I forced my eyes open. I was lying on the dusty ground, my head in Jesse's lap, and he was looking down at me. This close, I saw that his eyes were flecked with amber. Cool color. In a hot sort of way. Too bad it did nothing to brighten the worry that wedged a vee between his eyes.

Nice. It was nice to have someone worry about me. But even Jesse's apparent concern wasn't enough to deflect what my scrambled brain had decided was the most important thing for me to figure out.

"Where . . . ? What . . . ?" When I tried to sit up, he put a hand on my shoulder and gently pushed me back down. But not before I had a chance to take a quick look around.

I didn't see any sign of Goodshot or the other ghosts. And Jesse . . .

"You weren't here," I told him and reminded myself. "You . . . you drove away. And Goodshot came with me to Norma's, and he was here, but now he's gone and—"

A metallic noise to my left made me flinch, and Jesse shot a look that way.

"Sorry, Chief." This voice belonged to someone else, someone I didn't know. When I turned my head to see who it was, Jesse stopped me, one hand on my cheek.

"It's just the paramedics," he said. "They're going to take you—"

"Oh, no!" I might have been knocked senseless, but I knew enough to know I wasn't going to the hospital. Hospitals cost money and I was unemployed, remember. When Jesse put a hand on my arm, I slapped it away. Or at least I tried. The fact that I missed by like a mile said something about my current state of uncoordination. "I can't—"

"You've got no choice." He moved aside, carefully turning me over to the paramedics. "Head injuries are nothing to fool with."

"And this is a crime scene." This comment came from a middle-aged guy with a bushy mustache who bent over me and gave me an eagle-eyed look.

Sheriff by the look of his uniform and badge, and a rush of panic coursed through me. Maybe I wasn't going to the hospital. Maybe I was going to jail.

"I didn't go in the house," I said. It might have been a more convincing statement if my words didn't wobble and

I didn't have to press my eyes closed at the end of the sentence. It was that or watch my brain pop out my forehead and go bouncing through town. "I was just walking by and—"

"Didn't say nothing about Norma's crime scene." The sheriff gave Jesse a look that told me they had already discussed me, and the sheriff had expected me to come up with a half-baked story like this to explain what I was doing there. "Talking about *your* crime scene, Ms. Martin. Somebody assaulted you. Do you remember what happened?"

"No." I shook my head. Or at least I tried. Since the paramedics were in the process of slipping one of those goofy neck braces on me, it was kind of hard. Even that little bit of motion made my head hurt like hell. Maybe it was the pain that dredged up a memory. "Wait! Yes. I remember. It was Jimmy Choo. No, Jimmy Choo was my tote bag. It was Brian. At the stadium watching the baseball game. And in Norma's house. And—"

"And this Brian, he's the one who hit you over the head?" The sheriff had pulled out a little notebook and a pen and he stood above me with it, waiting for the details and looking a bit put out that he'd written down the whole thing about Jimmy Choo, then ended up crossing it out and starting again.

I hated to admit I didn't know anything for sure. Yes, I'd seen Brian in the house. But I hadn't seen who'd come at me with the California redwood that had smacked me over the head. Goodshot had been there, though. Along with his lady friends. I was sure of that, and I struggled to sit up so I could look around and find them and ask them exactly what had happened, but there was still no sign of the ghosts. "Goodshot . . . He was here," I muttered. "He must have seen everything. He could tell you . . . No, he couldn't tell you, he could tell me, because he can't tell you, of course. But if he told me, then I, I could tell you."

I saw the look the sheriff and Jesse exchanged, but before I had a chance to tell them I wasn't as crazy as their glances seemed to say, the paramedics lifted me onto a stretcher and I was so busy wincing from the pain that shot through my head and shoulders, I didn't have a chance to say anything at all. They wheeled me to a waiting ambulance.

"No, really." Maybe Jesse couldn't hear my feeble protest. Maybe that's why even though he was walking along beside me, he ignored me. "I don't want to go to—"

He squeezed my hand. "Don't worry. I'm coming with you to La Jara," he said, and when the paramedics slid the stretcher into the ambulance, he hopped in and sat down beside me.

It wasn't until we'd started on our way that I realized he was still holding my hand. My brain might have been scrambled, but I got the message. It went something like this: hand holding had to be some Southwestern touchy-feely police procedure designed to get a victim talking. Little did Jesse know, it wasn't going to work on this particular victim. "I can't tell you what happened because I don't know what happened," I said as if he'd been following what I was thinking. "I came around the corner and I didn't see—"

"Of course you didn't. The guy probably came up behind you. But you said someone else was there. Good-shot? Weird name. There's a story in my tribe. About an old-time Indian named Goodshot. He was—"

I pretended to drift off to sleep.

A good idea, yes?

Apparently not what the paramedic riding in back with us wanted to see. She put a hand on my arm. "I need you to stay awake, Ms. Martin," she said. "Just for a while. Are you dizzy?"

I tried to shake my head no, but since it made me dizzy, that wasn't very smart.

"But she is confused, right? I mean, she must be with the way she's talking." She was looking over me and at Jesse when she said this. "You said she talked about some-one else being there with her, but—"

"He was." If Jesse wasn't going to stand up for me, I had to do it myself. "Goodshot was there and Kitty and—"

"No footprints in the dust except Ms. Martin's and the attacker's." This from Jesse, and I had to give him credit, even though he was using all that police-y logic to prove I was talking out of my head, he didn't do it in an arrogant sort of way. Not like Quinn would have done. In fact, when Jesse looked away from the paramedic and back at me, there was a sort of hot chocolate warmth in his eyes that made the pain inside my head disappear. At least for a couple seconds. "You were probably seeing things. You know, because of that smack on the head."

"I didn't . . . I wasn't . . . He was there before . . ."

Before I was hit on the head. That was the last time I saw Goodshot clearly. Because after I was clunked . . .

Another wave of memory crashed into my brain. Ghosts popping like soap bubbles. Not out of existence. I may not be a philosopher, but I am enough of a thinker to know that my getting whacked on the head or not getting whacked on the head can't possibly affect the way the Other Side works.

It could, though, have an impact on how I see the Other Side.

Or didn't see it.

These thoughts spent some time swimming around inside my brain. They were on a third lap when I realized Jesse was watching me carefully, an expectant sort of look in his eyes. Like he was waiting for me to make sense. Or to not make sense. And like whichever way I went would help determine the outcome once we made it to the ER.

No-insurance girl did her best to get her act together.

"Goodshot was there before . . ." Had I been feeling more like myself and less like somebody with a head full of jelly, I might have remembered that there was no use arguing with Jesse, even when he was trying to lead me into talking by echoing what I'd said earlier. For one thing, he was Jesse, and it wasn't going to work. For another, I couldn't explain Goodshot and the other ghosts even if my head wasn't whirling.

It was best to change the subject. Easy. Even woozy, I had questions that needed to be answered. "You." Since Jesse still had a hold of my hand, it wasn't hard to tighten my hold as a way of letting him know this was important. "You were at the Laundromat. Oh, and my good jeans!" There was no way I wanted those jeans to spend the day in the dryer and maybe walk off with someone who wasn't me. I tried to sit up, to tell the driver we had to turn around and go back to the Laundromat so I could pop inside and save my jeans, but both Jesse and the paramedic pressed me back into place.

"You left," I managed to say when they got their way and I settled down. "You drove away, Jesse. I saw you. And . . . and you didn't know about Norma. How did you—"

"End up back in Antonito? Damned if I know!" He chuckled, but not like it was funny, more like something weird had happened and he didn't understand it, and didn't like admitting it. "I was on my way back to the pueblo," he said, "when a call came in on my radio. The call said that a woman had been attacked in Antonito and she needed help. The call requested backup from any police officer in the vicinity. Technically . . ." This time, Jesse glanced at the paramedic.

"I know I was out of my jurisdiction," he said, and even in my mushy-head state I knew this was so she didn't think he was butting his cop nose where it didn't belong. "But I'd just left you in Antonito." He swung his gaze back to me. "And you can say anything you want to say about what you're doing in this part of the world, but I know you're up to something you shouldn't be up to. So of course I figured the woman who'd been hurt was you. And that voice on the radio . . ." Jesse shook his head, trying to figure it out. "The man made it sound like it was really important that the local cops get some help. Naturally, I was worried. I turned right around and headed back to Antonito, and weird thing is, when I got to the address he gave—the place where I found you—I was the only one there. And when I called the local guys to ask where the hell they were and why they were dragging their butts, they didn't know what I was talking about. I got the call. They didn't. And that's strange because it came in on a frequency they should have been monitoring. I can't figure it out." Another shake of his head. "But I do know that you were in back of that house where no one would have seen you for who knows how long. You would have laid there forever if I didn't get that freaky call."

"Thank you, Goodshot." I whispered this because, let's face it, I didn't want Jesse to think I was any loonier than he already did. While I was at it, I looked around, too, as much as I was able because, let's face it (again), I fully expected Goodshot to be hovering in some corner of the ambulance, or floating above me, basking in Jesse's praise and feeling like the hero he was.

But again, there was no sign of him.

In spite of the warning look I got from the paramedic and the pressure of Jesse's hand against mine telling me not to budge, I shifted, suddenly aware that I was feeling something I hadn't felt in a long time.

Or I should say more accurately, I *wasn't* feeling something I had felt for a long time.

That little sizzle was gone.

The one I hadn't even realized had been a constant presence in my life since that day at Garden View when I fell and thwacked my head on Gus Scarpetti's mausoleum and first saw the ghosts.

* * *

A few hours later I was lying in bed in my motel room, glad that cooler heads had prevailed and nobody forced me to check into the hospital, grateful the docs hadn't found anything icky on their x-rays and CT scans of my brain, and—

Feeling really weird.

Yeah, that would explain why I couldn't get comfortable. Why my heart was doing a rat-a-tat inside my ribs. And my blood thrummed in my ears. And my hands were sweaty and my breathing was faster than a speeding bullet, and the quiet and blackness that closed around me felt . . . I dunno. Quieter and blacker than it had in a really long time.

Empty.

Believe me, I knew this had nothing to do with the crack on the head.

And everything to do with how my world had turned upside down.

"No ghosts."

I said the words out loud, just to try them on for size.

They felt all wrong.

Rather than lie there and try to make sense of the notion, I sat up, threw off the blankets, and slipped out of bed to pace my minuscule room. At least when Jesse called at three . . . (He had insisted, and since getting woken from a sound sleep beat the heck out of spending the night in the hospital, I had said it would be okay. Of course, that was when I thought I might actually be sleeping soundly at three, and before I realized that thinking about what happened to me—or might have happened to me—made me feel all antsy and nervous.) I'd be wide awake and perfectly coherent and could prove to him what I'd told him in the first place and shouldn't have had to prove: that I wasn't in desperate need of another ride in an ambulance.

Just the fact that my brain was ping-ponging like this says a lot about my mental state.

Was I relieved at my no-ghostly existence?

Worried?

Thankful?

Pissed?

At that point, I didn't know. I only knew that I wouldn't know what to feel, not for sure. Not until I got some answers.

The thought firmly in mind, I threw on my oh-so-ordinary jeans and a brown-and-black-plaid shirt that had the whole *Green Acres* vibe going for it, and slipped into the world's most adorable boots. The fact that the room spun a little when I bent down for the boots told me I needed to take things slow and careful, and slowly and carefully, I left my room.

It was dark and quiet in Antonito. But then, it was already after two, and even the bars were closed. Alone, I walked down the street, and yes, I did think about breaking into Tom's Laundromat to see if my jeans were there waiting for me, but I talked myself out of it. Some things, it seems, are even more important than favorite jeans.

At the cemetery, I took a careful look around.

I could detect no shimmer in the night-still air. No darker shadows in the shadows behind the headstones. No nothing.

No ghosts.

"Goodshot?" I was all by myself, and heck, Norma next door was the closest neighbor, and she was dead, so I didn't bother to keep my voice down. "Hey, Goodshot! It's me, Pepper. If you wouldn't mind just popping in for a minute, we need to talk. I want to thank you for that call to Jesse. And I need a little help!"

My only answer was the sound of the wind in my ears.

I considered my options and, because they were obviously limited, tried the same song and dance with Anarosa, Kitty, and Suzanna.

I got the same answer—nothing.

No ghosts.

The enormity of the realization rooted me to the spot. For exactly fifteen seconds. Then I realized that for the first time in years, I was free! No. More. Ghosts. In spite of my headache, my sore shoulders, and the worry at the back of my mind about the hospital bill and how the heck I was ever going to be able to pay it, I smiled.

No more ghosts meant no more being dragged into cases I didn't care about. No more cases meant no more getting shot at. Or knifed. Or slammed in the head and ending up in an ER in some no-name place I'd already forgotten the name of.

In fact, no ghosts and no more cases meant no more no-name places I had to visit in the name of investigating.

When I headed back to the motel, there was a spring in

my step. No small thing considering my head, and my shoulders, and my still-tender ankle. In fact, I just might have been skipping a little. Humming a happy little tune under my breath, I pulled out my suitcase and, one by one, I tossed in my clothes.

As for those wonderful, just-broken-in, fit-perfectly jeans . . .

I sighed.

And promised myself I'd buy another pair just like them once I got back home to Cleveland.

The prospect of a shopping trip further brightened my outlook, and when I dragged my suitcase to the door, I was humming just a little bit louder, but not so loud that I didn't hear my cell ring.

Jesse. Who else would be conscientious enough to actually mean it when he said he was going to call at three?

I answered with a perky, "I'm fine. I'm not unconscious. You don't need to call again. Bye!" and hung up. I didn't even notice—well, hardly—the little pang that stabbed my heart when I realized I'd never see Jesse again. "Not meant to be," I told myself. It was some consolation, sort of, and keeping it in mind so I didn't get mushy, I headed out to the parking lot, suitcase in tow.

I opened the trunk and plopped my suitcase in and I guess I couldn't help myself. Thinking about leaving this part of the world made me think about arriving there. And thinking about arriving there made me think about Goodshot. And thinking about Goodshot . . .

Just about to slam the trunk shut, I paused.

Thinking about Goodshot made me think about how all he'd ever wanted was for his bones to be buried on that pueblo of his.

And thinking about Goodshot's bones made me think about Dan. And thinking about Dan . . .

Well, it was easy to see where things were headed from there.

Ghosts or no ghosts, I was the only one who could help Dan, because I was the only one who knew he'd been kidnapped and that his kidnapping and Goodshot's bones . . . well, it was all connected somehow, only I didn't know the details yet. Just like I didn't know what Norma's murder had to do with the scheme other than that she took the bones and my tote bag along with them. I was also the only one who knew that Brian and his Cleveland Indians fans buddies were probably behind the whole thing. And that it all started because of some silly curse, and a baseball team that couldn't win.

What did it all mean?

That was a no-brainer.

I was the only one who could investigate, and whether there were ghosts in my life or not, I owed it to both the living and the dead to find out the truth.

Damn, but I hate it when my better self gets the better of me.

10

If I had my way, I'd just cut to the chase and get to the good part, namely, that as it turned out, I was glad I stuck around. The next day, I ended up in bed with Jesse.

As juicy as that part of the story is, though, I know it isn't fair to skip over everything that led up to it. I mean, really, that would leave out the second murder and the chasing and the running and the mayhem and, well, it's really not much of a story without all that, is it? And it's not like I'm going to divulge details, anyway, not about Jesse and me and what happened that night in that cramped and poorly decorated motel room.

So I might as well start with the murder and the mayhem, and the murder and the mayhem . . . well, that really started the morning after I'd been to the cemetery and made the discovery that in the world of private investigating for the dead, I was still investigating, but not for or with the not-so-dearly not-so-departed.

The first thing I saw (after the Tilt-a-Whirl moment when I dragged myself out of bed) was the note tucked under my motel-room door.

At least when I bent down to pick it up, the world didn't wobble as much as it had the night before, and my shoulders, though they still ached, didn't hurt as much, either. Things were looking up.

My outlook brightened even more when I unfolded the paper and read the message:

> *Thought it was a game and would be fun.*
> *Thought we'd be heroes for removing the curse.*
> *Not the way things are turning out.*
> *Meet me. 8 tonight. Tres Piedras.*
> *Where your tires were flattened, keep following the road up to Wind Mountain.*

This note wasn't cobbled together from words cut from newspapers. It was handwritten. By one of the kidnappers.

A kidnapper who sounded like he was ready to toss in the towel.

Oh yeah, I was jazzed, and in record time, I showered and got dressed and unpacked all the clothes I'd packed the night before. And I did it all with a happy heart.

With or without ghosts tagging along, I had a lead, but then the fact that I'd been able to do it on my own shouldn't have come as a big surprise. Except that they can be royal pains, endlessly annoying and day-and-night demanding, ghosts are never really all that helpful when it comes to my investigations, anyway.

Of course, now that I was completely on my own, the thought of going out to the middle of nowhere was a little creepier than usual. Tres Piedras. The place my tires were flattened. As far as I remembered—and I remembered pretty well—there would be no one within shouting distance if I got in trouble, and no place to run if this meeting turned sour. It wouldn't be bad to have a little backup, dead or alive.

I was just tugging a comb through my curls when the thought struck and I froze, realized keeping my arms up that high was making my shoulders cramp, and tossed down the comb. It landed on the dresser next to my cell, and automatically, I thought about the call I'd gotten from Jesse in the wee hours of the morning.

Dependable.

In my mind, it was a word that had never attached itself to any man—not my dad, who was doing time in prison for Medicare fraud, or Joel, my former fiancé, who hit the road when our family's reputation hit the skids, and especially not Quinn, who for all his deliciousness could be as much a pain in the butt as the ghosts in my life.

For one crazy moment, I thought of calling Jesse. He was dependable, and good in a crisis. I could still feel the warmth from where he'd held my hand all the way to the hospital. Oh yeah, Jesse would be good to have along when I went out to meet the kidnapper, all right. And he knew the lay of the land.

I already had my hand on my phone when a voice

started chattering inside my head. It went something like this:

You're on your own now. For real. No backup. No ghosts. And if you're going to prove that you can handle kidnappers and curses and anything else the Universe throws at you . . .

I didn't call Jesse. Instead, I checked the clock and smiled. I had until eight o'clock to get back to New Mexico.

That gave me plenty of time to head over to Tom's Laundromat and rescue my jeans.

I was bound and determined to solve this case on my own.

That didn't mean I didn't get the heebie-jeebies when I turned onto that rutted and rocky road to nowhere heading out to meet I-don't-know-who I-didn't-know-where. By that time, the shadows were long and the evening sky was darkening in the east to an inky color that reminded me of the jeans I'd retrieved from that dryer at Tom's. I will say this much for the folks of Antonito—they are an honest bunch. That, or maybe no one of my height who wore a size as small as mine had happened upon the jeans before I got back there to scoop them up. Either way, I was grateful, even though I hadn't bothered to change into them. I'd been in the foothills of Wind Mountain before, remember. Now that the jeans were safely back in my possession, I wasn't taking the chance of having anything happen to them in the way of dust, rips—or blood.

Not exactly what I wanted to think about so I was actually kind of grateful when a coyote streaked in front of my car and I had to grab on to the wheel with both hands and jam on the brakes. I can't say for sure, but I don't think the critter noticed (or cared about) the hand signal I gave it to show what I thought of its dirt road–crossing skills. It disappeared into the scrubby bushes, and a moment later, I heard it yipping. The sound was lonesome and way eerier than any of the ghosts I'd ever met, and it sent an icy shiver over my shoulders. I only hoped the coyote wasn't sending out a report to its friends about the fresh meat making its way up the mountain.

The terrain looked all-too-familiar. It should. I was just about at the spot where my tires had been flattened and I hoped while the cops were out there saving my car and towing it to the repair shop that had fitted it with new tires I couldn't afford, they'd gotten all the nails. Evidence, right? And cops are good about collecting evidence.

That didn't keep me from holding my breath. I didn't let it out again until I made it past the place where my poor car had spent that night.

I was on unfamiliar ground now. Here, the sloping contours of Wind Mountain were more imposing than ever. The closer I got, the more I could see that, like the landscape around me, the mountain was pocked with outcroppings of jagged rocks and decorated with shaggy gray sage bushes. I drove over a dried streambed lined with about a million little rocks, which made my car sway and lurch. I slowed down even more and kept both eyes on the road. When I maneuvered around a boulder bigger than my car, the shadows on the other side were thick. I turned on the Mustang's lights.

Up ahead, the road—and oh, how I use that word loosely—swung around to the left, through what looked like it might once have been a pasture and then through the center of more nothing. It shot off to the right, and I bounced along, heading up the side of Wind Mountain. Another fifteen minutes of inching along, and I was surrounded by scraggly trees. Piñon pines, I remembered someone in Antonito calling them, and don't picture Christmas trees when I say this. These pines were short, dark green, and as shaggy as that coyote I'd seen a while back. Their shadows hugged the road, and I cringed when their branches brushed the car like fingernails on a blackboard.

Another turn, and I was out of the trees and back to barren, rocky terrain. I edged around a rut that dropped off into a narrow gully alongside the road, turned one more time, and—

I was at a dead end.

Hoping kidnappers weren't into symbolism and this didn't mean more than it should, I slowed the car, stopped, and got out.

It was quiet up there near the clouds. So quiet that when a bird flew over, I heard its wings flap.

"Weird," I told myself, mostly just to hear my own voice and convince myself the altitude hadn't resulted in some sort of freaky deafness. While I was doing that, I took the chance to look around.

As rendezvous places went, this one pretty much had it all—there was an outcropping of boulders as big as houses about two hundred yards to my left, and a cliff directly ahead of me that looked to rise at least . . . I tipped my head back to see the top, but since doing that made my shoulders hurt, I decided it wasn't all that important to know how high the cliff was, and gave up.

Over on my right, the ground fell off into a shallow but steep arroyo. Oh yeah, as hard as it is to believe, I knew the word, all right. On our drive to New Mexico, Goodshot had pointed out that an arroyo is a steep-sided gulch with a flat bottom. In rainy weather, arroyos fill with rushing water. Not a problem. At least not for me. From the looks of the dust already coating my boots, I'd say it hadn't rained in those parts in about a hundred years.

By now, the sky to the west was an amazing mixture of reds and purples, and I stopped for a moment to admire it, wondering how the colors might translate to silk, if Saks ever carried anything in the same palette and if a redhead could get away with it. I was just envisioning a wrap dress with a plunging neckline and a sash belt when I heard the coyote start up again. This time, his mournful cry was echoed by his friends.

Out there, the *wide-open* part of wide-open spaces had a whole new meaning, and it was hard to judge distance by sound. Were the critters miles away? Or right around the corner? I couldn't tell, and I wasn't taking any chances. I decided to wait in my car. With the doors locked.

I was almost there when a man stepped out from behind the boulders. It was right at the spot where the last of the sunlight played with the shadows and I leaned forward, trying for a better look.

Short. Slim. Brown hair. Jeans. Yellow T-shirt with red letters on it: TAOS.

Nondescript. And it took me a moment to place the face.

Arnie.

The fact that it was one of Brian's friends who Quinn and I had met at the Indians game didn't come as much of a surprise. I called out and waved. Yeah, like he'd miss a redhead in gorgeous boots in the middle of the nothingness.

Arnie looked over his shoulder before he stepped toward me, but me, I didn't waste any such time. I'd already waited long enough.

I skirted a straggling sage bush and closed the distance between us. "Where's Dan? What have you guys done with him? And what about the bones? Norma had them, you know, and Brian must have known it because he went to Norma's, and he's got my Jimmy Choo bag, damn it, and I need answers, Arnie. Fast."

Unfortunately, fast turned out not to be fast enough.

Before Arnie could say a word, a sound like the pop of a giant champagne cork exploded in the quiet and echoed along the rocks that surrounded us. Startled, I jumped back, and it was a good thing I did. That way, when Arnie's eyes went wide, his arms flew out at his sides, and a spurt of liquid the color of the lettering on his shirt gushed out of him, I didn't get any on me. Before I could process what had happened, and even before I could scream, his body hit the ground.

Just a heartbeat later, a second shot pinged against a rock near my left foot.

"Hey, new boots!" I screamed in the nanosecond before I realized I didn't have to worry so much about the boots as I did about the body wearing them. It was too far to the car, and there wasn't nearly enough cover in that direction, so I darted toward the outcropping of boulders where Arnie had been hidden when I arrived. Protection from whoever was taking potshots at me, sure, but it took me about a second and a half to realize this wasn't the best place for me to hide. Those boulders were in front of me— between me and the shooter—but there was a steep, rocky rise to my right and, to my left, nothing in the way of cover.

If I stayed where I was and the shooter decided to come around at me from either side, I'd be trapped. Good strategy on the shooter's part. Not so good news for me, and I was just trying to decide what to do about it when a shower of tiny rocks skittered down the hill to my right. The dust flew and I squeezed my eyes closed. Too bad. I have a feeling I missed a pretty spectacular entrance.

"Get behind me, quick!"

Like anybody could blame me when my eyes popped open and I stared like a crazy person? What else was I supposed to do when Jesse slipped down that hill along with those pebbles? He shoved me behind him, leveled a rifle on his shoulder, and peeked around our rocky barricade.

"What?" I dared to try to look past those broad shoulders of his long enough to see that I couldn't see anything worth seeing. "What's going on?" I asked him.

"Just what I was going to ask you." Another shot clumped into the ground ten feet in front of where we were hidden, and instantly, Jesse returned fire.

I covered my ears with my hands, but that wasn't enough to block out the sound of the blast or the curse he mumbled. "Wherever he is, he's got great cover. I can't even see him moving." He took another shot.

When it stopped reverberating in my ears, I offered the tiniest of logical commentaries. "If you can't see him, what the hell are you shooting at?"

The smile he tossed over his shoulder was grim. "Just thought I'd let him know he doesn't have the upper hand. See, he figured you were back here all alone, and that you'd be easy to pick off. I'm just sending a little message, that's all." He took another shot, then glanced around, taking in the lay of the land. My guess was that he came to the same conclusion I had: if we stayed there, we were sitting ducks.

"You're going to have to make a run for it," he said at the same time he took my hand and tugged me closer to where the safety of our cover ended and the hey-I-dare-you-to-miss-hitting-a-redhead-in-all-this-nothing began. "See? Over there?" He cast a glance across what looked to be a hundred yards or so of barren space to another, much smaller, rocky outcropping. "On the count of three"—he put a hand to the small of my back—"you head that way. I'll cover you."

"What? We're in some bad Western movie now?" I slapped his hand away. I would have screeched with or without our attacker taking another shot, but when he did, and when the bullet pinged into the dust right where Jesse was asking me to go, I scuttled backward and folded myself into the farthest corner from the opening. "I'm not just going to run. Not out there. And you're not just going to cover me. There's a crazy person out there. A crazy person with a gun."

"Exactly."

The way he said it—so calm, so self-assured, so completely not as crazy and panicked as me—made me suck in a sharp breath. Maybe forcing me to stop and think was what Jesse intended all along. Or maybe he hoped to accomplish that with the look in those brown eyes of his. It was iron-willed, sure, but in a way that made a startling lump block my throat—one that had nothing to do with how freaking afraid I was.

It was the wrong place and really the wrong time for sexual tension, but if there was one thing I'd learned over the years, it was that these things aren't always convenient.

I did my best to ignore the heat. Not so easy considering that when I blinked myself back to reality and forced myself to concentrate, I sounded as if I had a five-pack-a-day habit. "You're . . . you're going to cover me."

It wasn't a question, but he nodded to assure me.

"And I'm . . ." I gulped and glanced at that rocky outcropping that looked so far away. "I'm going to wait over there for you. And you . . ." I think this was about when I realized I had one of Jesse's sleeves bunched in both my hands. "You're not going to let anything happen to you. Promise me."

A slow smile flickered in his eyes. "Because then you wouldn't know where to get the best boots."

"Don't be ridiculous. I already know where to get the best boots."

This time, the smile touched his lips. "Then maybe it's because you care."

I smiled, too. Or at least I tried. But then, like I said, I'd played this game before. He should have realized that and known I wasn't willing to let him have the upper hand. At least not yet. "Because then you wouldn't be able to tell me why you followed me and what the hell you're doing here."

Another shot, and he sprang into action. At the same time he pushed me forward, he wheeled around and squeezed off a few shots. And me? I scurried like a redheaded bunny, and if I looked like a goofball, darting and ducking, I didn't care. All that mattered was that I made it to that outcropping of rocks. As soon as I did, I dropped to my knees and prayed like I'd never prayed before that Jesse wouldn't get shot on his way over to join me.

It couldn't have been more than a minute but it felt like forever before he darted out from behind those big boulders, shooting and running. A few yards away from where I was huddled, he dropped to the ground and slid like a ball player nearing second base, and I swear my heart stopped beating. If he'd been hit . . . If he'd been shot . . .

When he rolled to his knees and scooted beside me, I pressed a hand to my very thankful heart.

He peeked over the edge of the rocks, and I could tell by the relentless way he scanned the landscape that he still didn't have a bead on the shooter. He took a couple shots anyway, just to show the guy he meant business. When he was done, he darted a look at me out of the corner of his eye. "So . . . you were going to tell me what you're doing here."

"Was I? I thought you were going to tell me why you followed me."

One corner of his mouth twisted into what might have been a smile. It was kind of hard to tell since his face was streaked with dirt and he wasn't the smiley sort to begin with. "Give me some credit. I didn't have to follow you."

Okay, so I was a bit off my game, what with the running and the being scared to death and all. I still didn't get it. "Because . . ."

"Because I got here before you did, of course."

My stomach jumped into my throat, and this time, it had nothing to do with the crazy attraction that sizzled in the air between us. If Jesse knew I was coming here . . . If he was here waiting for me . . . If this was some sort of ambush . . .

Pikestaffed by my own logic, I jumped to my feet and pointed a shaky finger at him. "You . . . you're one of the kidnappers!"

I found myself back on my knees just as quickly. But then, Jesse's hand was like a vise on my arm. "Stay down!" he yelled, just as another shot smacked into the dirt in front of us. And another.

Even that wasn't enough to make me crouch down and cover. I was too busy being outraged, staring at Jesse when he returned fire.

He shot me a look. "I'm not one of the kidnappers," he growled.

"But—"

"But nothing. There's more than one way to figure out what a person is up to, and you're not exactly Mata Hari."

"Who—"

"She was executed for being a spy during World War One. And that doesn't matter. You—" As if his words had been snipped with scissors, Jesse stopped. He tipped his head, listening. I guess he must have bionic hearing because after a minute or so, he slapped a hand to his thigh and stood.

"Son of a—"

That was when I finally heard a truck engine rev, somewhere far down the arroyo. "He's gone?"

Jesse's mouth pulled into a thin line. "He's gone." He offered me a hand up. "My cruiser's parked over that way," he said, and when he took off for it, he tugged me along at a double-step. "I've got to radio in and get somebody out here fast."

"Not before you explain." I braced my legs and refused to budge an inch and he had no choice but to stop and whirl to face me.

"Funny," he said, "that's exactly what I was going to ask you to do."

"You first."

"All right." He looked me up and down. "What were you doing at the cemetery last night?"

"That's not fair. I said you had to explain yourself first. Asking questions doesn't qualify as explaining yourself. And the cemetery—" I realized exactly what was going on, and my breath caught. "You've been watching me."

"Like a hawk."

"So when you called me last night . . ."

"I was sitting out in the parking lot. Under that one light that wasn't working. I guess it was a pretty good move because you didn't even notice my car when you dragged your suitcase out there. So now you can explain. You know, about why you decided not to leave, and why you had to go to the cemetery first, and what any of this has to do with kidnappers."

"No, no, no!" Okay, I stomped my foot in the dust. It was a childish thing to do, but justified. So was the fact that I raised my voice. Jesse obviously wasn't listening to a thing I said, so I figured I needed to be a tad more forceful. "You said you didn't follow me, but you obviously knew I was coming here. And you wouldn't know I was coming here unless—"

"I read the note, of course. The one from that guy." His brows low over his eyes, he looked over to where Arnie's body lay in a pool of blood. "The note he slipped under your motel room door."

This time, I couldn't even find the words to express my outrage so I stammered for a while. Finally, I propped my fists on my hips. "You read—"

"Oh, come on!" I could practically see the sarcasm dripping from those luscious lips. You didn't expect me to do nothing, did you? First you show up from out of nowhere—"

"Cleveland isn't exactly nowhere."

The city's reputation preceeded it. He rolled his eyes. "Then your car gets sabotaged way out here where you don't belong in the first place."

"I told you, I was—"

"Then you get smacked over the head outside the home of a woman who was just murdered."

"And I explained that, too. I said—"

"Then you start spouting off about somebody named Goodshot, and around here, that can only mean one person. Chester Goodshot Gomez is something of a legend in my tribe. He was a star in a Wild West show and people still tell stories about him. He's been dead for over one hundred years."

"I was a little woozy when I was mumbling about Goodshot. Hit over the head, remember?"

"And now this?" Jesse threw his hands out and spun around, as if that *now this* of his suddenly made more sense simply because of where we were. "That guy got murdered right in front of our eyes. And you were here to meet him because, at six o'clock this morning, he showed up at your motel room and left that note for you. Call me crazy, or maybe I'm just insightful, but I figured you weren't an early riser. I waited until he drove away and I got a slim jim out of my car. You know, one of those things you can slip down alongside a window and into a car door to unlock it. Perfect for sticking under a door"—he demonstrated with one hand—"and sliding out a note."

"So you read that note before I read that note?"

"And that's when I knew I had to get up here because I knew that whatever you're up to, you're in way over your head." He was wearing his Stetson, and he ripped it off and scraped a hand through his inky hair. "What's this about a curse? And what does it have to do with kidnappers? You thought I was one of them. You said so yourself. Whatever's going on"—another look over his shoulder to where Arnie lay—"it didn't exactly work out for him, did it? And you've got plenty of explaining to do. This is pueblo land, Pepper, and whatever's going on, those kidnappers are messing with me now." Another thought hit, and he groaned. "Shit, I'm going to have paperwork a mile high to deal with, and now that we've got a murder on our hands, I'm going to have to call in the FBI." He plopped his hat back on his head, gave me a disgusted look, took off the hat, and jammed it on my head. "And don't you know not to come out here without some sort of hat? It's one thing now that it's getting dark but when the sun is out—"

Okay, I shouldn't have started laughing. After all, he was being as serious as a heart attack. Blame it on the adrenaline shooting through my body. Or the relief I felt now that I realized we weren't going to get picked off like ducks at a shooting gallery. Maybe I just pictured myself out there in the middle of nowhere wearing off-brand jeans and a cowboy hat that was way too big for me and appreciated how ridiculous the whole thing was.

In the long run, it didn't really matter. My laughter shut him up, and side by side, we made our way to Jesse's cruiser and he put in all the calls he had to, and after that, he was too busy to bother me with any more questions. Backup arrived, and along with three other members of the pueblo police force, Jesse set up a few high-powered lights and a perimeter around Arnie's body and got to work. It was pitch dark by that time, and with nothing to do, I sat on a rock nearby (just in case the coyotes I could hear calling to each other decided to make an appearance) and learned to appreciate the glory of the Milky Way and stars the likes of which must shine over Cleveland, but I'd never seen before.

It was nearly dawn by the time everything was taken care of and Jesse followed me back to my motel, and I swear, though I'd reminded myself about a thousand times that my experiences with Quinn were enough to make me swear off cops for all time and that I'd never, ever go to bed with one again, what happened after that was completely out of my control.

Blame it on the adrenaline.

11

By the time I woke up, it was after noon, and Jesse was showered and sitting on the edge of the bed. He was dressed only in blue-and-white-plaid boxers, and his hair was loose. At the risk of sounding poetic (something I am so not!), it flowed over his bare shoulders like it had touched mine during our hours together, like black silk. For a few moments, I was distracted enough to forget about all the horrible things that had happened the night before and concentrate on the amazing stuff that went on between us when we got back to the motel. The look in his eyes cured me of that, and fast.

It was time for answers.

Weird thing is, for the first time since I'd been gifted with this Gift, I was actually ready to do something I'd never done with anybody—give them to him.

I plumped the pillows, propped them behind my back,

and made sure the threadbare blanket was tucked under my arms. No use taking his mind off the matter at hand. Not when we were about to have *the* talk.

"I see ghosts," I said, then corrected myself and barreled on before I could talk myself out of it. "At least I used to see ghosts. It all started back at home when I tripped and hit my head on a mausoleum. And since then, I've been . . . well, sort of investigating for the ghosts. You know, they ask me to right a wrong, or clear their names, or find their bodies . . . and I've been doing this for a couple years and that's how I got involved in this whole thing with Goodshot, because there are these crazy baseball fans and they're convinced Goodshot is cursing our team and they kidnapped Dan and he's a friend of mine, and I had to bring Goodshot's bones back here so I did. And it's not like they know I can see ghosts—I mean, the baseball fans, not the ghosts, because of course the ghosts know I can see ghosts. But the baseball fans don't know I see ghosts, they only know that Goodshot's bones were at the cemetery where I work. Only I don't work there anymore, but they figured even so, I still know people and still have access. Which isn't true, either. At least about having access because I had to steal the keys to Goodshot's mausoleum and that's what I did and I took his bones and I got here and I was all set to exchange the bones for Dan, but then the bones got stolen and I got hit on the head and I'm not sure, but I'm pretty sure . . ." I paused for a moment, waiting for the familiar surge of ghostiness to tingle along my skin, and when it didn't, I was convinced and went on.

"No, I'm sure. I'm sure after that whack on the head I

got over at Norma's, I can't see ghosts anymore because Goodshot and his girlfriends have disappeared, and see, I was really happy about that. The no-ghost thing, not the whack on the head. Because really, it's not like in the movies when people talk to the dead, and it's all interesting and like that. It's really more of a pain in the neck, and because of the ghosts, people keep trying to kill me. So I was glad. Who wouldn't be? And I was all set to leave, which is why you saw me out in the parking lot with my suitcase. But I couldn't. Leave, that is. Not when I thought about Dan and how if I don't help him, nobody will, and then that note came and I thought it was my big break in the case, so I went out to Wind Mountain and Arnie got killed and . . ."

It was pretty impressive, actually, not having to take a breath all that time, but my lungs finally gave out and so did my voice. Jesse reached over to the table by the side of the bed and handed me a bottle of water. Nice gesture, and I fully expected it was the last thing he'd do before he grabbed his clothes, and gave me the ol' *hasta la vista, baby*. That is, after he told me I was nuts.

I glugged down a gulp of water while he turned to give me a careful look. "It makes sense," he said.

"It does?" The bottle was at my lips and I froze. That is, until reality came crashing down around me. I capped the bottle and set it down. "No," I said. "It really doesn't. None of it makes sense, and I wouldn't believe it myself if someone told me what I just told you. It's weird. And creepy. Aberrant behavior. That's what Dan used to call it, and I never admitted it then, but I'll admit it now: he was

163

right." I threw my hands in the air, and when the blanket dipped, I tucked it back into place. "Don't you get it? I just told you I see dead people, and you just said—"

"You're the raven." He pursed his lips and nodded. "That's what Strong Eagle, the shaman, told me. He told me you see the living, and you see the dead. He knew. Even before I met you."

"And you believed him?"

He slid his gaze to mine. "Why shouldn't I?"

"Because it's crazy."

A smile sparkled in his eyes. "It is."

"And you're a cop. Cops are—"

"Logical. Rational. Reasonable."

"Logical, rational, reasonable people don't believe in ghosts."

"You do."

"Which might mean I'm not logical, rational, or reasonable."

He considered the possibility. "You know good boots when you see them. And you've got great taste in men." The sparkle made it all the way to his lips. "Sounds reasonable to me."

"But—"

"Welcome to the Great Southwest. The skies are wide open, and so are our minds. Anglos have been in these parts for a few hundred years. They're still getting used to the altitude, and the attitude. But my tribe has been here for much, much longer. Think how enlightened we are by now."

"That's great. But I just said—"

"That you walk with the dead. Yeah, I heard that part."

"And you just said—"

"That I believe you. There's no reason I shouldn't. You're an honorable woman. If you weren't, you wouldn't have come here in the first place. Bet you wouldn't have swiped Goodshot's bones, either. What you did, you did for a friend."

"But most people just don't come right out and admit—"

"Most people don't have your kind of Gift. And if they do, I think most of them aren't comfortable enough with it to tell anyone. You're honest and you're open and you trust me enough to share what's obviously a huge part of your life. Thank you."

I leaned forward, the better to give him a careful look. "If you're just saying this to get me back in bed—"

"You're already in bed." He leaned closer and the kiss he gave me was long and slow and searching. It curled my toes. When he was done, he sat back. "I'm saying it because it's true. It makes sense. And I believe you. What you just told me explains what you're doing here. It doesn't explain . . ." His mouth thinned. "Why didn't you just tell me in the first place? I don't care what kinds of cases you've investigated in the past, you can't just head out looking for kidnappers on your own. It's crazy, and it's dangerous. And you're not doing your friend Dan any favors. The smart thing to do from the start was to get law enforcement involved."

Quinn's face flashed before my eyes. "I haven't had much luck with law enforcement, not when it comes to explaining about this stupid Gift of mine."

"Is it?" Jesse chuckled. "Stupid? In my tribe, we'd consider it a great honor."

I rolled my eyes. "That's because there aren't dead people bugging you all the time. And bad guys shooting at you. Only"—I felt a stab of guilt, and I reached for his hand and squeezed it—"there was a bad guy shooting at you, and it was all my fault. You could have been hurt, or . . ." I couldn't go there. "Sorry."

"Hey, it comes with the job description." He twined his fingers through mine and his thumb played over the back of my hand. "So, what are we going to do?"

I patted the empty spot in bed beside me. "You want to—"

He gave me a quick kiss. "Yes, I want to. Later. And tomorrow. And the day after that." Another kiss and he got up and reached for his pants. "For now, we've got a kidnapping on our hands, and a lot of work to do."

It may have been the kisses that muddled my brain like mint leaves in a mojito. Or maybe I just needed some time to adjust to anyone who could think so far out of the box. I watched Jesse get dressed, staring all the while. "You believe me? Really?"

"Like I said . . ." A shrug of those broad shoulders. "Why shouldn't I? You're not the kind of woman who pretends things are real when they're not. At least . . ." He raised his eyebrows. "At least I hope not. Now get moving. We've got a lot to talk about."

* * *

It was something of a red-letter day—what with all that had happened in the wee small hours of the morning, my confession to Jesse, and the not-so-insignificant fact that when I told him about the ghosts, he didn't call the nearest loony bin and tell them to bring a straitjacket and a net big enough to snare a five-foot-eleven woman. What all that means is that I wasn't going to spend that particular day looking like a refugee from the New Mexican no-man's-land. I showered and dressed in one of the V-neck tanks I'd brought from home (creamy colored and with lace edging), my new boots (of course), and those jeans I'd retrieved from Tom's. Before we left the motel, Jesse insisted I take along a long-sleeve shirt and a jacket, too, and when I rolled my eyes, he reminded me that there was no telling where we might end up.

Where we ended up first was the Taopi Pueblo.

Here's the thing about pueblos, and it sure isn't anything I knew before that day: *pueblo* is a sort of all-purpose word in those parts. For one, it's a general name for the Native Americans in New Mexico. They're called Pueblo Indians. What they have in common with other Native Americans is that they were firmly established on the continent long before any Europeans showed up. What's different about them as compared to other tribes is that they were never forcibly removed from their ancestral lands. They were, however, conquered and enslaved by the Spanish, who swept through a few hundred years ago, and until this day, most of them still retain the Spanish surnames they were given at the time. The good news is that the Taopi, like the other tribes in New Mexico, still occupy lands that have been theirs since before recorded history.

So when I say *pueblo*, I'm talking about the however many thousands of acres that are owned by the Taopi tribe, but that same word—*pueblo*—is also used for the homes inside the original historic village. Think adobe condos, individual homes built side by side and some atop others. They have shared walls, but not doorways. Like I said, condos. Or cluster homes. The Pueblo Indians of the American Southwest were ahead of their times.

Yeah, I know, it's all very confusing, and on our drive from Antonito back into New Mexico, I told Jesse so. When it came to history and a little lesson in Taopi culture, though, he was not going to let me off the hook so easily.

According to him, about two hundred or so Taopi actually still reside within the village where their ancestors lived for about a thousand years. As far I was concerned, this was pretty odd because, as he went on to explain, there is no electricity or running water allowed within the village. Go figure. Most of the tribe live in regular ol' houses with regular ol' electricity and (hallelujah!) running water, still on tribal land, but outside the historic village.

That's where the Taopi Tribal Police Station is, too, and when we pulled into Jesse's reserved parking space and got out of the car, I checked things out and headed right across the street to a string of boutiques where silver jewelry sparkled in windows and leather was worked into boots and purses, and brightly colored dresses were shown to perfection in chic window displays.

Civilization! I couldn't have been happier. "Oh, shopping!"

Jesse caught me by the arm. "You can shop later. Business first."

I didn't grump—at least not too much. Instead, I went inside the modern, brightly lit police station, stood back, and watched Jesse in his element.

R-E-S-P-E-C-T.

That's what it was all about. Everyone we ran across on our way to Jesse's office was friendly, but the way they acted made it clear that he was the boss and they knew it, from the woman working the front desk, to the officers we passed in the hallway, to the maintenance man who greeted Jesse with a nod and me with an appreciative smile.

Inside his office, Jesse shut the door and changed into the clean uniform he kept there. When he was done, he sat down behind his gray metal desk, waved me into one of two guest chairs in front of it, and folded his hands together on the desktop in front of him.

"Explain," he said. "From the beginning."

I figured this was going to happen, and I was prepared. I hauled my purse onto my lap and took out the postcard I'd received back in Cleveland from Dan, the one with his picture on the front of it. I handed the photo to Jesse.

"Dan," I said. "And here that watchband that he's . . ." I was already reaching into the box for the watchband that had arrived with the first ransom note, when Jesse stopped me.

"We'll want the evidence techs to take a look at that," he said. "So leave that where it is. But this you got in the mail, right?" He looked to me for confirmation before he took the picture out of my hands.

I knew he was sizing up Dan, and sizing up done, he looked back at me. "He's a nerd, huh?"

"You can tell? From the picture?" I couldn't exactly argue the point so I gave in with the lift of one shoulder. "He's a paranormal investigator. A sort of egghead researcher. I guess that makes him a nerd."

"And he cozied up to you because he figured you could help him advance his research."

Yeah, that was one of the reasons. The other was that Dan had the hots for me and I for him. At least for a while. Rather than get into all that, I simply said, "You got that right."

"So that's how you got to know each other."

It wasn't a question, but I nodded, anyway. "And I got to know Dan's wife, too. Only she was dead at the time, and a royal pain if ever there was one. That's the last I saw him, after we wrapped up that investigation. But then I ran into Brian—he's the one I'm pretty sure kidnapped Dan—at a baseball game. Brian is a ghost hunter, too. I met him when I was working on another investigation." Jesse didn't need to tell me to back up and explain; I figured he'd have questions. I went through the story as logically as possible, and while I did, he scratched notes on a legal pad. I even told him how I broke into the mausoleum and . . . er . . . appropriated Goodshot's bones.

That's the point where he stopped writing it all down. "I'm going to ignore that part of the story," Jesse said. "At least for now. And when the Feds get here . . ." I guess the aforementioned G-men had an appointment because he glanced at his watch. "We have to call in either the FBI or the Bureau of Indian Affairs when we've got a felony on our hands," he explained. "And I guess we're going to have to tell them about the bones. But let me do the talking, okay? I'll vouch for you and we can always chalk the whole thing up to extreme emotional upset. After all, you were worried about your friend."

He took another look at the picture of Dan. "And you say you think they wanted Goodshot's remains so they could rebury them here on the pueblo?"

"Well, that's what everyone in Cleveland was talking about the night I ran into Brian and Arnie and the rest of them. They said that Goodshot cursed the city and the only way to remove the curse was to take his bones back to the pueblo. The hardcore fans, they think it's Goodshot's fault our baseball team stinks."

The somber expression on Jesse's face never cracked. "I guess when you could still see Goodshot, you should have just asked him to lift his curse."

Rather than confess I'd never thought of it, I wrinkled my nose. "Goodshot wanted to come back to the pueblo." There was a window behind Jesse's desk, and it looked out over a panorama of mountains and, in the distance, those ancient pueblo condos he'd told me about earlier. The sky was a shade of vibrant blue I'd never seen back in Cleveland, the sun glinted against rock and coarse-grained dirt, and the air was clear. It was only because I wasn't thinking about the dust, or the no electricity or running water thing. Or the coyotes. I mumbled, "I guess I can sort of see why."

"What I can't see . . ." All this time, Jesse was still staring at Dan's picture, and he stood and took it with him to the window where the light was better. He turned it this way and that, and I think the first I realized there was more going on than met the eye (well, at least my eyes) was when a muscle bunched at the base of his jaw. He strode to the office door, opened it, and called out, "Hey, Olivas, you out there? Come on in here."

Pete Olivas was young, short, and wiry, with the same dusky-colored skin as Jesse and hair that was buzzed so short, he looked like a Chia Pet with one day's growth. Jesse introduced me before he handed Dan's picture to Pete.

"What do you see?" Jesse asked.

"Looks like a nerd." Pete chuckled, then realized he might have offended me and swallowed his laugh. "And it looks like some sort of excavation. See? You can see the archaeological equipment and the tents and the tables and stuff in back of this guy."

I, too, had noticed all that back when I first got the picture, but since it was from Dan and I knew Dan was into all sorts of things like history and science and all that, it never really registered.

Jesse, apparently, was far more interested in what appeared in the background of the photograph than I had been. He leaned back against the windowsill, his arms crossed over his chest. "What else do you see?"

Apparently, this was some kind of test, and it was obvious Pete didn't want to embarrass himself. Or let down his boss. He swallowed hard and squinted for another look at the photo. "The background is . . ." Pete's mouth went slack and he looked up at Jesse, whose expression said it all. Pete had seen exactly what Jesse had seen earlier, and Jesse was just looking for confirmation.

I, of course, was left in the dust. I waited until Jesse told the kid to get on the phone and call the tribal governor and the war chief and his staff and get them down to the station ASAP before I popped out of my chair.

"Something's up."

"I'll say." Jesse flicked the photo with thumb and forefinger. "See that formation of hills in the background?" He tipped the picture so I could see it. "That's up on Wind Mountain. Way out in the backcountry. Deep in Taopi land."

I didn't know why he looked so grumpy. This was good news. "Then we're close!" I crooned. "Dan was here. Right nearby. And all we have to do is—"

"All we have to do is figure out what your friend was doing excavating an ancient site on our pueblo. I guarantee you, there were no permits issued. If there were, I'd know about it. And the place he's messing with . . ." Jesse's mouth thinned. His eyes hardened. "It's sacred land."

My stomach went cold. "What are you saying?"

Jesse dropped the photo on his desk and I looked down at Dan, who grinned up at me. "I'm saying if there's an excavation going on out there in the backcountry, your friend is messing with my people and their heritage and a place he has no business being in. That means he's messing with me, too. Once I get a hold of him . . ." At his sides, Jesse's hands curled into fists. "Once I find your buddy Dan, he's going to have bigger things to worry about than just being kidnapped."

12

A little while later, a dozen or so serious-looking men showed up at the police station to meet with Jesse, and I was asked to wait outside. No great shakes since, as far as I was concerned, *outside* included those boutiques across the street that catered to the tourists who came to explore not only the historical aspects of the pueblo, but the many talents of its current-day residents.

Sure, I was concerned about the things Jesse said, about how Dan might be doing something he shouldn't be doing somewhere he shouldn't be doing it, but I wasn't going to let that stop me. There is no better therapy for worry than shopping.

I bought a silver bracelet and earrings for myself, and a pot made of some kind of famous clay (the shopkeeper explained, I forgot) to send to my mother in Florida. I was tempted by a dress or two, but an unemployed cemetery tour guide has her limits. Even if she doesn't like them.

By the time I walked back into the station with my shopping bags, all those men I'd seen were leaving a conference room—and not looking any happier than when they walked in.

Jesse signaled me into his office, pointed to a corner where my bags would be safe, and without a word, took my arm. A minute later, we were in a convoy of three SUVs marked TAOPI TRIBAL POLICE and headed out. Someone had kindly tossed my long-sleeve shirt and jacket in the vehicle along with an extra department-issued Stetson, and though I had no plans to wear any of it, I was as grateful for their consideration as I was for the supply of bottled water in the backseat. It was hot and dry up there so close to the sun, and I slathered on lip gloss and watched the last signs of civilization disappear in the side-view mirror.

What had Jesse called where we were going? Backcountry?

He wasn't kidding.

Not far from the historic village and a couple streets of modern, well-tended homes on the far side of it, the road vanished completely, and along with the other two SUVs and the officers and tribal elders in them, we bumped over rocky terrain. Jesse was wearing sunglasses, but I didn't need to see his eyes to know he was royally pissed. His hands were bunched against the steering wheel, his jaw was tight, and every one of his movements was crisp and efficient.

Oh yeah, he was a man who could lose it at any moment. The fact that he didn't, that he stayed calm and professional, says a lot about him.

"Those men . . ." We'd been in the car maybe ten minutes and he hadn't spoken a word, so when he finally did, I jumped just in time to see him glance into the rearview mirror at the cars that followed us. "One of them is the tribal governor," he said. "He's the one who takes care of business and civil issues within the village. The war chief and a couple members of his staff came along, too. Their job is to protect the Indian lands outside the pueblo walls."

"And every single one of them is as honked off as you are."

"You got that right."

There was no politically correct way to approach the subject so I didn't bother trying to mince any words. "Have you considered that you might be wrong?"

He shot me a look. "About Dan? Or about where he's digging?"

"I'm pretty sure you're right about where he's digging. You recognized the place and so did Pete, and I'm guessing the others did, too, when you showed them the picture, or we wouldn't be here right now." I glanced out the window, mumbled, "Wherever here is," and went right back to talking to Jesse. "What I mean is, maybe you're not right about Dan. He's not the kind of guy who would be involved in anything underhanded."

"He better not be."

"And he's been kidnapped, remember. Which means he can't be doing anything at all. At least not up here on the mountain."

"Maybe."

"Not maybe. Definitely."

"He's definitely in that picture. And in it, he's definitely somewhere he shouldn't be."

"But that doesn't mean—"

"Yeah. It does."

So much for that conversation. Convinced Jesse wasn't going to listen to reason, I spent the rest of the trip staring out the window at the wilderness, which got rockier and more rugged by the moment. I am not the great-outdoors type, but hey, I am from the Midwest. At least in summer, my world is lush: trees, flowers, plenty of green grass. Here, there wasn't enough water for much of anything to grow. Those tough, hardy sage bushes were gray. The rocks were brown. So was the soil. There was a certain savage beauty to it, but it sure wasn't home.

By the time we stopped and parked near a pile of boulders much like the ones we'd hidden behind when we were attacked the night Arnie died, we were high up on the mountain and surrounded by a whole lot of nothing.

When he got out of the car, Jesse didn't say anything about me minding my own business so I took that to mean I could go wherever he was going. Along with everyone else who'd come along from the station, I circled the boulders and came up against what looked to me at first like a wall of solid rock. Jesse knew better. He was leading the way, and he cut to his left, climbed a shallow slope, and found a path between two steep-faced cliffs. Single file, we made our way through the rock walls that at a couple places were barely far enough apart to accommodate

Jesse's broad shoulders. Like I said, he led the pack and I was near the end of the line. Pete Olivas brought up the rear. The ground was uneven and the rocks on either side of us were rough and jagged. Within a minute, I'd broken a nail. Another minute, and both my arms were scraped. I didn't think this was the time to ask to go back to the car for that long-sleeve shirt.

Ahead of me, I saw Jesse scramble up a rock as tall as he was and offer the cop behind him a hand up. When it was my turn, I gratefully accepted the assistance of the silver-haired senior citizen in front of me and Pete behind, whose cheeks got as red as a New Mexico sunset when he put his hands on my butt to give me a push.

This was feeling a little too much like actual exercise so when I saw that, up ahead, the cliffs on either side of us were farther apart and the ground was flatter, I actually would have breathed a sigh of relief if I could have caught my breath.

"Here." From behind, Pete gave me a poke and handed me a bottle of water. "We're almost there," he whispered.

He was right. Just another minute or two and the cliff faces parted and we stepped onto what looked like a flat, broad plain, longer than two football fields and just as wide. Once the crowd in front of me parted, I saw that we were at the top of what Jesse would tell me later was called a mesa, a flat-topped elevation that soared even higher than the rest of the mountainside around us, with a killer view of the surrounding countryside and a front-row seat on what must have been heaven's front door.

To our left, one of those cliff walls we'd walked beside

only a bit ago rose to the sky, its surface decorated with pictures carved into the stone: curlicues and animals with long snouts and short legs, and people with flat-top heads and triangle noses. The wall was pocked with doorways carved into the stone.

Another pueblo. And from the looks of it, one that was far more ancient even than the village I'd visited earlier.

Tucked away in one corner of the mesa between the pueblo and the panorama beyond was a weird-looking structure. Think raised dinner plate shored by timbers that stuck out of one side of it like spokes. It was flat on top and low to the ground, and directly in the center of it was an entrance that led down into the floor of the mesa, into what must have been an underground cave.

"Kiva." Still behind me, Pete explained. "It's a sacred space. For sacred rituals."

Grateful for the update, I studied the kiva and the tents, tables, and equipment set up around it that I recognized as part of the background of that picture Dan sent me. All around the complex, the place was alive with workers, who scuttled back and forth like busy ants.

I had to give Jesse credit. He was itching to charge ahead. His shoulders were so stiff, I waited to hear the snap, crackle, and pop, and he whipped off his sunglasses, the better to take a gander of all that was happening. He held back, though, and we did, too, knowing he was the one who had to make the first move.

He didn't. While we waited for Jesse, he waited for the tribal elders to take the lead, and when they did, we all followed along. In fact, Jesse didn't even say a word. Not until we got as far as the outermost canopy, where a petite blonde who barely looked old enough to be out of high school was standing at a table cleaning pottery shards with a soft brush.

"Who's in charge here?" Jesse asked.

Young or not, one look at the cops and elders and she gulped and looked over her shoulder to where a short guy wearing thick glasses was looking at a rock through a magnifying glass.

"In . . . charge?" He was a gulper, too, but then, I don't suppose these science-y types are used to being surrounded by cops and stern-faced Indians. "That would be . . ." In a desperate search for salvation, he scanned the area. Apparently, he found what he was looking for because his eyes lit, and he pointed toward the kiva. "That would be Dr. Valenzuela. I'll . . ." He sidled out from behind the table where he'd been working. "I'll take you right to her."

Caridad Valenzuela was, as it turned out, a stunning brunette a whole lot shorter than me with the slim, lithe body of a ballerina, skin that managed to glow even in this harsh light, and dark, intelligent eyes.

Oh yeah, it was small-minded of me, but I couldn't help but glance at Jesse as we were introduced all around. Sure I understand that guys always appreciate a gorgeous woman. I just didn't want this particular guy to appreciate this particular gorgeous woman too much.

Not to worry. Jesse was all business.

When he explained why were we there, some of the sun-drenched color drained from Caridad's cheeks. "All the permits are certainly in order." I would learn later than

Caridad was originally from Spain, but all I knew at that moment was that her accent was as exotic as her looks. She swept out an arm, directing us to a tent at the farthest reaches of the mesa. "If you'd like to see them . . ."

It went without saying, and a few minutes later, we were all crowded around a folding table in what was obviously Caridad's private sanctuary. Don't ask me how it all got up there, but Caridad's quarters were equipped with a plushy oriental rug, a camp bed that looked plenty comfortable, and any number of storage cabinets designed to hold pottery and files and keep out the harsh elements all at the same time. She went to one of these, found the appropriate files, and handed them to Jesse, who handed them to the war chief, who looked through them, gave his head a curt shake, and passed them back for Jesse to study.

"They're signed by Michael Winter Day." Jesse glanced at the war chief beside him. "And you, sir . . ?"

Another shake of Michael Winter Day's head. "I might be old, but I'm sure not stupid. I never would have signed such papers, and if I did, I sure would remember."

His expression impossible to read, Jesse leafed through the file again. "They're also signed . . ." He tipped the folder toward Caridad and pointed. "By Dan Callahan."

That was my cue to move forward. "But Dan wouldn't—"

The briefest of looks from Jesse and I swallowed the rest of my words. But then, he already knew what I was going to say.

Jesse finished with the papers and signaled to one of the other cops for an evidence bag. He slipped the file inside. "We're going to need to take a much closer look at this," he said. "They're probably forged."

Caridad sank into the nearest chair. There was a turquoise, red, and purple shawl draped over the back of it, and the colors looked especially intense against the sudden ashen tone of her skin. "That . . . it is not possible," she said. "But Dan wouldn't—"

Exactly what I'd said, but I didn't bother to point it out. For one thing, Jesse was too busy to pay any attention. He was directing his officers to walk through the excavation and close things down. The tribal elders went along to see what damage might have already been done.

That left me and Jesse. Me, Jesse, and Caridad, and without being invited, I took the seat opposite hers, bit my tongue, and waited for Jesse to do his cop thing. He didn't waste any time.

"You want to explain?" he asked. "Or would you rather have legal counsel present when you do?"

Caridad lifted one elegant shoulder. "My goodness, no! We have done nothing wrong, I assure you." When she looked up at Jesse, those big brown eyes of hers were moist. "I did not believe we did. There must be some terrible mix-up. It is the only explanation."

"So Dan Callahan, he assured you all the paperwork was in order?"

She didn't so much shrug as she did twitch away the very thought. "Why would I question this? Dan is . . ." The smallest of smiles touched her full lips. "He is unconventional. You will hear that from everyone here you talk to. But he is professional. And honest. A good man. I did not ask him if the paperwork was in order. I did not need to."

I'd been quiet long enough. I leaned forward. "She's right. That sounds like Dan."

I'm not sure how anybody could miss a tall redhead out there on the side of a mountain, but I think it was the first time Caridad actually paid any attention to me. She swung her gaze my way. "You know Dan?"

"Old friends." It seemed sufficient. "He sent me a note and said he was coming to see me and—"

"Pepper?" Caridad popped out of her chair, hurried to the other side of the desk, and grabbed my hand to give it an affectionate pump. "But of course, I should have known instantly. Dan, he has spoken of you many times."

Any other situation, I might have blushed appropriately and said something about how I hoped everything he said was complimentary. This didn't seem like the time or the place.

"I'm Caridad." Like I'd forgotten—or I should have known more than I did—she pointed one finger back at herself. "Dan, if he was in touch with you, he must have told you all about me. Dan and I, we were married last spring."

So this was the news Dan was coming to Cleveland to tell me!

I sat for a moment, processing it, trying to decide if I was royally pissed Dan hadn't spilled the beans, surprised he'd found another woman to share his life with after the pain he'd gone through thanks to Madeline, or just plain disappointed. While I did, Caridad did an elegant little

184

two-step in front of me, barely containing her excitement. "He said he was going to speak to you and convince you to come here. He told me that's why he went to Cleveland. I did not know you arrived. But that means . . ." She scanned the excavation site. "But Dan, he must be here with you as well."

She didn't know about the kidnapping. Of course she didn't know. What wife would be out here playing in the dirt if she knew her husband was being held for ransom?

This news I was going to leave up to Jesse.

He told her. Unemotional, plain and simple. He told Caridad her husband had been kidnapped and that I was there in New Mexico because I had attempted to save him.

"Thank you." When she grabbed my hands again, there were tears staining Caridad's cheeks. "He said you were a good friend."

Apparently not good enough to hear the news of his marriage until months after it had taken place.

I wiped the sour thought away and concentrated on the matter at hand. "If we knew more about what's happening out here, maybe it could help us find Dan," I suggested.

She shook her head. "There is nothing I can tell you, nothing I know. If I did, I would most certainly do all in my power to bring Dan back." She was not the hand-wringing type. I knew that even though I'd only known her for only a couple minutes. That didn't keep her from clutching her hands together at her waist. Her bones were fine and sharp, like a bird's, and against the red T-shirt she was wearing with jeans, her hands looked as fragile as her composure.

It didn't take a detective to pick up on the vibes. It did, however, require a little woman's intuition. Good cop or not, I knew this was one area where Jesse wasn't going to be able to help. I slid him a look, and when he ignored it, I got up and pointed out to where I saw Pete walking along the face of the pueblo.

"Olivas is calling you," I said.

"I didn't hear him," he grumbled. "Besides . . ." He homed back in on Caridad. "We have a lot we need to talk about."

She nodded and, on shaking knees, made her way back around the table. There was a bottle of water nearby and she took a drink and pressed a hand to the small of her back. "I was digging yesterday," she said. "Perhaps a little too much." She sank into her chair. "It was Dan's idea," she said. "To excavate here. He told me . . ." For a moment, she dropped her head into her hands, but apparently, Caridad was something of a realist. She knew we wouldn't disappear. Not so easily or so quickly. When she raised her head again, she looked directly at Jesse.

"My husband," she said, "believes in some things that are . . . how shall I even begin to explain this? . . . things that are out of the intellectual mainstream."

"He's a paranormal researcher." Jesse nodded. "Yes, I know."

"And this site . . ." Caridad looked beyond the walls of the tent. "There are stories of spirits who visit the kiva, and legends of rituals and ceremonies."

"Rituals and ceremonies that are sacred to my tribe."

Jesse's words were as brittle as his composure. "You have no business here."

I wound one arm through Jesse's and swung him around to face the mesa. "You're not going to get anywhere hitting her over the head like this," I managed to mumble from between clenched teeth. "She's scared to death."

"She deserves it," he muttered. "They all do. And besides, that's the whole point."

"Not if you're looking for information that might actually help us figure out what's going on." My message to him delivered, I raised my voice. "See, you heard Pete that time, didn't you?" I gave him a nudge out of the tent. "They obviously need to talk to you about something."

"Yeah. I . . ." Jesse stepped out of the tent. "I'll be right back. And don't think we're not going to continue this conversation," he said just to make sure Caridad didn't think he was going to let her off the hook.

Once he was gone, I strolled back into the tent and sat down opposite Caridad. "Sorry," I said. "Cops are pricks."

"That one . . ." Her gaze followed Jesse across the rocky mesa toward the kiva. "He does not seem so bad. And I am sure he is only doing his job, but . . ." She spread her hands in a helpless gesture and gave me a watery smile. "I am usually not so emotional. I apologize."

"Give me a break!" I waved away her concern. "You just found out your husband . . ." Yeah, I choked on the word a little, but I recovered in a heartbeat. "You just found out Dan's been kidnapped. Of course you're upset. You'd think a cop would understand, but hey, you know how they can be. Hardheaded and hard-hearted." I didn't want to overplay the good cop/bad cop shtick so I decided to change the subject.

"What's really going on out here?" I asked her.

"I thought it was simply an excavation. But now . . ." She raised her hands in a helpless gesture. "I did not know. You must believe me. Dan, he has been obsessed with this site for some time now. You are his friend. You know how he can be. He talks about it day and night. He is the one who begged me to arrange the excavation. He said . . . he promised me he had all the proper paperwork. There must be some mistake." She turned pleading eyes on me. "You know he is a good, honorable man."

"I do know that." I wasn't bullshitting her. Not this time. I'd known Dan for years, and although he had the tendency to be too focused on science at the risk of neglecting the really important things in life like haircuts and basic fashion sense, he had never been dishonest. Well, unless the fact that he had kept his most recent marriage a secret from me counted.

Another wash of acid raced through my system, and I told myself to get a grip.

"We both know he's a stand-up guy and as trustworthy as all get-out. He'd never do anything underhanded," I said. "But then, how do you explain that phony paperwork? And what was he doing here in the first place? Dan is all into ghosts and stuff. This whole archaeology bit, that doesn't seem like his thing."

"He assured me this place was important to his work. And Dan . . ." For a heartbeat, a smile touched Caridad's lips. "He is difficult to say no to." I was glad she didn't look to me for confirmation because, if she had, I would have remembered that motel room outside Chicago where I was all set to say yes, yes, yes to Dan, and would have, too, if not for the fact that the creepy ghost who was his first wife swooped in and stole my body before I could.

"So Dan, he was the one who pushed you to excavate here?" I waited for her to nod to confirm what I'd said, and when she hesitated, I pushed. Just a little. "The cops are going to find out, Caridad. I'm sorry, but you know it's true. I understand that you're trying to protect Dan, but those Taopi Indians out there, they're plenty pissed. They're not going to let this rest. Not until they get to the bottom of things. And if you're keeping secrets from them, and if all this has something to do with Dan getting kidnapped . . . well, don't you see? If you don't tell us everything you know, you might be putting him in danger."

"Yes. Yes. I understand." A tear slipped down her cheek. "I will try to help as much as I am able. But I do not wish to get Dan in trouble."

"He's already in trouble. The kidnappers have him and they're waiting for me to find some bones so I can exchange the bones for Dan. Only somebody stole the bones, and I'll tell you what, I'm afraid if we don't do something soon . . ." I didn't have to elaborate. Caridad's breath caught on the end of a sob.

It took her a minute to compose herself. "I am an anthropologist," she said around the tears that clogged her voice. "I am not nearly as imaginative as Dan. I came to this place for the science, not the parascience. And now you're telling me that because of something we're doing . . . of something that's going on . . . you say that is why Dan has been kidnapped?"

"We're not sure," I said, because leaping in with the story of the baseball fans would only muddy the water. "The cops are doing everything they can to find out. That's why we need your help. Caridad, when was the last time you saw Dan?"

She considered it for a moment. "Two weeks or so. Yes." There was a calendar on her desk and she stabbed one finger toward a date a couple weeks back. "He was here, putting the final touches on the entrance into the kiva." After all Jesse had told her about the phony permits and the sacredness of the site, Caridad's cheeks got dusky.

"And when you didn't see him for two weeks . . . didn't that seem a little weird to you?"

"He told me he was going to Cleveland. To see you because . . . You must forgive me, Ms. Martin, I know this sounds bizarre, and as I said, I am a person of science. But you know Dan, so you will understand. You know he has a tendency to not only think outside the box but to sometimes not even know where the box is. He told me he needed your help on this project because you are able to talk to the dead."

This didn't seem like the right moment for me to mention that the talent had deserted me, so I went on with my questioning. "I'm going to guess the kidnappers haven't exactly given him access to his cell phone. Didn't you think it strange that he hadn't called?"

Another lift of those delicate shoulders. "Dan is a genius. You know this. He doesn't always follow rules. If he needed me, I knew he would call. If not . . . then I knew I would see him when he came back here to the mountain. Only now . . . now you tell me . . ." Her voice broke and she got up and went over to the camp bed and the small table next to it where there was a box of tissues. She dabbed one to her nose. In an elegant sort of way, of course. "Do you think this has something to do with the bones of Goodshot Gomez?" she asked.

I jumped out of my chair. "You know about Goodshot?"

"I see I have touched a nerve." Caridad swept back across the tent. No easy thing considering it was so small and the two of us pretty much filled it up. "Dan, he always told me that here the spirits could be called forth with the bones of one of the members of the tribe who . . ." She passed a hand over her eyes. "I am sorry. I do not remember very clearly except for this odd name, this Goodshot Gomez. When Dan speaks of the paranormal, I am afraid I do not always pay as close attention as I should. There is a legend about a sacred silver bowl with healing powers and the people who were once entrusted with the secret of its hiding place. This is the story Dan was drawn to, for the legend says spirits guard the bowl and they can be called forth by those who know how and that this, it has something to do with the bones of one of the old ones. I do believe he thought you were the one who would know how to make this happen. Perhaps it is true since you know about the bones, too."

"I was the one who brought the bones here to New Mexico. To ransom Dan."

"So the kidnappers . . ." Caridad's brow creased. "They know about the bones and about the ceremony to call the spirits? And they want to perform this ceremony so badly, they are willing to kidnap Dan to do it? It makes no sense."

She was right. It didn't. It didn't explain about the baseball curse. Or Norma's murder. Or why Arnie had been gunned down right before he could talk to me.

I told Jesse all that later when everyone was off the mountain and he was leading the way back to the car.

We'd just passed out of the narrow passage and he said, "I dunno. It actually makes plenty of sense to me."

By that time, it was nearly dark and I stepped carefully around the jagged rocks in my path. "Come on. You weren't listening to everything I told you. It really doesn't."

He was standing at the driver's door and he looked at me over the roof of the SUV. "Think about it, Pepper. Everything falls into place. That is, if your friend Dan is the one who forged those papers. And faked his own kidnapping."

13

It was bad form to argue with a guy who'd just gotten out of your bed—and had made the last few hours pretty spectacular.

That didn't stop me.

When Jesse walked out of the bathroom, showered and dressed, I was ready to pick up the conversation he'd started right before he went in there, the same one we'd had on our way down the mountain a couple evenings before.

"You're nuts."

Big points for him, we were on the same wavelength and he wasn't afraid to admit it. "Mine is a valid theory," he said.

"Yeah, if you're nuts."

"No, if you're not so involved with the suspect that you're unwilling to admit it's possible he could be a suspect at all."

"Except Dan and I are not involved." I emphasized that last word, just like he had. "We've never been involved."

"But you are friends."

"That doesn't mean—"

"Sure it does. You can't see the forest for the trees. You think Callahan can't be guilty because—"

"Because he's Dan. And he can't be guilty." I crossed my arms over my chest and the plaid shirt I was wearing with my no-name jeans.

Since that's exactly how Jesse was standing, we must have looked like a pretty pair. Apparently he realized it, because he'd left his boots by the side of the bed and he went over to slip them on. "Callahan's fingerprints are all over those forged papers," he said, and that wasn't exactly fair. He'd already dropped that bombshell the day before— two days after we'd visited the pueblo on the mesa and shut down the excavation there—and he didn't need to keep reminding me. "And you know what the workers from the site told me when I brought them into the station for questioning. There was never any doubt at the site about who was in charge of everything from who worked there to where they were digging—Dan Callahan."

"Of course he was in charge. Dan is smart. Smarter than anybody I know. If somebody was going to be in charge—"

"In charge of an illegal excavation on lands that belong to the Taopi nation."

I huffed. There wasn't anything I could say. Not about that.

194

Time to change the subject. A little, anyway. "But Dan was kidnapped weeks ago!"

Leave it to a cop not to be swayed by the passion in my voice. "There's no evidence to support that." He stood up. "You know that as well as I do. Come on, Pepper, look at the facts."

I'd tried. Honest. In the last couple days, I'd listened to every piece of evidence Jesse and his officers presented. To me, none of it added up.

Not the lack of anyone's fingerprints but mine or Dan's on the watchband that came with the ransom note.

Not the hunting cabin the pueblo police had found far out in the wilderness that looked like it had been recently occupied, but not like anyone had ever been kept there against his will.

Not a body. Thank goodness, not Dan's body.

It was frustrating. And confusing. And I groaned. "But why would—"

"Callahan fake his own kidnapping? To get the bones, of course. When you talked to her, Dr. Valenzuela told you that, more than anything, he wanted to excavate that site on Wind Mountain, right?" I guess Jesse took pity on me, because after staring at me for a heartbeat and knowing I wouldn't give him an answer because I didn't want to be forced to admit the truth, he barreled on. "She told me the same thing when I talked to her yesterday. Callahan knew the bones were an integral part of a sacred ceremony. He knew that ceremony called the spirits. That all checks out. The shaman confirms it. Follow the logic here, Pepper. If

Callahan is as obsessed with the paranormal as everyone says he is, and if he needed the bones to call the spirits of the ancient pueblo—"

"Then why not just give me a jingle and ask me to come out for a visit and, oh by the way, bring a dead guy with me?"

"I guess he knows you're more honest than that."

As compliments went, it was a good one. Too bad Jesse didn't cut his losses and stop right there.

"Callahan knew you needed a really good reason to break into a mausoleum and haul away a guy who'd been buried there for more than a hundred years," he said. "He found one. And I'm sorry to have to put it so bluntly, but I guess you're just not getting it. He played you. If you thought he was in danger—"

"Then what about Norma, huh?" A good question, and I gave him a sort of *aha* look along with it. "There's no connection between Dan and Norma."

"Number one, there's no connection between them that we know of. And number two, the sheriff here in Antonito is working that angle, and so far, he hasn't found anything. For all we know, Norma's murder may have nothing to do with any of this."

I had to give him that. Even if I didn't have to admit it. I lifted my chin. "Then what about Brian? You can't tell me it's just coincidence that he's in Antonito, Colorado, when I'm in Antonito, Colorado. I saw him at the grocery store, remember. I followed him and he flattened the tires on my car. I saw him at Norma's that one afternoon, and he's probably the one who whacked me on the head and knocked me out. Brian and Dan—"

"Know each other from the ghost-hunting community so it really wouldn't be any big surprise if they were involved in this together. And speaking of that . . ." He raised his eyebrows. "Did you ever get a hold of that guy you said you knew back in Cleveland? The one you were with the night you ran into Brian and his friends? You said he might remember Brian's last name."

Talk about touchy situations. New lover asking about old lover, only new lover didn't know old lover was a lover. Or a cop for that matter. No way I was going to mention any of that and have some sort of law enforcement bonding mojo going on. Once that happened, who knew what kinds of secrets Jesse and Quinn would share. I was in no mood to be the topic of their conversation. Or some weird game of macho one-upsmanship.

"I called when you asked about it," I reminded Jesse. "And again yesterday. He hasn't returned my calls."

"Busy guy, huh?" I didn't like the way Jesse said this. Like he already had his suspicions and he was just waiting for me to confirm them.

I guess it was just as well that my cell phone rang. "Quinn." I recognized the number so I was talking as soon as I answered. "You got my message?"

"That's not a very friendly hello from someone I haven't heard from in a couple weeks."

Quinn is not the chipper sort so when I realized there was a bit of a lilt in his voice, it made me paranoid.

I turned my back on Jesse. Yeah, like that would actually give me some privacy in a room the size of the walk-in closet I'd once had back home. "I'm working a case," I said.

"With dead people?"

"No." The whole truth and nothing but. "In fact, you'll be happy to know I can't see them anymore. The ghosts are gone and I'm on my own and—"

"Really?" Don't ask me why it interested him that I couldn't see ghosts. When I could, he didn't much care. "What are you doing about it?"

"I'm investigating without them."

"How's that working out for you?"

I actually might have gotten irritated if he didn't sound so damned perky. I know, I know . . . *Quinn* and *perky.* Two words that have never before been used together in the same sentence.

I crinkled my nose. "Are you okay?"

"Why shouldn't I be?" I heard him draw in a deep breath and let it go in a kind of whoosh that said that, at least to him, all was right with the world. "Why haven't you called?"

"Phones work both ways. Why haven't you called?"

"I actually did. A couple days ago. Before you called me, in fact."

A couple days ago, I was up on Wind Mountain at the site of the ancient pueblo. Not much oxygen up that high and, for sure, no cell service. "What did you want?"

"I was going to come see you."

"And I wouldn't have been there because, like I said, I'm

working a case. And for this case I'm working, I need some information. So that's why I called. I thought you could—"

"You don't have to wait for me to call you. You know you can call me anytime. Or hey, I could come over to your place right now. Then we can talk."

"We could, but I need information now and—"

"How about dinner?"

As if it would help me make sense of his rambling, I shook my head. "We can do that another time. For now, I thought you might remember something I can't remember. I need a name."

"You have one. Pepper."

I pulled the phone away from my ear and made a face at it. "You're still taking those painkillers, aren't you?"

"No painkillers." Across the thousands of miles that separated us, I heard the smile in his voice. "Got cleared by the docs today. They say I can go back to work."

That explained it! I actually breathed a sigh of relief. Now that I knew he hadn't gone off the deep end, it might be easier to get through to Quinn. "That's great. I know how much that means to you. And you can start right now. By helping me out. Like I said, I need a name." No more bad jokes so I added quickly, "Those guys we met when we went to the Indians game. Brian, the ghost hunter, and his friends. Do you remember—"

"Brian, John, Gregory, Arnie. Of course I remember. First names and last names. You think you're dealing with an ordinary mortal?"

I knew for a fact I was not. Like I said, old lover, and a damned good one.

"So . . ." Of course, I had no idea what Quinn was really doing, but he sounded so self-satisfied, I pictured him strapping on his shoulder holster and admiring himself in the mirror while he talked. "You're in New Mexico, right?"

It took me a moment to find my voice and stammer, "How . . . how did you—"

"Come on, give me some credit. Arnie got murdered out in New Mexico . . . what, three or four days ago? You didn't think that would make the news here? He's from Cleveland, after all. And now you're calling and telling me you're working a case and you need last names because you can't remember. And one of the people who's name is mentioned is the victim. So, who's your suspect? Obviously, not Arnie."

"Obviously."

"I'm thinking Brian."

"Because . . ."

I pictured him giving me one of his patented, blasé shrugs. "Brian was obviously the spokesman for the group so he was obviously in charge so if there's something suspicious going on . . ."

"Brian, yes."

"Ran him through the system as soon as I heard about Arnie. Brian Reynolds. Nothing there. No priors. Clean."

"Brian Reynolds. That helps." I looked toward Jesse when I said this, and he got the message and got right on his phone to start digging from this end. "Only the cops out here—"

"Cops, huh?" Oh yeah, I knew Quinn plenty well, and

I knew there was a green spark in his eyes when he said this. "Any of them good looking?"

I couldn't help myself. I glanced at Jesse. Like I needed the reminder that *good looking* didn't even begin to describe Jesse? I shook away the thought. "Does it matter?"

"It does. You have a thing for cops."

"Not all cops."

"Yeah." He chuckled. "Good thing it's just me."

"Good thing."

"And that's the other cop I hear talking there in the background, right?" There was no use denying it so I didn't bother to answer. Though he wasn't talking loud, Jesse had a deep voice and it rumbled through the room like thunder. "You must be at the station."

Dang, but I hated lying to Quinn. But not nearly as much as I hated the thought of dropping the truth on him without the proper chance to cushion the blow.

I coughed from deep in my throat and hoped it sounded enough like static to justify me saying, "We're breaking up."

"You mean our cell signal?"

"Yeah. Of course. What else would I mean?" I mumbled a few unintelligible sounds just so he'd believe me. "We'll talk. Soon."

It wasn't until I hung up that I realized Jesse was off his call, too. "So how does he feel about that?" he asked.

I tucked my phone into my purse. "About . . ."

"He's the one . . ." Like Quinn was actually standing there, Jesse poked his chin in the direction of my phone. "You said you never had any luck with law enforcement, explaining about the ghosts. He was the one who didn't believe you."

"He's not as open-minded as you."

He grabbed his hat from the bedside table. "I'm jealous."

"You shouldn't be. There's nothing going on between Quinn and me. Not these days."

"Not what I'm talking about." Like I said, the room wasn't big, and it didn't take Jesse more than a couple steps to walk over to me. No lead-in. No explanation. He just took me in his arms and kissed me, long and hard, and when he was done, he looked into my eyes. "Because he knows you better than I do," he said.

I wrapped my arms around his neck. It was nice and cozy, and besides, the way he kissed me made my knees weak and I needed the extra support. "We're working on that."

"We are." He backed way. "And we can keep working on it in the car. Come on." Jesse opened the door. "I've got a lead. Norma's ex."

"And you think—"

"I don't know what to think." He clapped his hat on his head. "That's why we're going to talk to him."

Turns out Will Kettle, Norma's ex, was Taopi and he lived on pueblo land. Within an hour of leaving Antonito, we were outside the rusted trailer he called home sweet home.

He didn't ask us in, and I was relieved. From the brief

glimpse I got when he opened the door, I saw that the inside of the trailer was cramped, dark, and packed with more junk than any one person should be allowed to own. There was mighty loud music coming from inside, too. Will snapped the door closed behind him, muffling the head-banging noise, and led the way to the other side of the trailer, where there were a couple battered lawn chairs set up under a torn green-and-white-striped canopy.

Will was a short guy. Blotchy skin, stringy hair, as wiry as the stunted tree that grew over near where Jesse had parked the SUV. He lit a cigarette and dropped into a chair next to a propane grill that had seen better days. "Didn't have nothing to do with Norma dying," he said.

"Didn't say you did." Jesse had refused the offer of a seat. He stood to my left, opposite Will, loose-limbed and comfortable, as much a part of that land as the dust that kicked up in a hot breeze. They must have known each other, Will and Jesse. It made me wonder how Will could look so darned unconcerned. Or maybe he just didn't notice the hawk-like sharpness of Jesse's eyes.

"Sheriff from Antonito, he already talked to me," Will added.

"So I hear." Jesse studied him for just long enough to make Will squirm. "Where were you when Norma got killed?"

"At work. Over at the perlite mine. You can check with my supervisor."

"I don't need to." I wouldn't be so bold as to call Jesse's expression a smile. "Sheriff already did."

"Then you know there's nothing I can tell you."

Jesse hitched his right hand over his gun. It wasn't a threatening gesture. But it got Will's attention. "I heard Norma broke up with you."

Will shifted in his chair. "No loss."

"You might not have thought so at the time."

"Shit, I was already seeing somebody else by the time Norma sprung the news on me that she'd fallen in love." He gave the words a twist that told me Will didn't believe in love. "Imagine the little bitch dumping me before I could dump her! No loss. I got Gabriella Montoya to help me forget. You know her, Jesse. Everybody knows her. Gabriella, she's got a reputation." A smile spread over his face like oil on water. Will had bad teeth. "Everything they say about Gabriella is true. Which means I ain't exactly missing Norma."

"What happened?" Jesse wasn't talking about Will and Gabriella, thank goodness. No way I wanted to know that story.

He pulled in a lungful of smoke and blew it out in a long puff of indifference. "Norma was all right. If you know what I mean. But a guy like me . . ." Will's gaze slithered in my direction. "I'm not a one-woman kind of guy, but when Norma said she was seeing someone else, well, I don't put up with that kind of crap."

"The someone else, that had to be Brian." I said this before Jesse shot me a look that told me not to say anything at all.

He swung his gaze back to Will. "So Norma was seeing someone else, and that made you hopping mad."

"Like I said . . ." Will finished his cigarette, dropped it

on the ground, and mashed it with the toe of his sneaker. "I already had Gabriella to help me forget."

"Except it doesn't look as if you have forgotten. Not completely. Last night . . ." There was a folded piece of paper in Jesse's back pocket and he pulled it out. "Heard you got picked up in Antonito, Will. Outside Norma's house."

"That was bullshit!" Will jumped out of his chair so fast it tipped and hit the dirt. "I was just walking by is all."

"Not what the sheriff says."

"All right, so I was looking in the window, okay?" Will had stalked as far as the trailer and he came back the other way. "I left my guitar there, you know? When me and Norma, when we split. I left my guitar at her place, and hell, what was going to happen to it now that she's dead? I didn't know, but I sure didn't want to see it in some estate sale one of these days. Then I got a call, you know, about picking it up."

Jesse cocked his head. "A call? From who?"

Will shrugged. "Sheriff's department. That's what the guy said. Said if I stopped by last night, the house would be open and I could come in and get my things. Hey, I paid a hundred bucks for that damned guitar. Then I get over to Norma's and it looked to me like the place was shut up tight and I thought—"

"You thought about breaking in."

"Yeah, maybe. But thinking about it and doing it are two different things, and since I never did it, it's not exactly a crime, is it?"

Jesse took a couple steps closer. "You got a sheet, Will.

You can't afford to get nabbed again, or you're going to be facing some serious time. Good thing that deputy drove by and spotted you and stopped you from doing what you shouldn't have been thinking about doing in the first place."

"Yeah, well, a lot of good that deputy did me. He told me to get a move on, and I would have, too, if he stuck around to watch me leave. But he got a call, something about a big accident over on 285. He headed out fast. And I was all set to leave, too. That's when I looked in the window . . . you know . . . just to check for sure about the person who was supposed to meet me there and let me in. And that's when I realized there was already somebody in the house." Will spat on the ground. "Now that's the real crime. Calling somebody else and telling him he could come in and pick up stuff and then not letting me in to do the same. That damned guitar better still be there, or I swear—"

"Another person? In the house?" Jesse aimed a laser look at Will. "If you're lying to me, Will—"

"Ain't lying. Even thought of calling over to the sheriff's department about it, but well . . ." Will crossed his arms over his scrawny chest. "After the way they treated me, I figured the hell with them. Going to file a complaint, though. About that call, and not being able to get my guitar."

I thought about the day I, too, had peeked into Norma's window and saw Brian there with my Jimmy Choo bag. "Big guy, right?" I asked. "Sort of dorky looking. Close-cropped hair. Tattoo on the inside of his left wrist."

"Dorky, all right. But not all that big." Will squeezed

his eyes shut, remembering. "And he had shaggy hair. Brown. And wire glasses."

I sucked in a breath of superheated air just as Jesse took a copy of a photo out of his pocket—the one that I'd first seen back in Cleveland the day the ransom note arrived. He showed the picture to Will.

"That's him." Will pointed a finger at Dan's nose. "That's him all right. When I got to Norma's last night, that guy, he was already there inside the house."

14

"Don't touch anything."

I wasn't planning on it, but Jesse's order brought out the stubborn redhead in me. We were just about to walk into Norma's adobe next to the cemetery and my hands were in the pockets of my jeans. That is, until he had the nerve to say what he said, and I took out my hands and waved them around, just so he'd get the message.

He did. At least I guess that's what the eye rolling was all about.

"You know I didn't mean it like a threat or anything," Jesse grumbled. "So don't take it so personally. The sheriff called me in just as a courtesy, and I want to make sure we don't get in the way. Besides, the last thing we need is your fingerprints contaminating the scene. I'll bet anything your friend Dan's are already doing that."

"My friend Dan's." He'd already walked into the house

ahead of me and was greeting the sheriff and the deputies at work in there, so I don't think Jesse heard either my mumbling or the sarcasm in my voice. Like I'd told him on the way from the pueblo back to Antonito, no way Dan was involved. And if Will Kettle said he was, then Will was just crazy. Or so eager to deflect any guilt away from himself that he was willing to point the finger at Dan. Or more specifically, at Dan's picture.

"I wasn't planning on touching anything," I said, stepping into the pint-sized living room. There was a middle-aged guy with a bushy mustache in there shaking hands with Jesse. He looked familiar, and I remembered the last time I'd been at Norma's, the day I got conked on the head and ended up in the ER. Mustache Man was the sheriff, of course, and it wasn't until he looked at me and shook his head in disgust that I realized I was holding on to the front door.

I dropped my hand and wiped it against the leg of my jeans. Yeah, like that would somehow magically erase any fingerprints I'd already left.

"Don't touch anything," the sheriff said. Delivering the message, he didn't sound nearly as menacing as Jesse had when he said the same thing. In fact, the sheriff sounded as if he'd had to give this sort of warning far too many times, and he was just plain tired of it. "And don't go getting yourself knocked over the head again, Ms. Martin. I got too much on my plate to have to handle another assault report. Why don't you just . . ." He flattened his hands and pushed them, palms out, toward me. The way a trainer would who wanted a dog to sit and stay. "You just stay put and don't get into any trouble while I show Jesse what we're up to here."

What they were up to was dusting for prints there in the living room and in Norma's tiny bedroom with the magazine pictures of tropical islands pinned up on the walls. I watched them for a while—hands in pockets—but let's face it, I didn't like to see anyone work more than they had to. And these guys?

"They're wasting their time." In the interest of not embarrassing Jesse, I kept my voice down, but I wanted to make sure he knew I wasn't buying this Dan-as-guilty-party hogwash. "I could just save them the trouble and tell them Dan wasn't here. How could he be if he's been kidnapped?"

"Maybe." Jesse's arms were crossed over his chest. He slid me a look. "Maybe not. Either way, it would be irresponsible of them not to follow a lead." Since one of the deputies was bustling past, Jesse's voice was just as low as mine. He stepped forward so that the deputy could sidle through, then stepped back the other way so another deputy with a case full of fingerprint powder and brushes could get past us. Whoever said three was a crowd must have been thinking of Norma's house.

And I guess Jesse was, too. He looked toward the kitchen and the backyard beyond. "Maybe you should—"

"Go wait outside?" I wasn't exactly as upset about this dismissal as I tried to sound. It wasn't terribly cheery in there. Especially when I thought about how Norma had been murdered there in her own home and how now the cops were hell-bent on trying to pin the whole thing on

Dan. "I'll wait out back," I told Jesse. "Only you'd better hope while I'm out there, no one hits me over the head and knocks me out."

I decided to believe that the sleek smile that was his only response meant he didn't want me to get hit over the head, either, and I meandered through the deputies in the living room and walked into the kitchen. That's when Norma's bulletin board caught my eye.

It was one of those French boards, the kind that are covered with fabric and crisscrossed with ribbons. In Norma's case, the fabric was a tropical print complete with pink flamingos and fiery sunsets, and the ribbons were yellow, orange, and lime green. It wasn't the colors that caught my eye, though.

I glanced over my shoulder to make sure the coast was clear and closed in on the board. There was a recipe for sloppy joes attached to one of the orange ribbons, and a coupon for some off-brand laundry detergent attached to one of the yellow ones. Small, everyday things, and in light of what had ultimately happened to Norma, strangely moving. Rather than get all slushy about it, I looked at what was hanging on to one of the lime ribbons.

A photograph. Or at least all that was left of a photograph. Most of the picture had been ripped away, leaving only one corner that was hardly big enough to reveal why Norma prized it. I bent closer for a better look and made out one little sliver of sky with something brown silhouetted against it that might have been a rock. Or a distant mountain. Or a bowl of chocolate pudding.

No way to tell where the photo was taken or what—

or who—might have been in the center of it. No matter. That wasn't what made my detective instincts tingle. No, that was taken care of by the paperclip that had been used to attach the picture to the ribbon. The one bent into a weird, drunken figure eight.

Exactly like one I'd seen before.

"Hey, Jesse." He was just walking past the door so it wasn't hard to get his attention. But just to make sure, I grabbed on to Jesse's arm and tugged him into the kitchen. "Look." I pointed to the bulletin board and the scrap of photograph. "Brian was here. This proves it. And it proves he had a relationship with Norma, too."

Of course he didn't follow my logic, so I explained. About the first night I came to Antonito, and the aliens over at Taberna. About the one alien mask that had been held together by a weird, twisty paperclip.

When he still didn't look convinced, I stepped back, my weight against one foot. "Come on. You have to admit, it's a good catch."

"It's a great observation. You've got a good eye. But that doesn't mean—"

"Of course it does. Brian was the one wearing that alien mask. It had to be him. You said it yourself, Brian was obviously the spokesperson for the group." Too late, I remembered it wasn't Jesse who'd said that at all, it was Quinn. No matter. It's exactly what Jesse would have said if he'd been part of the conversation. Cop brotherhood and all that.

As if proving the point, Jesse launched into the same lecture I knew Quinn would have given me if he'd been there. "Even if it's true that Brian was wearing the mask that day—and there's no way to prove it, of course—all the paperclip tells us is that Brian was here."

Since that was my whole point, I perked right up.

Until Jesse shot my theory to the ground with, "Or that Brian gave Norma a paperclip. Or that Norma once saw Brian bend a paperclip a certain way and she liked the way he did it so when she needed to bend a paperclip, she did the same thing. See what I'm getting at here? No way this kind of evidence stands up in court."

"But—"

"Like I said, great observation." Something told me if he thought he could get away with it, he would have given me a pat on the head. Big points for him for knowing he couldn't get away with it. "So weren't you on your way—"

"Hey, Chief!" The sheriff stuck his head into the kitchen. "Got that call from the crime-lab guys in Albuquerque." Shaking his head, he tucked his cell into his pocket. "You're not going to believe this. They finished up examining the evidence, you know, from Norma's murder. Turns out they found some skin under her fingernails. You know, like maybe she fought with her attacker. They ran it through a database and it's Brian Reynolds's DNA, all right."

"That proves it." It wasn't polite to gloat, but let's face it, I had every right. I did restrain myself, though, and didn't give Jesse a boff on the arm. Not in front of his fellow cops. "It's just like I said. Brian must have been the killer."

"A killer without a rap sheet." Jesse wasn't convinced. He crossed his arms over his chest. "Why?"

Whatever Jesse was going to ask, the sheriff apparently had the same questions for the guys in Albuquerque. He was ready with the answers and nodded knowingly. "Turns out Reynolds was down in Daytona Beach, Florida, back in 2008. There was a serial killer on the loose down there, and the police were taking DNA swabs from everybody they detained. Reynolds wasn't their guy, of course. In fact, he was picked up for nothing more than a drunk and disorderly after some spring training baseball game, and they never did charge him. But since the cops were swabbing everyone, they swabbed him."

"He's our killer." Yes, I sounded thrilled, as thrilled as I suddenly felt. And relieved, to boot. Maybe now Jesse would stop looking to prove that Dan was somehow implicated in this crazy business. "All we have to do—"

"Is get our hands on him." Jesse sounded certain, but not particularly pleased at the prospect. And the deputies never stopped doing what they were doing, which told me that though they knew they had a solid suspect in Norma's murder, they weren't completely convinced Dan wasn't involved.

"Humph." That was me, grumbling as I turned to push open the back door with one shoulder so as not to leave any fingerprints. I walked outside, and from where I stood, I had a clear view of the cemetery next door, and I ambled over that way. "Boy, Goodshot, I could sure use some help." I waited for an answer. Or a little twinkle of light.

Or anything that might prove that some of the old magic was still at work, and when I didn't get it, I grumbled on. "They think Dan is involved. And they know Brian is for sure, only they don't know where Brian is, and if you were around, I could send you out on a sort of scouting party and maybe you could locate him for me. Then Brian could admit the whole thing. You know, about kidnapping Dan and about the excavation at the pueblo . . ." A shiver scooted over my shoulders and I shook it away.

"Okay," I said to the thin air around me, "so I don't understand what the excavation has to do with Brian and it does sound like Dan was the mastermind there and I don't know how the whole thing can be connected, but still . . ."

I was getting no answers from the dead, so I kicked my way through the dust over to the lopsided building behind Norma's house. Too small to be a garage. Too big to be a toolshed. My guess was that she used it for storage and I had no doubt the cops had been through it the first time they came to the house to investigate Norma's murder.

"You know, Goodshot . . ." Too antsy to stand still, I kicked the toe of one boot against the door of the shed. "They're being pigheaded about this. Even Jesse. I'm sure they'll look for Brian. I mean, now that they've got his DNA and all. But I think at this point, Jesse's more worried about what happened over at that old pueblo than he is about Norma. I guess that's his job." I sighed. "Norma's murder is the sheriff's problem, but still . . ."

I glanced over my shoulder to see if anything was happening in the house—anything that didn't look like a Dan

Callahan witchhunt, that is—and when there wasn't, I made up my mind. The motel wasn't far away, and my car was parked there.

"If they're not going to start right now and look for Brian . . ." I said into ghost-less silence.

"Then you know what? I'll just find him myself."

Just to show I meant it, I gave the shed door another kick.

And I guess that did the trick.

Because the shed door plopped open and I found what I was looking for when Brian's body dropped into the dirt at my feet.

I'm beyond screaming when I find a body. I mean, really, been there, done that. But I'm human, after all, and I do have a certain sensitivity when it comes to things like bloated flesh and bulging eyes and gaping, bloody wounds.

I might have shrieked. A little.

Like anyone can blame me?

The result, of course, was that everyone who was in the house came running, and ten minutes or so later, they were engrossed with this new turn of events. For my part, I think it's safe to say that I was just grossed out.

"How you doing?" I was standing at the wooden fence (badly in need of painting) between Norma's property and the cemetery when Jesse came over. "If you need to go back to your motel—"

I cut him off with a quick shake of my head. "Not the first time," I confided. "Hope it's the last."

He followed my gaze over to where the deputies were emptying Brian's pockets and searching the area around his body. "Every time, we hope it's the last time. But finding that body . . ." He swung his gaze back to me. "That's not what I was talking about."

"But Brian, he's dead and—"

"And you were out here trying to communicate with Spirit." If it were me, I would have taken credit for a little hocus-pocus mind reading. The flush that darkened Jesse's cheeks told me that as much fun as that would be, he was more honest than that. "Norma's house isn't all that well insulated," he said. "I don't think anyone else was paying much attention, but I heard every word, loud and clear. Did you get an answer?"

Another shake of my head.

"So my question stands. Damn, Pepper, it's such an awesome ability. To be chosen by Spirit for such important work . . ." He tipped his head back, obviously considering my Gift with far more reverence than I ever had. But then, he wasn't the one who'd spent the last few years dealing with annoying people of the not-so-alive persuasion. "Now that it's gone . . . I mean, your whole life has changed. How does that make you feel?"

I shrugged, then remembered this was the man who that morning—it seemed a hundred years ago—had confessed that he was jealous because he didn't know me as well as Quinn did. Well, if he wanted the whole package, this went with the territory.

"I was happy the other night when I first found out. Today . . ." I looked toward the cemetery. There wasn't even a hint of a supernatural sparkle there. Not for me. "I sure could use Goodshot's help," I admitted. "And . . ." I don't know why I bothered to lower my voice since it seemed obvious nobody on the Other Side could hear me. "I actually kind of miss him. He was a great guy."

"Taopi." Jesse nodded like the fact that Goodshot was great and the fact that he was a Pueblo Indian were one and the same. For all I knew, they were. "Maybe you can get your Gift back."

This time, my shrug wasn't as helpless as it was un-sure. "I'm not sure I want it back. I mean, a life without ghosts . . ." I drew in a deep breath of sage-scrubbed air. "No more trouble, no more hauntings, no more investi-gations. At least that's what I told myself when I first re-alized I couldn't see the ghosts anymore. But I'm still investigating, huh? I guess I just wish—"

Even though it was my wish, I wasn't sure what I was going to say, so I was glad one of the deputies came scram-bling up. "Sheriff wants you to see this," he told Jesse. "Dead guy's got a thousand bucks in his pocket. Cash. And this." He handed Jesse one of those plastic evidence bags with a scrap of paper inside it.

Jesse took a close look, and I did, too.

"Phone number," Jesse said. "We'll have to check it out."

And I knew they would, too. And that it wouldn't take them long to find out who the phone number belonged to. Which is, honestly, the reason I kept my mouth shut. I mean, besides that, Jesse never asked if I recognized the phone number so, technically, I wasn't obligated to tell.

"I think you're right," I said, pushing away from the

fence and heading out to the street. "I am going to go back to the motel for a while and rest. Finding a dead body . . ." I looked over to where Brian lay in the dust, daring Jesse to tell me I shouldn't be upset. "I'm going to . . ." I poked a thumb over my shoulder. "I dunno. A shower and a nap maybe."

"I'll call you," Jesse said, and he headed over to help out the other cops.

Just as well. It would keep him busy, and right now, I needed him busy for a little while.

At least until I could figure out what Brian was doing with Dan's cell phone number in his pocket.

15

Charming bistro tables and chairs. Terra cotta–tiled floor. Pots overflowing with flowers in every shade of a New Mexico sunset.

Ah, signs of the good life!

All set to step onto the outdoor patio of the Taos Inn, I paused, pulled in a deep breath fragranced with salsa and limes, and smiled the smile of a person too long relegated to dry desert air, dust—and murder.

Soft music playing in the background, the purr of voices out on the sidewalk just on the other side of the iron fence that surrounded the patio, the artistic vibe of Taos with its galleries, shops, and boutiques . . . after all I'd been through since I arrived in the Great Southwest, this was exactly what I needed, a real city with people and elegant hotels. Oh yes, and running water, too.

For a moment, I stood in the sunshine, drinking in the

warmth and the atmosphere, enjoying what felt like a moment in the spotlight.

I was so ready for it! Yes, I was a tad overdressed for a weekday evening. No matter. There is, after all, no value that can be placed on self-confidence, and in my good jeans, sandals with five-inch heels, and a spaghetti-strap lace cami the color of a blush, I not only felt on top of the world, I looked good, too.

And later that night when we got back together, I was counting on Jesse noticing.

For now, I had other things on my mind. I snared the nearest waitress, ordered one of the Cowboy Buddha margaritas I'd heard the inn was famous for, and made my way over to a table by the fence where Caridad Valenzuela was waiting for me.

In a lemon-colored tunic top, she looked like a pretty little canary. She apparently ate like one, too. Even as I gratefully accepted my margarita and ordered nachos with the works, I watched Cardidad pick at a plate of orange slices.

"We've got a problem," I said, but not until after I took a sip of margarita and sank back in my chair, quenched and satisfied. "How does Dan know Brian?"

"This Brian, he is the one the police have asked about, isn't he?" Her voice was husky, and when Caridad looked up at me, I saw that her big brown eyes were rimmed with gray. This was not a smoky-eyed fashion statement, but a testament to sleepless nights. Though she tried to cover it with foundation, her nose was red, too. Her trembling hands? That was something she couldn't disguise. They fluttered over the orange pieces. "I am so . . ." She pulled her hands onto her lap. "I am confused."

"You and me both." Another sip of margarita and maybe I couldn't feel the confusion clear completely, but I could at least imagine there must be an answer to all this craziness. "Truth is, I think the cops are, too. You know what that means, don't you? If we don't help Dan, nobody will."

I hadn't meant to get the waterworks going again, but then, I guess a woman whose husband is facing as many serious questions as Dan was could hardly help herself. She sniffed delicately and plucked a tissue from her purse. Like a heroine in some old, mushy movie, she dabbed it to her eyes.

"You are a good friend to Dan. When I see him again . . ." The words caught in her throat and she coughed, and took a sip of water. "He told me. How in Chicago, he thought he was making love to you. How Madeline, she ruined this for the two of you." Caridad reached across the table and patted my hand. "I am embarrassing you. I am so sorry."

"Not embarrassed. Honest." It was true so it was no big deal admitting it. "Dan and I . . ." Since there was no easy way to explain, I simply shrugged and took another sip of my drink, and when my nachos were delivered—glorious, steaming, and cheesy—I offered some to Caridad. She refused, so I got to work on them myself. I scooped up cheese and salsa with one perfect chip.

"It wasn't meant to be," I said, "And it's not like I'm brokenhearted about it or anything. I'm glad Dan and I are still friends. Only, I've got to ask, when he told you about me and Madeline's ghost and all . . ." Another bite of nacho gave me the strength to go on. "Didn't you think—"

"He was crazy to be talking so of ghosts? Oh, yes!" Caridad threw back her head and laughed, and I'd bet anything it was the first time she'd allowed herself to let go and relax since that day on Wind Mountain when Jesse and the elders closed the excavation and Caridad's world came crashing down around her. "But he is Dan. And Dan is . . ." It didn't take her long to find the words. "Dan is honest and genuine and so serious when it comes to his investigations. It was not long after we met that he trusted me enough to confide this information about Madeline and how her spirit occupied your body."

"And you believed him."

It wasn't a question. She nodded anyway. "That is what love is all about, isn't it?"

It took dying to convince Quinn. And he still wouldn't talk about it.

So unlike Jesse, who'd taken the news of my former Gift not so much in stride as he did like it was some kind of honor. Go figure.

I snapped out of that thought to find Caridad watching me carefully. She nodded and said, "You do know what I mean, Ms. Martin. I can tell this from the look in your eyes. You know about being in love and how love gives you the ability to trust. And to believe."

"Maybe." It was as much of a commitment as I was ready to make in front of an almost total stranger. "I can tell you love and trust Dan and that's great. Unfortunately, cops are a whole lot less understanding. Things aren't looking good for him, Caridad."

"It is all a terrible mistake. It must be!" Though it was soft, her voice rang with certainty. "The police think Dan had something to do with the illegal permits for the excavation. They think he knows this Brian and that they are somehow involved in . . ." A helpless lift of her shoulders said it all.

That wasn't all the cops thought about Dan and Brian. For one thing, they knew for sure that Brian and Dan knew each other. For another . . . well, for now, I was keeping the news of Brian's murder to myself. Caridad was already on the verge of hyperventilating. If I hoped to get any information out of her, I couldn't afford to upset her even more than she already was.

"I suppose they have their reasons." It seemed a nice, middle-of-the-road way to avoid dropping the news of the murder on her like a ton of bricks. "Could they be right?"

"There is no way Dan is guilty."

We were on the same page. When I left Norma's, high-tailed it back to the motel to change clothes and get my car, and called Caridad here at the inn, where Jesse had told me she was staying, I'd hoped we would be. In addition to being gratified, I found myself warming up to Wife No. 2. Which is saying a lot since Wife No. 1 tried to make me disappear forever into nothingness and Husband No. One and Only could have found a better way to let me know about his recent nuptials.

But that was sour grapes for another time.

"We . . ." Caridad leaned forward, every bone showing when she latched her fingers together on the table in front of her. "I believe we are the only ones who can help him. To prove he is innocent. It is what you are thinking, isn't it?"

"That, yes. And I'm thinking we need to find him. But to do that, we're going to have to try and figure out what's really going on. So first things first. If Dan didn't forge those excavation permits, who do you think did?"

Her shoulders were so slender, when she shrugged, I hardly noticed.

"Don't get pissed, but I've got to ask—do you think it could have been Dan?"

Another shrug.

Yeah, I was surprised. I tried really hard not to show it. I didn't need her to get all defensive. "So you think it could have been him?"

"You know he is not that kind of man."

"I do. But if it wasn't Dan—"

"The others on the excavation, they're all graduate students. None of them would have had the knowledge or the nerve."

"Which brings us back to Dan."

"Or me."

Don't think this wasn't something I hadn't thought of. I sipped my drink and studied her over the sparkle of salt on the rim of my glass. Pretty, professional, obviously very smart. Dan wouldn't have fallen in love with her otherwise. But sparkle or no sparkle, it was time to get down

to brass tacks. I set down my drink and leaned forward.
"Did you?"

She rearranged the orange slices on her plate. "I am an anthropologist. I study people and their cultures, and my specialty, it is Pueblo Indians. Most people believe this makes me a very dull individual. Yet here I am . . ." She held out her arms and looked around, taking in Taos and all of the surrounding countryside. "Here I am in the middle of this mystery. When I came here to New Mexico with Dan, my goal was only to assist him in his studies and to attend the San Felix de Gerona festival day later this week. This is the special feast day of the Taopi Pueblo and I was eager to study the people and their traditions and their celebration. Now . . ." She shook her head sadly. "I cannot show my face at the pueblo. Not after what has happened. Not after the place that is sacred to the Taopi has been desecrated, and I have been a part of it."

This was a roundabout answer to my question. Maybe. Or maybe it was a dodge. Either way, it wasn't helping, so I asked again, "Did you forge those papers, Caridad?"

With one finger, she traced an invisible pattern on the table. "I have thought of telling the police I did. Just to convince them that Dan did not, that he isn't hiding from them, and that they should go out and try to find him. But really . . ." She bunched the tissue into one hand and held on for dear life. "I believe they would ask me how I accomplished this forgery and I would not know what to tell them. Instantly, they would know I was lying." She picked up an orange slice, set it back down. "Would you do such a thing?" she asked. "Would you lie to protect the man you love?"

I'm not exactly the philosophical sort so, rather than think about it, I played with the little plastic straw in my drink. "That's a tough one," I said.

"It wouldn't be. Not if you loved someone as much as I love Dan."

"So what you're saying is that you have been lying to the police. To protect Dan."

She didn't answer.

"Look . . ." I rested my elbows on the table. "We're dealing with an awful lot of dead people here, Norma and Arnie and . . ." I decided to throw caution to the wind. "Brian is dead, too," I told her, and watched what little color there was in her cheeks fade away. "I found his body this afternoon. Dan's cell phone number was written on a piece of paper in Brian's pocket."

She went as still as stone.

"You're not surprised."

When Caridad pulled in a breath, it was so sharp, I swear even my lungs hurt. A fresh cascade of tears started, and this time, she didn't even try to dab them away.

"Caridad, if you know Brian and Dan were working together, you have to tell the police. They're going to find out anyway, and—"

Her spine went poker straight. "Then they do not need to find out from me."

"If you keep secrets, it's only going to look worse for Dan. And if you run . . ." I caught the little movement when she braced her hands against the arms of her chair to push it away from the table. "That's not going to look good, either, and they're going to find you. The only thing that's going to help Dan now is you coming clean and telling the cops everything you know. Then they can find Dan and we can get this whole mess cleared up."

"You are working with them."

"The police?" I was chewing a mouthful of nachos when I said this, and it came out sounding like . . . well, like someone trying to talk while chewing a mouthful of nachos. I swallowed. "The police? No, not officially. But if you tell me something, Caridad—"

"You cannot tell them! Swear to me, swear to me you will not."

"But if it's important to the investigation—"

"You must swear!"

I struggled with the ethics of the situation. For maybe three seconds. Then I pulled my hands onto my lap, crossed every finger I could, and gave her the earnest look of a truth-teller. Who says years of dating had never prepared me to be a detective? "I swear."

She took my vow at face value. Thank goodness. "A few weeks ago . . ." Antsy, Caridad rubbed her right hand up her left arm and along her shoulder. "We were at the excavation. I was actually down in the kiva. It is . . ." For a second, her expression was transformed. The worries of the last days disappeared, her eyes cleared, and a smile touched her lips. "It is an amazing place. Even I, who do not believe as Dan does in the world of spirits . . . even I could feel a presence there in the darkness of the kiva. I was down there alone. Only, I was not alone." She snapped out of the memory and shot me a look.

"I am sorry. To you, this is an everyday thing. Dan says you see and feel and talk to the spirits all the time. To you, my musings must sound sophomoric."

Since I didn't even know about my Gift in high school, I wasn't sure what she was getting at. Since I didn't have it anymore, anyway, it hardly seemed to matter.

"So you were down in that kiva thing." In spite of the late afternoon warmth, a shiver crawled over my shoulders. "Isn't it creepy?"

"I imagine I find such cultural treasures as fascinating as you find the mausoleums and gravestones in the cemetery where Dan tells me you work."

I imagined not.

I shook away the thought. "So you were down there in that kiva . . ."

"And when I came again out of it, I saw Dan near our tent. He was talking to a man."

I didn't need a road map to see where this story was leading. The only way to counteract the sudden sourness in my stomach was a nice, long sip of margarita. "Brian," I said when I was finished.

"Yes." Caridad shook her head. "Dan, he introduced me. The man's name was Brian, Brian Reynolds."

"And did Dan explain what Brian was doing there?"

"Dan told me they had business together."

"The bones."

"We do not know this. Not for certain."

"But if we're going to get anywhere in our investigation—"

"You promised. You swore you would not tell the police what I have revealed."

"Yes, I did." Notice how I did not add anything like *and I'm not going to*. "That's not what I was going to say." This much was the truth. "I was going to say that if we're going to get anywhere in this investigation and find Dan, then let's just play with some ideas. Let's say Dan is the one who wanted Brian to get the bones. I mean, just for argument's sake."

She nodded. The movement sharp and quick. "For argument's sake."

"According to the legend, if there's a ceremony at the kiva, and if the ceremony somehow uses the bones of one of the people entrusted with the location of some magical, mystical something . . ."

"A bowl, yes. A silver bowl." She filled in the blanks of my memory. "The bones, the sacred ceremony . . . these are what call the spirits. And these spirits, they will reveal where the silver bowl has been hidden for more than one hundred years."

"So I get why Dan would be interested. It's the whole woo-woo thing. He'd want to perform the ceremony and call the spirits. But why would he care about this silver bowl?"

"This I do not know." I could tell from the way she shook her head sadly that she wished she did. "Maybe it is because this bowl, it is old and valuable."

"We both know money doesn't mean that much to Dan."

"Then maybe it is just to prove that the spirits are real."

She warmed to the idea, and sat up a little straighter. "If Dan, he says he performed the sacred ceremony and the spirits showed themselves, then everyone, they will just shake their heads and say yes, yes, that is Dan, believing too much in the paranormal. But if Dan, he can say that those spirits showed him where to find the bowl . . ."

"Then that would prove he had information he couldn't have gotten in any other way. I like it. It works."

Except it worked in all the wrong ways. But before I even had a chance to cringe and kick our argument in a direction that wasn't Dan's guilt, a flash of movement out on the sidewalk caught my eye.

Buckskin dress.

Feathered headband.

Long, dark braids.

While I was still processing the details and wondering why they looked so familiar, Caridad was tisking. "Obviously she knows very little," she said. "The woman is dressed all wrong for a Pueblo Indian. This is the costume of a Plains Indian. If you ask me, she isn't even a Native American. She is playing at it. No doubt if we gave her a chance, she would start talking about corn ceremonies, as if she were some expert."

Corn ceremony!

The pieces clicked into place, and just as they did, I took off and raced out of the bar. It didn't take me long to get out onto the sidewalk, but by then, Morning Dove—the woman who'd been at the Indians game back in Cleveland and wanted me to arrange for her to get into the cemetery to remove Goodshot's curse—was already gone.

16

I never did find out who San Felix de Gerona was exactly, except that he was the patron of the Taopi people, and that every year at the end of June, they had a huge to-do in his honor. That, and that he apparently didn't have any pull when it came to determining the weather for his big day.

The morning of the feast dawned cloudy and cool. From what I heard from the crowds of people who milled around me when I arrived at the pueblo, this was unusual. Thank you, San Felix. So much for showing off the cute little lemon-colored, square-necked tank I was wearing with an adorable A-line batik skirt in blues and greens and accents of the same fresh yellow. When I got out of the Mustang, I grabbed Quinn's blue windbreaker from the backseat. Not that I had any intention of wearing it. I just figured if I carried it along, maybe the weather gods would get the message, the clouds would part, and I'd get to bask in a little Southwestern sunshine.

The pueblo was packed with tourists, vendors, and Taopi, who, I found out later, always returned for the celebration, even if they'd moved to faraway places. I sidestepped my way through the plaza over to where I saw a yummy-looking guy in a uniform watching the crowds from behind his sunglasses.

"Hey, Officer!" I made sure my smile was as sunny as my tank top. "How's it going?"

I didn't have to see Jesse's eyes to know he slid me a look. I could feel the heat everywhere his gaze touched. It slipped from my tank top, to the skirt that ended three inches above my knees, to the open-toed, high-heeled sandals I was wearing with it. And all the way back up again.

"Nice," he purred.

"I hope you're not talking about the weather."

He twitched his broad shoulders. "Not much I can do about that. But at least everything else is going well." Another officer walked by and Jesse signaled for him to keep an eye on things and led me down a short street alongside the buildings that faced the plaza. He took off his sunglasses. "I'm sorry I'm not going to be able to spend much time with you today," he said. "We'll have thousands of visitors coming and going all day long."

"Not a problem." It really wasn't since I wasn't planning on hanging around long. "I'll take a look around and then I'll get back to work. Still no word on Dan?"

A shake of his head was all the answer I needed.

Just what I was afraid of. Which was why I had a plan.

"I'm going to go back into Taos and see Caridad again. I got her talking once, maybe she'll open up some more."

"Oh, no." As if he thought I was going to take off right then and there, Jesse put a hand on my arm. "Today is the feast, and you're not working. Besides, my parents want to meet you."

I took a moment to process the information. Processing done, I found myself feeling a little off-kilter—and completely terrified.

"Dinner," Jesse said, before I could come up with an excuse that would satisfy him. And his parents. One that was good enough to keep me from being thrown into a situation that made me woozy just thinking about it. "Feast day dinners are very important. And my family still owns one of the pueblos in the old village so that's where we'll be eating. It's an honor to be invited."

"I'm sure it is, but—"

"I told them all about you."

I hoped he wasn't being literal because if *all* really was *all*, then it would include all we'd been doing together the last couple weeks. And I didn't want to go into a first meeting with the parents with that on my mind. Then, of course, there were the ghosts. Or at least there used to be the ghosts. If Jesse's parents thought like him and actually believed that talking to the dead was some kind of privilege, and they expected me to have some kind of wacky Gift, they might be disappointed to learn the truth. Or they might think I was crazy. Or . . .

I swallowed hard. "You told them all about me, huh? Is that good news or bad news?"

One corner of his mouth pulled in a wry smile. "You've got nothing to be nervous about."

"I'm not nervous." I folded my arms over my chest, and when that didn't do anything to kill the chill that made my knees knock together, I took drastic measures: I slipped on Quinn's windbreaker and hugged it tight around me. "I'm just thinking . . . you know . . . that we don't have any time to waste. You know, when it comes to the case. And finding Dan. And the murderer. Somebody needs to talk to Caridad again. Right now."

"Brian's murder is a problem for the sheriff up in Antonito. He's a good man, and he's on top of things. Trust me."

"I do." Through my flash-frozen terror, I somehow managed a smile. "It's just that—"

"My parents and my two brothers and my sister . . . they're all going to love you." The quick kiss he gave me told me he had to get back to work. "Just like I do."

Yeah, that's how he left it. He turned right around and walked away with those words still hanging in the air.

Just like I do.

What's a girl supposed to think?

I wasn't sure, but I did know that, after that, I wasn't quite as chilly anymore.

There's a lot that goes on at a pueblo feast day celebration, and a whole lot of it has to do with centuries-old traditions and ceremonies. Which means most of what happens isn't exactly secret—because visitors are welcome to respectfully watch—but there are no cameras allowed, no cell phones, no recording devices, no talking during sacred dances or clapping after. I can't say for sure, but my guess is the Taopi don't mind if visitors head home and tell their friends and neighbors what they saw at the feast, they just don't want the whole thing treated like some kind of stage performance.

To the Taopi, this is sacred stuff.

This whole keep-it-secret vibe actually worked out pretty well as far as I was concerned. Though I watched the dancers in their brightly colored costumes, I really didn't understand most of what I saw so there was no way I was going to remember much of it, anyway.

In fact, the only thing that really made an impression were the *koshari*. That's a word that means sacred clowns. I'm not kidding. The clowns are men whose faces and bodies are painted with elaborate black and white stripes. They wear outlandish hats and beat drums, and for reasons I never did find out, they eat watermelon. Watching them, bewildered and kind of scared by their bizarre behavior, I heard people around me say that the *koshari* play tricks, act out pantomimes, and mimic people in an effort to teach lessons about the proper—and improper—way to behave.

Hmmm . . .

Aside from that strangeness, the feast was interesting enough. I ate some really good cookies full of cinnamon, watched a race and a pole-climbing contest, and saw Jesse long enough for him to remind me about dinner with his family. Gulp. I strolled through the booths of vendors and, for lunch, had something called posole, a sort of pork soup that was better than I expected it to be. While I was minding my own business, I wondered if I could slip away long enough to do some investigating in Taos and get back to the pueblo before Jesse even noticed.

I was going to do it, too, and was on my way back to the car when I heard a familiar voice.

"The corn ceremony was very important to the Taopi." The words whooshed their way to me on the end of a chilly breeze. "If you come this way, I'll tell you all about it."

The *this way* was actually that way, back across the plaza, and I turned in that direction just in time to see a troop of tourists following a costumed guide.

Buckskin dress.

Feathered headband.

What was it Caridad had said? The clothes were all wrong for a Pueblo Indian.

I wouldn't have realized it without Caridad's expert input, and maybe these tourists didn't, either, because en masse, they followed Morning Dove. I slipped in at the back of the crowd, and we trooped to a less-crowded corner of the pueblo, where the Native American who I would bet wasn't proceeded to talk (and talk and talk) about the importance of the corn ceremony in Taopi culture. When she was done (finally!), she gladly accepted the tips the unsuspecting tourists offered. I waited until the last of them was gone before I stepped forward.

"Hey, Morning Dove, fancy seeing you here."

It took her a minute to figure out who I was, which was actually pretty bad PR on her part since she was the one who wanted to get into the cemetery where she thought I worked so she could do her corn mojo. I knew exactly when she recognized me because two spots of bright color popped in her cheeks.

"What are you doing here?"

I shrugged my shoulders inside the blue windbreaker. "Same as you, just enjoying the feast. Only . . ." She had a wad of dollar bills clutched in one hand and I gave them a knowing look. "Only that's not exactly what you're doing, is it?" Since I knew she wouldn't come right out and admit it, I went on. "You think any of those visitors have any idea that you're just a regular ol' woman from Cleveland and not one of the Taopi?"

"I never pretended to be anything I wasn't." A gleam in her eyes, Morning Dove hiked up her buckskin dress (she was wearing jeans under it) and tucked the tip money in her pocket. "All I said was that I was going to tell them about the corn ceremony. And I did. If they want to show their appreciation to me for sharing my knowledge, that's their business."

I nodded like I understood this crazy way of thinking. "Might be the business of the pueblo police, too," I said in that oh-so-casual way that always catches people off guard. "The chief just happens to be a friend of mine."

She narrowed her eyes. "What, you want a cut of my tips or something?" A toss of those so-dark-it-had-to-be-a-phony-color braids. "You don't know the police chief here."

"Slept with him last night."

I guess I must have had the look of a woman who'd had

239

great sex in the last twelve hours because her face turned the same color as her pale buckskin dress. "You wouldn't—"

"Tell him? That depends."

Like she expected the cops to be hiding behind the nearest rocks, she shot a look from side to side. "On . . . ?"

"On you telling me the truth. Seems strange finding you here. You know, since the last time I saw you, you were standing outside of the stadium in Cleveland talking about removing that curse Goodshot put on the team."

She remembered, all right. "So? Is there something wrong with me trying to do the city a favor?"

"There is if it involves kidnapping somebody, then asking for Goodshot's bones as a ransom."

I'll say one thing for Morning Dove, she was either a really good actress, or worse at hiding her emotions than anyone I'd ever met. The trick, of course, was to figure out which. Her mouth fell open. "Goodshot's bones got stolen? Back in Cleveland? And then—"

"Brought here to pay the ransom, yeah. And then they got stolen again. And three people got murdered. And the kidnapped guy is still missing. And . . ." I pulled in a deep breath. "And now out of the blue, here you are."

"That's nuts." She back-stepped away from me. "That's just crazy. If you think I had anything to do with that . . . that's just . . . it's nuts, and I'm not going to stand here and listen to it."

"You are. Unless you want me to get my honey over here so you can explain why you're taking money from tourists who assume you've got the tribe's seal of approval."

She stopped dead in her tracks. "I don't know anything about Goodshot's bones."

"Prove it."

"I can't. I don't know how." She ran her tongue over her lips. "I came here for the feast. I always do. Every year. I go around to a bunch of the pueblos on feast days. You know, to take people around on tours and stuff."

"And take their money under false pretenses. Yeah, I get that part. And now you're going to tell me you weren't here on . . ." I did some quick mental calculations and came up with the day Norma had been killed. "You were here then."

She shook her head so hard, her braids whipped her cheeks. "Just got here."

"I don't believe it. You were around a couple nights ago. In Taos."

"Yeah, sure. I mean, I just got here for the feast. I wasn't—"

I mentioned the date of the evening when Arnie was shot and Jesse and I were used for target practice. "You going to tell me you weren't here then, either?"

"I wasn't. I swear." Maybe buckskin is hotter than regular fabric. Even though I shivered in the next cool breeze to blow the dust around my feet, there was a sheen of sweat on Morning Dove's forehead. "I don't know how I can prove it except . . ." Again, she hitched up her dress and reached into her pocket. She shoved an airline ticket at me. "There. Check it out. My ticket from Cleveland. I got here two days ago."

Yeah, that's what the ticket said. "That doesn't mean you weren't here before that, left, and came back."

She wasn't prepared for a detective's insight. "But I didn't," was all she had to say.

Like I said, sincere as hell. Or a really good actress.

"Prove it."

Thinking really hard, Morning Dove squeezed her eyes shut. "I . . . I . . . I know!" Her eyes popped open. "You can call my supervisor at work. He'll tell you I haven't taken a day off in months. I save all my vacation time. You know, for the various feast days. I work at Big Daddy Burgers."

Big Daddy, a place I'd once flipped burgers in an effort to get a suspect to talk. "I don't suppose you know Ray Gwitkowski," I said.

"He's my supervisor. And if you know him, you know he's an honest guy. You can talk to him and—"

If she expected me to take that at face value, she was sorely mistaken. I reached for my cell phone, then remembered the tribal rule about phones at the feast. "I'll call him later," I assured her. "And here's what you're going to do. First, you're going to let me know where you're staying in Taos."

She did.

"Next you're going to tell me if you even think about leaving."

She swore she would.

"And third, you're either going to take off that costume because you know it's all wrong and you don't look like a

Taopi Indian, anyway. That, or you're going to leave the pueblo right now. Choice is yours. And if you don't—"

"Going." She shuffled through the dust like her feet were on fire. "I'm leaving. I won't be back. I swear."

Had I just let a murderer slip through my fingers? Give me a little credit here! I went over to the police station and called Ray Gwitkowski. He was a buddy of mine, a volunteer at Garden View, and he sort of owed me since I'd once rescued him from the clutches of an annoying-to-the-max woman who had the hots for him. Ray confirmed Morning Dove's story—damn it—and that her real name (I knew I was right about the non–Native American thing) was Marlene Fritella. But that didn't mean she was off the hook. A person clever enough to engineer the kidnapping and the murders would also be devious enough to figure out a way to make the timeline work. Just to cover my bases, I also called the sheriff in Antonito and gave him Morning Dove's info. Like Jesse had mentioned, it was his case, and if I wasn't going to be able to follow up immediately, somebody had to.

Feeling righteous and warmer after having spent fifteen minutes inside the station, I walked back outside, stuffed my hands into the pockets of the blue windbreaker, and stopped dead in my tracks.

There was something dry and rough in my pocket.

I pulled it out, gasped, and instantly stuffed it back where it came from.

Goodshot's skeleton hand.

I thought back to the night of the body snatching and

how I'd found myself holding the hand when the bier collapsed and the coffin shattered. All this time, the skeleton hand had been with me and I hadn't remembered it. Then again, I'd been a little busy looking for the rest of Goodshot's body.

"Weird," I mumbled to myself, then got a move on before the cop who just walked out of the station could wonder why I was talking to myself.

Looking to kill some time, I headed for the plaza and the ancient pueblos beyond, and that's when it hit. The idea, I mean. The best idea I'd had in as long as I can remember.

"Goodshot wanted his bones buried on the pueblo." Yes, I was talking to myself again, but since there was another dance going on a few hundred yards away, and more drumming, I figured nobody heard me. "I can't bury all his bones but . . ."

I spun around and hurried in the other direction, away from the dancing and the drummers. Away from the sacred clowns with their watermelon and off to the loneliest edges of the old village. I got to a spot far from the crowds, looked around to make sure no one was watching, took off the windbreaker, and set it down on a nearby rock.

"You wanted to be buried on the pueblo, Goodshot?" Okay, I admit it. I paused after I said this, half hoping that I'd get some sort of response. But even here on the sacred grounds of the pueblo, the old magic was gone. No time to second-guess how I was feeling about it. I knew what I had to do, and I had to do it before anybody showed up and saw what I was up to.

"All right, Goodshot," I said into the chilly nothing. "I don't know where the rest of you is, but this . . ." There was a stick lying in the dirt nearby and I grabbed it and started scratching at the soil. "This is the least I can do for you."

Lucky for me, skeleton hands aren't all that big, and I didn't need to make the hole too deep. I scraped away at the rocky soil with the stick, and when I'd loosened enough of it, I scooped it out of the hole with my hands, thinking as I did that in addition to getting filthy, I was probably violating every tribal law, federal regulation, and local ordinance there was. Messing with tribal land—literally. I was just as bad as those excavators up at the ancient pueblo. But for all different reasons.

This did not deter me in the least. I scraped and dug and scooped the hard, dry ground, and after fifteen minutes, I was glad I'd taken off the windbreaker. I swiped my arm over my damp forehead and studied the hole. Another couple inches and I was home free. I could take the skeleton hand out of the pocket of the windbreaker and put it in the New Mexico earth where it belonged. Satisfied, I sat back on my heels for a well-deserved breather.

Too bad breathing was something I never got the chance to do.

Before I knew what was happening, and long before I could react, a rope looped around my neck and the person holding it—someone I hadn't heard come up behind me—tugged and twisted. Hard.

I gagged and fought for a breath that wouldn't come. That's when instinct and panic took over. My hands shot up and I struggled to wedge them between the rope and my neck, but my attacker's hold was too strong. I thrashed and flipped, and behind my eyes, stars exploded and sparkled like a thousand supernovas. The last thing I remember seeing were the black-and-white stripes painted on my assailant's legs.

That and the hole I'd dug in the dusty New Mexico earth. The one I landed in, face first.

17

Sputtering is not attractive. Then again, being choked to death isn't all that good for a girl in the looks department, either, so I guess the fact that I was sputtering—and alive—was a big plus. So was Pete Olivas, who was standing over me when I came to. Apparently, he'd already used his radio to make the call about the well-dressed woman unconscious on the ground, and clearly, Jesse knew *well-dressed* could only mean me.

When I pulled myself out of the dirt and sat up, Jesse was sprinting in my direction. He was winded, his hat was missing, and when he saw me breathing and conscious, a look of such relief swept over his face, I swear if I hadn't already fallen for him, it would have happened right there and then.

He was on his knees beside me in an instant, directing

Pete to get the paramedics over there at the same time he gently fingered the abrasion on my neck, checking for damage. It hurt like hell and my guess was that what felt like a rug burn all along the front of my neck didn't do much for the overall look of my outfit. But then, neither did the coating of New Mexico dust I was wearing like a second skin. I scraped my hands over my arms, brushed my skirt. Trying to swallow was another matter.

"Water," Jesse instructed Pete, and when he gave me a bottle of it, he looked into my eyes. "Can you tell me what happened?"

Water, huh? It felt like fire going down, and I coughed and forced myself to take another sip. In the great scheme of things, the pain gave me the chance to develop my strategy because, let's face it, the truth wasn't exactly going to put me in a shining light, law enforcement–wise. "I was . . ." Another sip, another cough, and lucky for me, a couple paramedics showed up just at that moment, and while they checked me out, it gave me a little more time to stall.

Thank goodness, this time no one insisted I go to the ER. They cleaned up my neck and put some ointment on the abrasion, then they transported me back to the police station in an ambulance. I think this last bit was because Jesse insisted more than because anyone thought I really needed it. His arm around my shoulders, Jesse walked me to his office. More water, and thank goodness an officer (it was a woman, of course, because only a woman would think of it) gave me some wet paper towels. I did as much damage control as I could without the benefit of running water, shampoo, and a hot oil treatment, and by the time I was done, Jesse had made me a cup of tea and added a couple spoonfuls of honey.

"It will help soothe your throat," he said.

I smiled my thanks but the expression didn't last long. It hurt. And besides, it was time to explain.

"I found Goodshot's hand," I said. "His skeleton hand. It was in the pocket of the—"

I looked around the office. The blue windbreaker wasn't there.

Yeah, there was still fire in my throat. But now, it shot through my veins, too, I jumped out of the chair. No easy feat considering I'd just nearly met my maker at the end of a rope.

"The windbreaker." Holding on to the chair for balance with one hand, I pointed with the other at the nothing that should have been on the chair next to me. "Pete . . . the paramedics . . . did they . . . what did they do with my windbreaker?"

Jesse called Pete into the office, and Pete swore that when he found me, there was no windbreaker anywhere nearby. Just to satisfy my sputtering protest that he must be wrong, he even went back to check out the dusty corner of the pueblo where I'd been attacked. A few minutes later, his voice crackled over the radio. "Nothing here, Chief. No windbreaker."

The fire faded and ice settled in my stomach. Jesse was standing nearby and I grabbed his hand. "You know what this means, don't you?"

He raised an eyebrow. "You get to go shopping for a new blue windbreaker?"

I forgave him for being obtuse, but only because I'd seen how upset he was when he thought I was in real trouble. Of course he wasn't thinking clearly.

"Forget the windbreaker! I hate that windbreaker!" I didn't need to muffle my screech since my throat was raw and it came out sounding froggy. "It's not the windbreaker that guy was after, it was what was in the pocket of the windbreaker."

"You said . . ." Jesse plunked down on the edge of his desk. "Goodshot's skeleton hand. But why were you out there with the bones and what—"

"Long story." I waved away the question as if it didn't have federal-penitentiary significance. "The night I . . . er . . . borrowed the bones, the hand ended up in my pocket, and I forgot all about it, but I found it this afternoon and I took it out . . . you know, just to look at it . . ."

"And if whoever has the rest of the bones knew the hand was missing and was following you in the hopes of finding it . . ." Three cheers for Jesse. He'd gotten to the heart of the matter and done it in a way that avoided the whole messy tampering-with-Taopi-land thing. He was already at the door and had already told Pete to get together whatever officers could be spared from the feast before he turned back to me. "He's got the entire skeleton."

Yeah, exactly what I was thinking.

"And now," I said, "he can perform that magic ceremony and call the spirits out of the kiva."

"Calling the spirits, huh?" Jesse put on his Stetson. "Sounds exactly like something Dan would do."

He just wasn't going to let it go.

I forgave Jesse. But that was only because we were already racing out of the office and there wasn't time to bicker.

For the second time, we made the trip out to the ancient pueblo. The route was just as dusty, just as rocky, and bumpier than ever thanks to the fact that Jesse drove it at as much of a breakneck speed as he was able. No doubt he felt the same sense of urgency that was pounding through me. And the same gnawing frustration. What with the crowds at the feast and the fact that another sacred dance had started just a few minutes before we set out to gather everyone Jesse wanted to bring along, it had taken more than an hour to locate the elders and Strong Eagle, the shaman.

What that meant, of course, was that the person who attacked me and took Goodshot's hand had the jump on us.

By the time we arrived at the entrance to the steep, winding path through the two cliffs, the clouds had parted. Just what I'd been waiting for, except that the sun was already sinking over the horizon, and it was chillier than ever. Not that I missed the blue windbreaker or anything, but I was grateful when Pete reached into the back of the SUV and tossed me a Taopi police officer's jacket. It was too big, but at least it was warm. Good thing I'd stowed my cowboy boots in the Mustang before I left the motel and had time to retrieve them while Jesse was gathering his troops. No way I ever would have made it up the trail in my high-heeled sandals. Then again, I wasn't sure I was going to make it, anyway. Jesse set a punishing pace and I stumbled along behind him, watching the bobbing beam of his flashlight as he led the way.

By the time we stepped out onto the mesa, the sky above us was the color of grape juice and dotted with a million stars. Directly above us was the smudge of the Milky Way. Too bad I didn't have time to be awestruck. At least not by the Milky Way.

But then, I was pretty busy being awestruck by what was happening over on the flat-top roof of the kiva. One of the excavation worktables had been set there and turned into a makeshift altar with chunky candles burning on either end of it. The flames flickered in the breeze, tossing flapping shadows on what was laid out on the table—a human skeleton.

Goodshot.

There was a bowl of sage next to the bones. The tips of the branches were smoldering, and the smoke from them swirled around the altar like restless banshees.

Maybe it was the smoke that got into my brain and made me see things. Maybe that's why I was suddenly feeling even more winded than I had on the mountain path, and a lot like I'd been kicked in the stomach.

Maybe that explained why I saw Dan Callahan standing at the altar.

Big points for Jesse. When he turned around to give me a look, he didn't say, "I told you so." In fact, the only emotion I saw in his brown eyes was concern. "Are you going to be all right with this?" he asked me.

"All right?" It wasn't my raw throat that caused me to sputter over the words, it was the lump of emotion that blocked my breathing. A lump that dissolved in a flash thanks to what felt like a wallop to my midsection.

Oh yeah, there's a lot to be said for anger. It's a great alternative to the pain of betrayal.

I was headed over to the kiva before anyone could stop me.

"You son of a bitch!" I guess my throat wasn't hurt so badly after all, because I managed to bark the words at Dan and I watched him flinch and spin to face me. "That whole baloney about you being kidnapped . . . that whole thing about how I had to dig up Goodshot's bones and bring them here to save you . . . and what happaned to Norma and Arnie and Brian . . ." I was nice and close now and I took advantage of the fact that Dan was still so surprised to see me, he hadn't moved. I punched him right in the nose. "You son of a—"

No way Jesse was going to let things dissolve into a ruckus. I would have given Dan another well-deserved smack if Jesse didn't come up behind me and grabbed hold of my arm. "You're Dan Callahan," he said. He was just being official, I think, since the fact that I'd thwacked Dan probably told Jesse all he really needed to know.

Dan had snapped out of his daze the moment my knuckles met his nose, and from behind his now bent wire-rimmed glasses, he blinked like a stunned owl at us and the Taopi who gathered around us. "Pepper? What are you . . . How . . ."

"Oh, no!" I was in no mood to be placated. Or held on

to. I ripped my arm out of Jesse's grasp, the better to point a finger directly at Dan's already puffy nose. "Don't you try to play innocent," I growled. "All this time, I've been desperate to find you. And I've been defending you up one side and down the other. And all this time, you're the one who's been behind it all."

Dan fingered the bridge of his nose. "I don't know what you're talking about. You don't mean . . ." He looked over his shoulder toward the skeleton. "If you're talking about this, I've got to admit, I don't understand it, either. There's a legend about the bones of an Indian who knew the secret hiding place of the sacred bowl, but these can't be them. I mean, how could they? Those bones are buried back at Garden View. You've got to believe me, Pepper, I'm just as confused as you are."

"Oh yeah?"

So okay, it wasn't exactly a stinging comeback, but apparently Dan didn't notice because he snarled right back at me, "Yeah."

Not the tender reunion scene I had always envisioned having with Dan someday. But still too leisurely for Jesse. In one smooth movement, he stepped behind Dan and slapped on his handcuffs.

"Hey! What's going on?" Dan actually might have tried to wriggle away if Jesse hadn't had such a tight hold on him. "I'm the victim here. These four guys kidnapped me and—"

"Save it." It wasn't until he finally spoke that I realized Jesse was even angrier than I was. There was a knife-blade edge to his voice, and his eyes glinted in the light of the flickering candles. "You can tell your story to the tribal council. And the FBI. And a couple federal prosecutors. Maybe by then you can figure out a way to explain how you forged those phony excavation papers."

Sure, the light was bad. That didn't keep me from watching Dan turn as waxy as those candles. "Don't be ridiculous. Come on, Pepper, tell this guy you know me and you know I wouldn't do anything like that. The permits were legit. They had to be. Besides, I never signed them. That was all left up to—"

He swallowed the rest of what he was going to say, and come on, it doesn't take a detective to figure out why. Too bad I never had a chance to astound the Taopi with my keen insights. Before I could utter a word, a couple things happened. A movement across the mesa caught my eye and I saw Caridad step out of her tent. That is, right before she took off running.

Like skinny little Caridad actually thought she could outrun the Taopi Police, the shaman, the elders, me, and oh yeah, Dan? He wrestled his way out of Jesse's grasp the moment he saw Caridad, and it helped that Dan was familiar with the terrain. Even with his hands cuffed behind his back and in the twilight that swallowed us as soon as we were a few feet from the candles, he knew his way. The rest of us raced after him.

Something told me Caridad wouldn't have stopped at all if she hadn't run out of breath. Good news for us because Dan caught up with her, we caught up with Dan, and Pete Olivas put him in a hold there was no way Dan could escape. Once the running was over, we found ourselves near a gigantic boulder that stood guard at a spot where the mesa ended and the awesome nothingness of the New Mexico night sky began.

"Caridad? Honey?" Dan called out to her. "What's going on here? These people are saying crazy things. Do you have any idea—"

"Of course I do not." Caridad gulped in breath after shallow breath. She was dressed in jeans and a light-colored jacket, and in the high beams of the flashlights aimed in her direction, I saw her raise her chin and throw back her slender shoulders. When she looked at the half circle of people gathered around her, her eyes sparked. "What are you doing here?"

"That's exactly what we'd like to know." Yeah, that was me. It was what Jesse was bound to ask, anyway, so I didn't feel guilty about stepping on his procedural toes. "You were told to stay off the mountain."

"Yes, and of course, I would have done this. But Dan . . ." Caridad turned to me, her eyes big and moist and pleading, her breathing ragged. "You remember what we talked about, Pepper? You remember how I asked if you would do anything for the man you loved? When my husband called me and told me he needed my help, of course I came here to the mountain. To him."

"Me? Called you?" Dan did a little squirming, but in spite of being short, Pete was no pushover. A bit of arm twisting and the squirming stopped. "Caridad, honey, I'm completely confused. You called and said—"

"You see what those kidnappers, you see what they have done to him?" When she looked at her husband, her smile was bittersweet. "He is confused. I believe this is from lack of water. Pepper, she was the one who told me you had been kidnapped, Dan. I was worried. So very worried. And then I arrived here this evening to pick up a few things, and I found Dan here. The kidnappers, they must have left you here, though I do not understand why."

Dan tried to step toward his wife, but by now, Pete had hold of his one arm and another of the cops had his other. He wasn't going anywhere. "But that's not how it happened! I mean, yes, some of it is. I was kidnapped." As much as he was able, Dan turned to Jesse. "Brian Reynolds, he's this ghost hunter I know from Cleveland . . . he and these three friends of his, they showed up here at the excavation last spring on their way home from Indians spring training in Arizona. You know, just to visit. It was great to see him. And I thought that was that. But then they showed up again a couple weeks ago and I was showing them around and . . . I don't know, they must have knocked me out or something. One minute, I was here at the excavation, and the next thing I knew, I was in some cabin somewhere and they were talking about bones." He looked over his shoulder toward the altar and Goodshot's remains. "That's not really Goodshot Gomez, is it? How could it be? He's buried back in Cleveland."

The fact that Goodshot had made the cross-country trip might have been something of a bit of news to Strong Eagle and the elders. Rather than let them get all discombobulated about it, I decided to gloss over the *how* and get right to the *why*.

"The kidnappers wanted the bones in exchange for

you," I told Dan. "Only then Norma stole the bones and she got killed and Arnie did, too."

Dan nodded. "So that's what happened to Arnie. He left the cabin one evening, see, and he never came back. The other two guys—John and Gregory—they got all upset. They insisted something was wrong, that Arnie had gone to the cops and that they were all going to end up in big trouble. They argued with Brian. He wanted to stick around. They weren't paying attention to me, and I managed to loosen my ropes and slip out of the cabin. Lucky for me, city guys aren't as used to roughing it as I am. I spent the night in the wilderness, hiked down the mountain the next day, and called—"

There it was. Another one of those too-obvious-to-be-overlooked hitches in Dan's explanation. Like I could stop myself? I turned to look exactly where Dan was looking.

And Dan was looking at Caridad.

"Of course you called her first," I said. "She's your wife. And you figured she was worried about you. Worried sick. But you're not going to say that, are you, Dan? Because you know what it means." A quick look at him before I turned back to the missus. "He's trying to protect you."

This shouldn't have come as a big surprise to Caridad, but her eyes snapped to mine, anyway.

"Come on, Caridad, give the guy a break," I told her. "The next thing you know, Dan is going to confess that the kidnapping was all a hoax designed to get a hold of Goodshot's bones. Just so nobody figures out that you're the one who did it." I swung back around in Dan's direction. "I'm right, huh? You're keeping quiet, Dan, about who was in charge of those permits, and about who you called after you escaped. That's because it was Caridad. And if you talk, it's going to make her look as guilty as sin."

Dan's chin quivered. "Don't be silly. How could you possibly—"

"There's the old legend for one thing." I glanced toward Strong Eagle, a sturdy, middle-aged guy with kind eyes and big, tortoiseshell glasses, and since a walk on the woo-woo side was no longer my stomping grounds, I let him take over.

"The legend says that the bones of the last person who knew the location of the sacred silver bowl needed to be brought here to the pueblo," he said. "The story tells us that once the bones are here and the prayers are spoken, the spirits will appear. They will show us where the bowl is hidden."

"Yes." The other Taopi gathered around nodded and murmured. "That is so."

"And that silver bowl . . ." I watched Caridad carefully. "That silver bowl has magical healing powers. That explains it all, doesn't it? I should have seen it from the start. But I didn't. Not until right now. Not until I watched you huffing and puffing your way across the mesa."

Caridad was still breathing hard, so it wasn't very convincing when she grumbled, "I do not know what you are talking about."

"She got Brian to kidnap Dan because she knew I'd

bring the bones to ransom him," I said for the benefit of the elders. "And Brian needed Norma's help. Poor Norma, that pretty much sealed her fate."

"But if Brian wanted the bones, why pretend they'd been stolen?" It was a good question, and I acknowledged it with a nod toward Pete.

"Because the guys Brian brought here to New Mexico with him, they were true Cleveland Indians fans. They believed Brian when he said he was doing this for the team. They thought that once they had the bones, they really were going to bury them here on the pueblo. That would have been perfect because not only would it lift the curse on our baseball team but it would put Goodshot right back where he belonged. Only Brian never had any intention of burying the bones, did he, Caridad?"

She tossed her head and aimed a laser look at Jesse. "I cannot believe you, a professional, would let this . . . woman . . . make these ridiculous accusations. You cannot listen to her. She does not know what she is talking about."

"Hello, I'm talking about how you're the one who really wanted the bones." Since Caridad was ignoring me so she could try her best oh-poor-me look on Jesse to gain his sympathy, I waved my hands in front of her face. "And Brian couldn't let his buddies know that. That's why the bones had to get stolen at Taberna. And that's why somebody had to keep Norma quiet about her part in this whole thing. Was it you who killed her? Or Brian?"

"This is insane!" Caridad made a move to get past us, but one of the elders stepped in her path and that gave me the opportunity to keep putting the pieces together. Now that I knew Caridad was the spider in the center of the web, the rest made perfect sense.

"Once Norma was out of the way, I'll bet you and Brian thought everything would be A-OK. He was going to sell the bones to you. That was when Arnie and the others realized they'd been double-crossed. They weren't going to save their favorite baseball team. So Arnie contacted me and then . . . Poor Arnie never stood a chance, did he? Once you bumped him off, you were free to do the deal with Brian. You paid him for the bones. That explains all the money they found in his pockets. And man, you must have been pissed the first time you tried the ceremony and nothing happened. That's when you realized Goodshot's hand was missing, right? And I'll bet anything the ceremony requires all the bones, not just most of them. That's probably when you started following me to see if I had the hand. It's probably why you killed Brian, too. You figured if I didn't have the hand, it meant he held out on you."

I didn't hold it against Jesse for coming up with a logical protest. After all, this whole mess was about to get sucked into the legal system, and there would be more pointed questions to come. "But the person who killed Arnie had to be an expert shot," he said. "Arnie got hit on the first try, and Pepper, we never got hit at all. The shooter just wanted to scare us away."

"She just wanted to scare us away." I turned again to Caridad. "You want to just come right out and confess?

Then we can all get out of here and get back to the feast. I wouldn't mind a couple more of those cinnamon cookies."

Caridad didn't say a thing. She didn't need to. It was Dan who spoke, and when he did, his voice was low and so full of pain, it hurt to listen to him. "She was on the Spanish Olympic team." He did his best to move closer to his wife, but no way Pete was going to let that happen. "Caridad, they're going to find that out, they might as well know right up front. She's an expert marksman, rifle and pistol. But that doesn't mean anything." When Dan looked at me, there was pain in his eyes. "Pepper, you've got it all wrong. That doesn't mean—"

"Let me guess . . ." I wasn't trying to be mean, but I had to get Dan to face the truth. "When you escaped from Brian and his buddies and finally got off the mountain, Caridad was the first person you called?"

"Of course. She's my wife, and she was so relieved to hear from me—"

"That she told you to lay low, stay out of sight, and not contact the authorities." This from Jesse, and I wasn't surprised. He was smart, and he knew exactly where I was going with this.

Dan swallowed hard. "She said there was some confusion about the excavation permits, that the cops were looking for me, and until things were straightened out, it was better if nobody found me."

"Which also gave her time to follow me and see if I had the skeleton hand. I did. But Caridad, you didn't know that until today at the feast. You must have seen me take it out of my pocket and when I tried to bury it—"

"You were burying a hand? On the pueblo?" The elder closest to me didn't sound happy so I decided he needed to be reminded that I'd nearly been choked to death. Maybe if he realized I'd risked my life for the sake of a pueblo legend, he'd look a little kinder on me.

"You came up behind me and wrapped that rope around my neck. What stopped you from finishing the job, Caridad? Somebody was coming, right? And you couldn't afford to stick around and finish me off."

Her laugh echoed against the cliff walls. "How foolish you all are," she said, glancing around at the Taopi. "To listen to this woman. Why would I want to perform this ceremony? I am a scientist. If you're looking for someone who believes in these silly, paranormal things, you know you must look at Dan."

His mouth fell open. "Caridad, how could you say such a thing?"

"He's the one who believes in magic," she said, swinging an arm in her husband's direction. "He's the one who wanted to prove the existence of the spirits. And he told me, many times . . . he told me he would do anything to make this happen."

"Yeah, I bet he did. But you . . ." I took another step closer to her. "You're the one who wanted the magical bowl, because according to the legend, the bowl cures sickness and you need it, don't you, Caridad?"

"Caridad?" The single word from Dan wasn't as much as question as it was a wail.

"It explains everything," I said matter-of-factly. "The sore back. The dark circles under your eyes. You running out of breath when you tried to take off on us. And it explains you not ordering one of those crazy Cowboy Buddha margaritas because, let's face it, they're fabulous and nobody but a recovering alcoholic could resist. You weren't drinking because you're on some kind of heavy-duty medication. And it isn't working, is it? If it was, you wouldn't need the ceremony or the magical healing bowl."

"I do not believe in these things." She stomped one foot in the dust. "I am logical. Rational. It is Dan." She pointed a finger at him. "He is the one. It was his idea."

"We'll sort it all out at the station." Jesse moved forward to take hold of Caridad's arm, but I was quicker.

"We can find out sooner than that," I said, shooting forward. I knelt down and pulled up Caridad's pant leg.

"Black-and-white stripes," I said, looking at the pattern painted on her leg. "Just like the sacred clown who attacked me."

It was one of those moments great movie endings are made of, and it might have been remembered that way, too, if I hadn't been caught off guard and Caridad's arm didn't go around my throat. Before I could regain my balance, she dragged me to the edge of the mesa.

"I'll push her," she said, mostly to Jesse because he was the one who moved first. "One step closer and I'll push her over the side. By the time she hits each of those rocks on the way down, you'll be lucky if you find one strand of that phony red hair."

"The hell it's phony!" I would have squirmed if I dared. The way it was, I could feel the wind that shot up from the bottom of the canyon that surrounded the mesa. It was as cold as death. I guess it was a good thing it was dark. Something told me it was a long way down. It was the same something that told me I didn't want to find out firsthand.

"I want your guns. Here." Caridad tapped the ground with one foot and waited until Pete, Jesse, and the other cop tossed their weapons on the ground and kicked them nearer to her. "Dan was right, by the way . . ." Still keeping a firm hold on me, she bent and grabbed Jesse's gun. She kicked the other two over the edge of the mesa. "I am an excellent shot. So you will let me by, and you will wait here for one hour. You will give me time to get down to the canyon and get in my truck and leave this place. And if you don't . . ." Her hand bunched in the back of my jacket, she hauled me to my feet. "If I hear one movement of anyone coming after me, I will surely kill Ms. Martin."

I'd already decided what I was going to do so this last threat didn't exactly help me make up my mind. It did scare the living daylights out of me, though, so before I could let that stop me, I shrugged out of the sleeves of the too-big jacket and took off running. Yeah, I hid behind Jesse. It was the sensible thing to do and he didn't seem to mind. In fact, when I peeked out from around him to see what Caridad was up to, he pushed me back.

"You've lost your hostage and you've got no way out." When he took a step toward Caridad, Jesse's voice was calm. He held out a hand to her. "Come on. We'll figure out what happened and we'll work things out. It's the only way out, Caridad."

"The only way? I don't think so."

I figured she wasn't being literal and I'll bet nobody else did, either.

That would explain why nobody but Jesse had time to move. He shot forward, but he was one step too late when he reached out to grab Caridad just as she hurled herself over the edge of the mesa.

18

We spent the night on the mountain. For one thing, it was a crime scene and Jesse said it had to be secured. For another, Strong Eagle refused to be rushed through the removal of the bones and the reconsecration of the sacred kiva.

Jesse insisted I stay in Caridad's plushy tent, and even though the thought gave me the heebie-jeebies, I gave in. I was bone tired, the skin on my neck stung, and besides, even the tent of a recently deceased murderer beat outside. Plus it wasn't like I was going to sleep, anyway. I sat in the chair by her desk, and every time I closed my eyes, I saw Caridad disappear into the dark nothing that surrounded the mesa one second and the look of bleak misery on Dan's face the next.

By the time the first light sent the stars packing, I'd had it with fighting the losing battle. I stepped outside just in time to see Jesse heading for the tent where Dan had spent the night. No doubt, poor Dan had been handcuffed to the tent's main support post to make sure he didn't try to take off. Yeah, he was stupid. I mean, about Caridad and all. But I couldn't stand the thought of Dan like that. Pete had a pot of coffee going in the tent the grad students had once stayed in, and I got a cup for myself, one for Jesse, and another one for Dan.

When I stepped into Dan's tent, he was sitting on the edge of a camp bed much like the one in Caridad's quarters. His glasses were off and his eyes were red-rimmed and puffy. So was his nose. When I handed him his coffee, it was my way of saying I was sorry. Not that I regretted punching him in the nose if he really had something to do with those phony permits and all. But hey, the guy had watched his wife take a header off the side of a cliff. The least I could do was offer what comfort I was able.

What I didn't get was that Dan wasn't handcuffed. I guess the look on my face must have said it all because Jesse spoke right up.

"I've just been expressing my sympathies to Doctor Callahan, and telling him how much I appreciate all the help he gave us."

Good thing there was a chair nearby. I dropped into it. "Help?"

"Sorry." The single word was apparently supposed to convey Jesse's whole message. Yeah, right. I waited until he was done gulping down his coffee and that was long enough.

"You're sorry because . . ."

"Because we had to keep you in the dark." With a look, Jesse showed that the *we* meant both him and Dan. "Doctor Callahan and I figured it would be easier this way."

"Doctor Callahan . . ." I swung a no-nonsense look in his direction. "Doctor Callahan better start talking. Were you in on this, Dan? With Jesse?"

"Not exactly." Dan's shoulders were stooped, and when he shook his head, it was as if it cost him every last ounce of energy he had. "But the chief here, he had this theory about Caridad and—"

"You knew?" Sleep-deprived or not, I hopped out of my chair and, fists on hips, faced Jesse. "You knew Caridad did it? And you never told me? And you . . ." This time, I turned to Dan. "You knew it, too?"

Jesse scratched a hand along the back of his neck. "I wasn't sure. But as soon as I learned she'd been on the Olympic team and was an expert sharpshooter—"

"You knew that, too?" I sank back down in my chair. "Somebody better start explaining. And quick."

Jesse did. "Give me some credit," he said. "I am a cop, after all. I located Doctor Callahan a couple days ago and yes—" He held up a hand to stop me when I opened my mouth to protest. "I could have told you, but I decided it would be safer if you didn't know. If the doc here was our murderer, I didn't need you marching in to confront him. But I had this theory about Caridad."

"And I didn't believe a word of it." Dan stared into his coffee cup. "Then Jesse convinced me there was only one way to find out. If we confronted Caridad together—"

"You could both get the proof you needed." I understood, I just wasn't sure I liked it. "Only, Dan, I'm betting that you didn't think there would be any proof. You went along with Jesse because you thought his suspicions were all wrong, and that he'd find out Caridad was really innocent."

"Yes." He looked up at me, his face lined with grief and worry. "She's the one who forged those permits," he said. "I saw them initially. I handled them, sure. I mean, before they were ever signed. Jesse says that explains my fingerprints on them. But I never signed them. When he showed me my forged signature . . . well, even then, I didn't believe it. But after everything Caridad said last night . . . after everything she did . . ." His voice broke over a sob. "I'm sorry, Pepper, I was blind. And it nearly got you killed."

"But how . . ." I blamed my confusion on not sleeping and hoped Jesse didn't hold it against me. "When . . ."

"When I finally found Doctor Callahan staying in a little motel outside of Taos, he had this with him. He grabbed it from the cabin where the kidnappers had kept him." Jesse reached around a nearby file cabinet and pulled out my Jimmy Choo tote bag.

Only it wasn't.

Jesse caught on to my dubious look. "You know something's wrong."

"That bag's a knockoff." I knew it instantly, but then, I have a keen eye for that sort of thing. "The glaze isn't shiny enough, and there's too much space between each of the studs on the handle. But if this is the bag that was at the cabin with Brian, that means the bones were in it, and if the bones were in it, why did he need to go to Norma's to look for the real thing? Oh wait!" It was so clear, I would have slapped my forehead if I wasn't afraid it would leave an ugly mark.

"It was because my bag *is* the real thing. The knockoff belonged to Norma, right? And she took one look at my real designer bag and saw a dream come true. She knew Brian would never be able to tell the difference, so she put the bones in the knockoff and gave that bag to him. Only . . ." The rest had me stumped, so Jesse filled in the blanks.

"After Brian had the bag of bones he took from Norma's, he must have seen this." He opened the bag enough for me to see the tag inside that showed Norma's name and address. "Even though they looked the same, Brian knew the purse wasn't yours. He must have figured that Norma kept your bag and if yours had a nameplate in it like hers did, he was afraid someone might find it at Norma's, then track you down and put two and two together. He couldn't take the chance. That's why he was at Norma's that day you got knocked on the head."

"So I'll get my Jimmy Choo back?"

Jesse was the picture of stony-faced patience. "After the case is wrapped up."

It was some good news, at least. "And Dan?" I asked.

Pete Olivas showed up outside the tent, and even though Pete didn't say a word, Jesse stood up like he knew he had someplace to go. "Doctor Callahan has cooperated fully," he said. "I'll be sure to make note of that when I talk to the prosecutor. Now . . ." He motioned us to follow him. "Strong Eagle is ready to begin."

Pete walked side by side with Dan over to the kiva, and Jesse and I followed.

"Strong Eagle is going to do the ceremony that calls the spirits." I didn't need to be a detective to figure that out; I saw that the bowl of sage on the altar was smoldering, just as it had the night before when Caridad was going to get Dan to perform the ceremony. "He's going to find out the location of the sacred bowl."

"That's the idea." We were nearly to the kiva, and Jesse put his arm around my shoulders and gave me a quick hug. "The ritual is secret, but Strong Eagle is allowing Dan to attend in the hopes of easing his grief. And of course he wants you to be there. We couldn't have done any of this without you."

I'm not a ceremony kind of girl. After all, before ghosts first butted their ectoplasmic noses into my life, I wasn't even sure I believed in spirits or the Other Side. But here's the thing: as soon as we took our places around the altar and Strong Eagle started chanting words I couldn't understand, I felt . . . something. Electricity crackled in the air. A vibration flowed from the ground. The colors of the rocks and the sage and the carvings in the cliff face were more intense, and the sound of the shaman's voice was as clear as crystal.

There was magic on the kiva that morning, and as the sun peeked over the mountains, it filled the air and danced over my skin like the fresh morning breeze.

That same breeze blew the smoke of the smoldering sage branches into big, gray puffs and the scent filled my lungs and stung my eyes. I closed them for a moment, and when I opened them again, there were men and women standing at the altar with Strong Eagle.

The Old Ones.

Don't ask me where the words came from, but there they were in my head, and I knew they were right. These were the spirits of the Taopi who had lived in this pueblo a thousand years before. They were small people, and their eyes were filled with wisdom. As if they were no more substantial than the smoke that drifted around the altar, they swayed in each passing breeze, faded, floated, and came back into focus again. Strong Eagle nodded to acknowledge them. He said a few more words in the ancient language, and the next thing I knew, Chester Goodshot Gomez was standing next to the shaman.

I would have raced right over there if Jesse didn't put a hand on my arm to stop me. In a heartbeat, I saw why. This was the moment the Taopi had been waiting for for more than one hundred years; Goodshot put a hand on Strong Eagle's arm, and together, the two men walked to the entrance of the kiva and disappeared inside.

I was all for going after them to see what was up, but hey, I am not completely dopey when it comes to these sacred, woo-woo things. Jesse and the elders and the other cops stood with their heads bowed. So did Dan. I knew this was one time it was better to stay put—and keep quiet.

Not that it was easy. Standing there with the silence pressing in on me, I just about thought I'd burst. That is, until Strong Eagle and Goodshot emerged from the kiva and walked back toward the altar. By then the sun was above the mountains and it glinted like a million stars against something in Strong Eagle's hands.

The sacred silver bowl.

When Strong Eagle set it on the altar, I got a good look at it. The bowl was maybe a foot across and just as tall, hammered silver decorated with the same sorts of symbols that adorned the cliff face of the pueblo. Pretty much the only thing I know about silver is that it's pretty and I like it for earrings and jewelry. But I knew this: the bowl was very old, and very special. Once it was on the altar, I realized that the humming vibration I'd heard ever since Strong Eagle started to chant wasn't coming from the ground or the rocks or the cliffs. It was coming from the bowl. Like music.

Okay, I'm not a crier. I mean, not for stuff like this. But hey, it was hard not to be moved by the magic of the moment and the look of gratitude in Strong Eagle's eyes. A smile touched the shaman's face. I didn't understand the words, but when he spoke, I knew he was thanking the spirits and promising that Goodshot's bones would be buried with honor on the pueblo.

Strong Eagle bowed to all the Old Ones, and I knew what that meant, too: the ceremony was nearly over, and Goodshot was about to disappear forever into swirling smoke and the stuff of legends.

He'd already started to fade when he looked across the altar and caught my eye. I didn't see him move, but the next thing I knew, Goodshot was standing directly in front of me.

"The Taopi owe you their thanks," Goodshot said. "They can now use the silver bowl in their sacred ceremonies."

My smile was watery.

"I owe you my thanks, too. You brought me back to this place where I belong. Strong Eagle, he understands this, and he will explain it to the elders. Don't worry." His eyes sparkled as much as his smile. "I've convinced him that you shouldn't do time for snatching my bones."

"Thanks." I'd always been lousy when it came to good-byes and I scrambled for a way to make him stay, just a little while longer.

I didn't need to. Goodshot wasn't done. "I have been thinking," he said. "About your Gift, and about how it deserted you when you were trying to help me and rescue your friend. I've asked the Old Ones to grant me a special favor, and they have agreed. The spirits are gone from your life, Pepper. You can live the rest of it in peace, without ever having to worry again about dealing with them. Or . . ." Goodshot looked into my eyes. "If you want, you can have your Gift back."

"Really?" It was a dumb question because, of course, he was serious. I knew ghosts wouldn't bother to come back from the dead at magical ceremonies just to hand me a line. Funny thing was, I didn't even need to think about it. "Yes," I said. "I would very much like my Gift back."

Goodshot glanced toward Strong Eagle. "She is the raven," he said. "The one who walks with the living, and the dead. This is one dead guy"—he gave me a wink—"who will always be grateful."

A breeze kicked up. It extinguished the candles on the altar and blew the smoke into the morning sky.

And when it was gone, so was Goodshot Gomez.

It took a couple days for the excitement to die down and for Jesse to get all his reports written and his phone calls made. We decided to celebrate with dinner on the patio at the Taos Inn, and I wore my newly dry-cleaned batik skirt and yellow tank in honor of the occasion. I knew it was worth getting all dolled up when I saw the appreciative grin on Jesse's face. He was off duty, and he was wearing butt-hugging jeans and a black T-shirt. He was even more delicious than the Cowboy Buddha margarita I found waiting at the table.

He stood up and pulled out my chair. "I ordered appetizers. I hope that's okay."

It was sweet. I only hoped my stomach would settle down enough to eat. Me, nervous? It was so not my style, but on the way over, I'd made a big decision, and it was time to share it with Jesse. In anticipation, my heart was beating a cha-cha against my ribs.

"I'm afraid I'm going to have to cut tonight short." Jesse didn't have to say he was sorry because I could see it in his eyes. "A couple FBI agents are on their way up from Albuquerque. Said they'd be in this evening. I've been keeping them informed every step of the investigation, but we've still got a lot to talk about."

Not exactly how I'd dreamed of spending the evening. And it meant I didn't have time to stall. "Listen . . ." I plunked my elbows on the table and took a sip of my drink. "I've been thinking."

"Yeah, me, too." Jesse had a glass of ice tea in front of him, and he added sugar and stirred. "There's something I want to talk to you about."

"Good." Another drink did nothing for the cha-cha, but it did taste good. "I've got something I want to talk to you about, too."

Stalemate or the opening I was looking for?

I didn't find out because that's when Dan showed up.

"Sorry to butt in." Dan stood next to our table, shifting from foot to foot. He'd gotten a haircut since last I saw him, but he still looked like a shaggy puppy. He still looked miserable, too. Maybe that's why Jesse took pity on him and waved to a nearby open table.

"Pull up a chair," he said. "Join us."

"No. I'm going to head over to the pueblo for that meeting we have with the FBI this evening." Dan held out some papers toward Jesse. "I just wanted you to know that Pepper was right. I found these in with Cari—" He coughed and cleared his throat. "I found these medical reports in with Caridad's things. She had lung cancer." His voice was clogged with misery, but he went on. "I can't believe it. She never said a thing to me about it, she just decided to handle things on her own. But that was Caridad. She was a strong woman. Like . . ." He poked his hands into the pockets of his jeans. "Like you, Pepper."

I gladly accepted the compliment. After all, after nearly

getting marooned in the desert, choked to death, and thrown off a cliff, I deserved at least that much. I sipped my drink, thinking, and yes, gloating just a little.

"Here's something I don't get," I said, sipping done for the moment. "Will Kettle told us he saw you at Norma's house. But why—"

"I think I've got that figured out." Jesse sat back in his chair. "Caridad called you and told you to come there, didn't she?" he asked Dan, who nodded in reply. "Because . . ."

"She said I'd find the bones there, and since I knew they were a real treasure to your people, I had to go look. Can you believe what a fool I was?"

Neither Jesse nor I was cruel enough to answer.

"She set me up," Dan said. "She called that other guy and sent him over, right?"

"Yeah." Jesse confirmed. "We checked Caridad's cell phone records. She's the one who called Will Kettle and told him he could pick up his guitar."

"Just so this Will guy could see me there and that would make me look even more guilty." He was still having trouble processing it; Dan shook his head and looked at Jesse. "Everything else?"

"All confirmed. John and Gregory, the other two kidnappers, they've been picked up back in Cleveland and they're talking their little hearts out. They did it for the baseball team, you know. All so that the curse could be lifted and the team can start winning again."

After all I'd seen in the Great Southwest, this sounded less crazy to me than it would have back home. "Goodshot's buried," I said. "Maybe they will start winning again."

"Maybe." Dan back-stepped away from the table. "Pepper, I just want to tell you . . ."

"Yeah, I know." I waved away his concerns with one newly manicured hand, partly because I felt sorry for Dan, but mostly because I knew if I didn't cut this short, I was going to lose Jesse for the rest of the evening, and I might never again have the nerve to bring up what I was going to bring up. What I hoped he wouldn't think I was crazy for bringing up. "You were finally going to admit you have lousy taste in wives."

For the first time since that night on the mountain, Dan grinned. "Yeah," he said. "Something like that. And I was going to tell you that you're a good friend, and I appreciate it. I was going to say, too, that the next time I'm in Cleveland . . ." He made a face. "You know, now that I think about it, I probably won't call you the next time I'm in Cleveland. Seems like every time I do that, I put you in some kind of mortal danger."

He didn't say good-bye before he walked away. I was grateful. I also appreciated that, even though he didn't know it, he'd given me the perfect opening.

I swirled the little plastic straw in my drink. "Speaking of Cleveland . . ."

"Exactly what I was going to say." It wasn't my imagination. Jesse was just as nervous as I was. Before I could even wonder why, he said, "At the pueblo. You know, when Strong Eagle performed the ritual . . . I was wondering, did you see anything?"

Not exactly what I wanted to talk about so I sighed. Better get it over with. "You're telling me you didn't."

"I saw Strong Eagle. And a beautiful morning. And the smoke from the sage."

"But no ghosts?"

"I felt . . ." Like he could still feel it, Jesse scraped his hands over his arms. "I felt something in the air. Like the electricity before a thunderstorm. I didn't see a thing, though, but I was watching you. You were talking to somebody."

I grinned. "Goodshot says thanks for all your help."

A smile brightened Jesse's expression. "You did see him. Does that mean . . ."

"Ghosts are us. I'm back in business."

"Is that good news or bad?"

I thought about it while I sipped my drink. "I'm not sure yet. In fact, there's only one thing I am sure of."

He reached across the table and took my hand. "Yeah, me, too."

"And Jesse, I have to go back to Cleveland, and I've been thinking . . ."

Apparently, I hesitated just a tad too long because at the same time I finally said what I'd been bracing myself to say, "I'd like you to come with me," Jesse blurted out, "I want you to stay here."

We laughed. At least until we realized what the dead-lock meant.

"It's great here," I said, lying just a bit—I mean about the dust and the fact that there's not always running water, and the lousy cell phone service and the coyotes and such. "It's beautiful and you're here and . . . but, well . . ." I held tight to his hand. "It isn't home."

"And Cleveland wouldn't be home for me, either. My family is here, and I'm not used to cities. I like the wide-open spaces, the mountains, and the sage."

"We could grow sage in the garden."

He appreciated my attempt at being funny and squeezed my hand. "My people are here. And yours are there. I was afraid this was how tonight might end."

Our waitress brought over tacos and burritos and set them down.

"Hey, don't look so gloomy," Jesse said. "We've got time."

"Yeah." I pushed the closest plate away. "And I'm suddenly not all that hungry anymore."

Jesse stood up and pulled me out of my chair. "I've got two hours," he said. He tossed up a room key and caught it in one hand. "And I know exactly how I'd like to spend them."

19

It was a great two hours, and sometime during that time, we decided it would be easier—on both of us—if we just said our good-byes there in that room at the Taos Inn. So it was no wonder I was surprised when I was putting my suitcases in my car back at the motel in Antonito the next morning and Jesse pulled up in the Taopi Police vehicle.

I slammed my trunk closed. "I already spent the night being miserable," I said as soon as he was out of the SUV. "So if you haven't come to tell me you're hopping in the Mustang and heading east with me—"

He stopped me with a kiss. "Wish I could. I've got"—he poked a thumb over his shoulder back toward New Mexico and the pueblo—"meetings coming out the yin-yang today," he said. "Everybody from the elders to the FBI. But I couldn't let you leave without giving you this."

He opened his hand and the morning sunlight winked

against a silver chain with a small silver charm on it, a bird. "It's a raven," Jesse said, carefully looping it around the still-red skin of my neck and fastening it. "And every time you look at it, I want you to remember that he is your spirit guide. He's strong. Like you. And brave. Like you. He welcomes new experiences, but remembers the past."

"Like I'll always remember my time here." I closed my palm around the charm, and I know it sounds crazy, but I could swear I felt the warmth of the raven's body and a sort of hum from deep inside it, the twin of what I'd felt from the sacred silver bowl. This was no ordinary bird, and it was no ordinary guy who'd given it to me.

"Strong Eagle blessed it for you," Jesse said, reading my mind. "He tells you to be safe, and to always remember that your Gift is special."

"Thanks." It was my turn to kiss him, and when we were done, I knew I had to move, and fast. I got into the Mustang and wheeled out of the parking lot and I was almost strong enough to just keep going. Even though I knew it was going to make my heart crack in two, I couldn't help myself. As I headed north out of the parking lot, I looked over my shoulder.

Jesse was smiling.

Without Goodshot, the ride back to Cleveland wasn't nearly as interesting as the ride out West. I made it in four days and could have done it faster except for that outlet mall in Nebraska. Shopping always helps, right? Well, it always had before. I tried my best, but by the time

I got back to Cleveland, I was already missing Jesse and feeling blue. I was just headed past Garden View Cemetery and toward my apartment when my cell rang. Ella needed to see me ASAP.

About a thousand reasons floated through my head— one of Ella's teenaged daughters was in trouble, there had been a murder and nobody could seem to get a handle on it, Ella needed fashion advice.

In fact, I thought of everything in the book except—

"It's good news and bad news, Pepper." Since there were tears streaming down Ella's face, it was hard to decide which was which. Her cheeks were a cherry red that matched the suit she was wearing. "We've had quite a bit of commotion around here today, Pepper. Jim . . . our administrator . . . well, of course you know Jim. He was the one who instituted all those austerity measures. Staff doing landscaping work, and going through the trash for recyclables and—"

"Picking staples out of old memos so we could reuse the paper." I'd never forgive Jim for the damage he'd done to my nails. "Of course I remember all that, Ella. Jim's budget cuts, that's why I lost my job."

"Jim's budget cuts . . . Well, it turns out . . ." We were the only ones in Ella's office, but she lowered her voice, anyway. "We were operating in the red because Jim was cooking the books. He had an off-shore account some-where and was planning on disappearing with all the cem-etery's money."

Not something I was expecting and I dropped into Ella's guest chair, my mouth open.

My question was only natural. "You're sure?"

"There's been a big investigation and the news came down this afternoon. Jim's outta here." To demonstrate, Ella zipped a finger across her neck. "The police took him away an hour ago."

"That's terrible," I said.

"It is." Nobody is as sympathetic as Ella. Except that she was smiling. "But the good news is . . ." She drew in a deep breath. "The board of directors has asked me to take Jim's job. Pepper, I hate to take advantage of another's misfortune, but . . ." Her grin was as bright as the New Mexico sun. "After all these years of hard work, I've been promoted. I'm the new administrator of Garden View Cemetery!"

It was well deserved and I jumped to my feet and gave her a hug. "But who—"

"Community relations manager, yes." Still smiling, Ella circled around her desk and sat down. "It's a big job. Not only is that person responsible for our tours, but for our newsletter, for being a liaison with the media, for our speakers bureau and public relations. I know you can do it."

"Me?" Yeah, I was sitting again, but that was because my knees had turned to rubber.

The phone on Ella's desk rang. "Jennine was supposed to ring me when the board was reconvening so I've got to go. They'll want an answer. What do you say, Pepper?"

I looked around her office—my new office—and I didn't have to say a thing. Humming, Ella scurried out.

And I got up, walked around to the other side of the desk, and sat down.

Just like that, I was back at Garden View. Working with the dead.

Right where I belonged.

FROM
CASEY DANIELS

A HARD DAY'S FRIGHT

A Pepper Martin Mystery

Cemetery tour guide and reluctant medium Pepper
Martin is enjoying quite a reputation on the ghostly
grapevine. So when a free spirit from the sixties needs
closure, she knows just who to haunt . . .

PRAISE FOR
THE PEPPER MARTIN MYSTERIES

"Pepper is a delight."
—MaryJanice Davidson, *New York Times* bestselling author

"Gravestones, ghosts,
and ghoulish misdemeanors delight."
—Madelyn Alt, national bestselling author

"Entertaining . . .
Sass and the supernatural cross paths."
—*Publishers Weekly*

penguin.com
facebook.com/TheCrimeSceneBooks

SIXTH IN THE PEPPER MARTIN
MYSTERIES FROM

CASEY DANIELS

TOMB WITH A VIEW

**Cemeteries come alive for amateur sleuth
and reluctant medium Pepper Martin.**

Cleveland's Garden View Cemetery is hosting a James
A. Garfield commemoration. For Pepper Martin, this
means that she'll surely be hearing from the dead presi-
dent himself. And when she's assigned to help plan the
event with know-it-all volunteer and Garfield fanatic
Marjorie Klinker, she'll wish Marjorie were dead . . .
too bad someone beats Pepper to it.

penguin.com